Torn

A novel by Neva Bell

Cover Design by Barbara Schwenzer.
olibeebees@gmail.com; IG: @olibees

For my Aunt Cindy, who loves a good paranormal read, but also gives amazing advice and guidance. Love you!

Chapter One

"Chloe, if you don't put on more sunscreen, Willa will fire me."

"Again?" I whine. "I just put some on."

"That was two hours ago." Jessica chucks the bottle of suntan lotion at me.

"You should put more on," Whitney agrees. "You don't want a sunburn at your party tomorrow night."

I sigh, but do as I'm told.

The girls are right. My fair skin, blue eyes and blonde hair are not made for a day in the sun. We set up camp at 11 a.m. on the roof of the building and haven't moved since. A pitcher of lemonade, a pile of magazines, and a package of Oreos seal the deal.

Whitney flips the page of a *Cosmopolitan* magazine. "What time will James be home?"

I lather on a pound of sunscreen. Better safe than sorry. "Around five."

Jessica smiles. She looks adorable in her red bikini and white sunglasses. "I'm sure you're excited to have him back."

That's an understatement. "Text messages and Facetime are okay, but it's not the same."

"What will you do when he's Pack Leader?" Whitney asks, her aviators tilting down her nose so I can see her emerald green eyes.

I hesitate. "We haven't figured that out yet."

"You have time," Jessica assures me.

In the five months since we defeated Julian and the rogue wolves, James and I have struggled to figure out the logistics of our relationship. He spends the bulk of his time with me in New York City, but he goes home for a week every month. Those seven days are miserable.

I read and train as much as possible to distract myself while he's gone, and my new duties as the Verhena-in-training keep me busy. But sleeping alone in my bed stinks. What's worse, I have no idea how James and I will handle the inevitable separation our leadership roles will bring.

Whitney breaks my train of thought when she announces, "I'm going home after your party."

I raise an eyebrow. "Are you really going this time?"

Jessica snickers.

Whitney feigns shock. "Why Chloe, whatever do you mean?"

She knows exactly what I mean. Whitney has gone back and forth about her future for months. Ivan pushed hard for her to return home, but she decided to stay in New York City. She applied to a few fashion design schools and got into two of them, but she hasn't committed to either one.

"What about school?" Jessica asks.

"Oh, I'm coming back."

"So just a visit then?"

"Yes." Whitney frowns. "I'm breaking up with Brandon and I want to do it in person."

I can't help it, I slap my forehead with the heel of my hand. The Brandon rollercoaster continues. "I thought you were giving it another shot?"

Whitney purses her lips. "We were. He did pretty well for a few days, but now it's back to the same old stuff. Not calling or texting me, disappearing on adventures with his friends. How can I ever have kids with him?"

I almost spit out my lemonade. "Kids? You're already thinking about kids?"

Whitney shrugs her shoulders. "I want kids. Don't you?"

"I do," Jessica responds. "I want three or four."

"Three or four?" I ask shocked.

"Yep. I'm an only child and I always wanted a brother or sister."

I sit back in my lounge chair. I don't know if I want kids or not. I haven't spent much time thinking about it. When we were young, Chelsea was the one into baby dolls. She loved feeding them with plastic bottles and changing their little diapers.

Not me. I was much happier throwing them into the air to see if I could bounce them off the ceiling.

"Does James want kids?" Jessica asks.

"I have no idea," I answer honestly.

Whitney smiles. "He does, he told me."

I gulp. "He does?"

"Yes. He hopes we live close so our kids are friends, not just cousins."

My stomach sinks. James wants kids?

How many?

And more importantly, how soon?

God love her, Jessica changes the subject. "You psyched for tomorrow night?"

I grin. "I can't wait!"

Tomorrow is my 21st birthday. It's hard to believe it's been a year since my Branding Day. My whole world has changed in those twelve months.

To celebrate, Willa is throwing me a huge party. She reserved a hotel ballroom to accommodate the estimated five hundred guests who are attending. Including my parents and my former coven leader Samantha, I will know ten of those people. High ranking coven members and Willa's friends will fill the rest of the seats.

"Is everything ready?" Whitney asks as she grabs another Oreo. She twists the cookies apart and licks the cream from the middle.

"Everything but my speech."

"You have to give a speech? About what?"

I roll onto my stomach. "Willa wants me to tell the story of the rogue wolves firsthand, then tell the crowd a little about myself."

I doubt people are coming to my party to listen to me talk. I'm pretty sure they're coming for the free food and booze. But what Willa wants, Willa gets.

"It's going to be a supernatural shindig," Jessica says with a smile.

"Yeah, especially now that the vampires are coming."

Whitney sits up, her face pale. "What?"

Poor Whitney. Still the last to know everything. "Willa invited two of her vampire friends, and they RSVP'd last week. I've been reading about them ever since."

"I thought they stayed in Europe."

"They usually do, but Willa and these vampires go way back."

Whitney is not comforted by Willa's stamp of approval. "How many are coming?"

"Two."

Unlike Whitney, Jessica's eyes glisten at the idea of our vampire guests. "You know what's crazy? They'll look exactly the same as they did when Willa met them sixty years ago."

Before I can say that Willa was my age when she met Baxter and Elias, Whitney interjects.

"Tell me everything you know about them," she says panicked.

I frown. My friend is genuinely concerned, not that I blame her. Before my research in the library, I knew little to nothing about vampires. They seldom visit the U.S., and my coven rarely spoke about them.

"Whitney, it's okay," I assure her. "I was nervous too, but they aren't a threat. If they were, they wouldn't be invited to my party."

Whitney hugs her knees to her chest. "I don't like it. Maybe I should stay somewhere else."

"You're safer here than anywhere else," Jessica reasons.

"She's right Whit. And besides, most vampires don't drink human blood anymore."

"They don't?"

"Nope. They eat raw animal meat and organs."

Whitney crinkles her nose. "Eww."

Undeterred by the vampire diet, Jessica asks, "Is it true they avoid sunlight?"

I shake my head. "No, they are perfectly fine in the sun. They're great at blending in and adapting to their environment. You won't be able to spot them in the crowd tomorrow night."

"What about immortality? Do they really live forever?"

I consider Jessica's question. "They're not technically alive."

"What do you mean?"

"It's hard to explain," I pause. "Witches and werewolves are human. Our bodies operate almost identically to the average person's. We just have abilities above and beyond it. But vampires are different. They aren't living beings, they are dead."

Whitney shivers. "If they're dead, then how are they walking around?"

5

I wiggle my fingers at her. "The same way I can shoot fire from my fingertips. Some things aren't explainable Whit."

"Yeah, I guess you're right," she concedes.

I'm about to change the subject, but Jessica continues her line of questioning.

"Do they sleep?"

"They rest, but they don't actually sleep. Their senses are stronger than ours. It prevents their minds from turning off."

"Super senses, huh?" Jessica says as she scans the city skyline. "Interesting."

"Sight, smell and hearing. Not sure about taste, but they aren't eating much anyway."

"Yeah, just blood," Whitney chimes in.

Ignoring her, I continue. "They're also superfast. Most video cameras can't capture their movements."

Whitney groans. "Great…"

"Whitney!" Jessica protests. "You're awfully judgmental for a werewolf. People say all kinds of bad things about werewolves, and most of it isn't true."

Whitney frowns. "You're right." She grabs another Oreo. "But I'm sleeping in a turtleneck while the vampires are in town."

Jessica and I both laugh.

I check my cellphone.

"Well ladies, it's time for me to head downstairs." I stand and grab my towel. "I need a shower before James gets back. I smell like sweat and sunscreen."

"What time is it?" Jessica asks.

"4:15 p.m."

"Shoot!" She jumps up and gathers her things. "I need to get a move on. The tailor closes at five and I have to pick up your dress for the party."

6

Whitney stretches on her chaise lounge. "I'm going to lay here a while longer."

Of all of us, Whitney needs the least amount of sun. Her golden brown skin gleams in the sunlight. She is already tanner than I will ever be in my life.

Jessica and I leave Whitney to her sunbathing and head inside.

"I feel bad she's so upset about the vampires," Jessica says as we hit the stairs.

"They won't be here long. She probably won't even talk to them."

Jessica smiles. "I think it's kinda cool. All these storybook monsters coming to life."

"Hey! I'm not a monster!"

She giggles. "I don't mean you! I meant werewolves and vampires."

"Were you scared when you found out they're real?"

"No, not really. Mom told me about them when we moved into the building. Were you?"

"A little," I admit. "Our coven made the werewolves sound like awful people. They were our sworn enemies for so long."

"I never heard bad things about them growing up here. Ivan was nice to me when he came to visit, and Willa says nothing but good things about the vampires."

"It's too bad you haven't met the vampires yet. You could give me the inside scoop."

Jessica laughs. "If Willa trusts them, I trust them."

"Right, but Willa thinks everyone is great."

"True."

Jessica and I say good-bye outside the door for my floor. It's still a bit bizarre to say I have an entire floor to myself, but I'm getting used to it. It feels more like home. Jessica and I filled one of the empty rooms with office furniture and equipment. We haven't had the chance to decorate or paint in there because we've been too busy, but it's a start.

I also turned one of the empty rooms into a guest space for my mom and dad. They've been to the building twice now and I'm hoping they come to see me more often.

I walk into my suite and frown. It's a bomb-hit-it. I could blame its messy state on the long hours in the library and the new duties Willa gave me, but in reality, I'm just lazy.

I run around and clean before James gets here. He doesn't need to know what a slob I am. Once all my laundry is picked up, I grab a drink from the new mini-fridge in my room. It's not a major addition, but it's definitely convenient. I don't have to go all the way down to the kitchen when I need something to nosh on.

I step into the shower and relax as the water runs down my skin. Nothing quite like a nice, hot shower.

I'm about to turn off the water when strong hands grab me from behind. Panic washes over me until I realize I know these hands. I know these hands very well.

I smile and lean back into my intruder's arms. "You're home early."

James kisses the back of my head. "By a few minutes. Couldn't wait to see you."

I turn around in his arms, lift up on my toes, and plant my mouth on his. It's been too long since I felt his lips against mine. It's simultaneously comforting and exciting. I run my hands down his t-shirt....

Wait? His t-shirt?

I step back and laugh. James is fully clothed. Shoes and all.

He smiles. "I told you I couldn't wait to see you."

The water soaked his clothes. His blue shirt clings to his skin and shows off his well-defined torso.

8

"No clothes allowed in here," I tease.

James pulls his t-shirt over his head and throws it into the tub. He kicks his sneakers out of the shower, then puts his hand on the wall for balance as he takes off his pants.

He smirks when he's done. "Better?"

I lean into his body. "Much."

Jessica

I have forty-five minutes to get to the tailor before the shop closes. I should have left sooner, but I was having too much fun sunbathing with Chloe and Whitney.

The three of us don't have much time to hang out these days. I thought Chloe's schedule would open up once she defeated the rogue wolves, but the opposite happened. Willa is stepping back and putting more on Chloe's plate, and in the process, mine as well. We are getting a taste of what it will be like when Willa officially retires.

Chloe is constantly on the phone or returning emails about coven issues. She's also working with Frank to create and implement updated policies for the Guard and the witch community at large.

In the meantime, I run around the office like a maniac setting up meetings, making sure we have plenty of supplies, and juggling the calls Chloe doesn't have time for. I'm on full speed from the time I get up until we shut off the office lights.

It's hectic, but I'm thankful for it. Before Chloe came, I was bored. Now my days are full and they go by quickly.

There are times I question Willa piling so much on Chloe. Chloe is still training every day and improving her magic. I'm worried about her daily stress levels, but I keep my concerns to myself. Chloe would just tell me she's perfectly fine, and who am I to question Willa? She is the Verhena, and I'm not even a witch.

Despite her workload, Chloe's power has increased exponentially. Her tattoo was blinding on the roof today, its gold feathers shooting off beams of light when hit by the sun. She is already as powerful as Willa, if not more so. When I sit in on her training sessions, my jaw hits the floor.

What's truly amazing is Chloe's attitude hasn't changed since the day she got here. She isn't affected by her power. If anything, she's oblivious to it. She's grown up a lot, but she still has that loveable innocence I saw the first day we met. Working for Chloe is like helping a friend. The fact that I get paid to do it is an added bonus.

I change out of my bathing suit and into a pair of cutoff shorts, a purple tank top and a pair of black flip-flops. I do what I can to fix my pixie cut and grab my purse. I need a shower, but I don't have the time. It will have to wait until I get back.

I push the down button for the elevator and run my to-do list through my head. First stop, the tailor. Depending on how heavy Chloe's dress is, I may be able to run into the office supply store to buy binder clips. I just bought a pack of fifty last month, but we're already out. Where they go, I have no idea.

The elevator bings and the doors open. I'm about to rush in, but stop when I see Frank standing inside. My stomach drops. He looks up from a stack of documents and does a double take. We stare at each other a moment, neither knowing what to say. The spell is broken as the elevator doors start to close.

Frank extends his hand and pushes the doors back. "Going down?"

I nod.

Frank steps to the side and I walk past him, taking a spot in the back corner. We are silent as the elevator begins its descent. I knew I'd have to see Frank again, but I didn't expect it to be this quickly. Or in a confined space.

"Where are you heading?" Frank asks without looking at me.

"The tailor. Picking up Chloe's dress for tomorrow night."

"Ah."

I can't come up with anything to say. Instead, I play with the zipper on my purse like it's the most fascinating thing I've ever seen in my life.

"Your mom make it to the airport on time?"

I smile. Mom left early this morning for a three-week vacation. She ran around like a mad woman before she left, worried she would miss her flight.

"She did."

Then we're silent again. Could we at least get some elevator music in here? After what seems like an eternity, the elevator opens to the lobby and we both step out.

"See you later," I say as I make a break for the front door.

"Jess, wait."

Dang it!

I glance over at the receptionist's desk. A Guard member is sitting sentry, but we're not close enough for him to hear our conversation.

"Frank, not to be rude, but I really need to get to the tailor. She closes at five."

Frank checks his watch. "One minute. Please?"

I give in. "Okay."

Frank's face is solemn. He's wearing his usual outfit of khakis and a polo shirt – blue today. He balances his stack of documents on one arm as he runs his other hand through his short, military-style haircut.

"About last night," he starts to say.

I put my hand up. "We don't have to do this."

"Yes we do," he insists.

"No we don't. What else is there to say? You're dedicated to your job and don't want to pursue this any further."

11

He frowns. "I feel awful. I want you to know that."

"I wish you felt differently, but you don't." I fight back tears. "So stop twisting the knife, okay?"

He nods. "Okay."

I turn away from him. He walks over to the receptionist's desk and I head out the front door. I breathe a sigh of relief as I step outside the building. I've done it. I saw him, I talked to him, and I didn't cry. It will only get easier from here.

At least that's what I'm telling myself.

As I weave through the city crowd, I can't help but think back to a few months ago when Frank asked me out on a date. During a sleepover party with Chloe and Whitney, everyone in the Guard Operations Center heard me say I have a crush on Frank. The men up there gossip more than your average high school girl and told Frank about it right away. After the rogue wolves were taken care of, he summoned up the gumption to ask me out.

I smile as I remember his awkward invite. He shifted his weight back and forth, not looking me in the eyes. "I was, um, wondering if, um, you'd like to go out sometime."

Of course I said yes.

Our dates were a secret from Chloe. I wanted to tell her, but Frank asked that we keep it between us. He didn't want Chloe to think he was slacking off. I thought this was a bogus reason at first, but I quickly learned work means everything to Frank.

We had plenty of opportunities to sneak out without Chloe noticing. We waited until she and James went up to her suite for the night, then we'd make our escape. It's a miracle the other Guard members never clued her in. Frank must have paid them off, or threatened them with death.

Despite his tough exterior, Frank is fun when he's off the clock. We went to the movies several times and held hands in the dark theater. My favorite thing we did was walk around Central Park getting to know each other. He made me laugh out loud several times and it felt good to be with him.

Things were heating up. I thought we were heading toward something serious. Until last night, when he abruptly ended it.

I stop my memories there. I watch the crossing signal at an intersection and glance around at the people standing next to me. Typical New Yorkers - an eclectic mix of business suits, summer dresses and workout clothes. The summer heat and humidity make everyone a bit more irritable than normal, but I love it. I despise bundling up in the winter.

"We can't do this anymore Jess." Frank's words ring in my ears despite my efforts to forget them, and the awful scene replays in my mind.

We were locked in a kiss on the sidewalk, just outside the range of the building's cameras, when he pulled back.

"What? Why?" I asked surprised.

Frank put his hands in his pockets. "It's too much for me."

I didn't know what to say, the carpet pulled out from underneath me. "I thought things were going so well," I finally stammered.

"They are. That's the problem."

I shook my head, trying to clear the confusion.

"Jess, please understand. I like you a lot. You're a great girl."

"You're a great girl" is not what women want to hear when they are being dumped.

"Yeah, right." I started walking back to the building, but Frank grabbed my arm gently.

"Seriously Jess, I like you a lot. I just can't right now."

"Is it because of Chloe?" I asked, venom in my voice.

It was wrong of me to bring Chloe into it. I know there is nothing going on between her and Frank. Chloe is with James. Period. End of Story. And from everything I've seen, Frank and Chloe are like brother and sister.

But I wanted to take a jab at him, I wanted to piss him off.

Frank stepped back, annoyance on his face. "No, it's not about Chloe. It's about me and my job. And how dedicated I am to it."

I swallowed my pride, apologized for my Chloe comment and told Frank I understood.

"I'm really sorry Jessica. I wish I was the right man for you."

"It's okay," I managed to say. "I appreciate your honesty."

I wanted to ask why he bothered going out with me in the first place. Why start something when you know you can't commit to it? But I didn't ask. Why prolong the agony?

Instead, I turned and walked away. I wasn't ready to go inside the building, so I walked around the block instead. Warm tears slid down my cheeks.

Let it out now, I told myself. You can't let anyone see.

Frank was gone by the time I came back. I squared my shoulders and walked in the building like I hadn't just had my heart ripped out.

I shake the cobwebs from my mind as I approach the tailor's shop. I check my watch – ten minutes to spare. Bells chime as I walk in. It's a small shop that once housed a dry cleaning business. The dry cleaner's lobby is still intact, white tile flooring and a large counter cutting off the front of the shop from the area in the back. The overhead racks, once filled with the clothes of working New Yorkers, are now empty.

"Hello?" I call out.

A surly woman I recognize as the tailor who poked and prodded Chloe with pins emerges from the back.

"Hi Jane," I say with a warm smile, hoping to make up for my tardiness. No one likes a customer coming in ten minutes before closing time on a Friday afternoon.

Jane grunts in response. She's around my mom's age with steel blue eyes and curly blonde hair that's in need of a touchup around her roots. Her black tank top says, "Not today" in white letters and her jeans are torn at the knees. What Jane lacks in bedside manner she makes up for tenfold with her sewing skills.

She grabs a garment bag from a rolling rack near the register and hands it over the counter to me. "Here you go. They're both in there."

"Both?" I say before Jane can walk away. "Chloe was only measured for one dress."

"Right, but then an older woman dropped off a dress the next day and asked me to alter it according to Chloe's measurements."

I'm confused. "Really? Who?"

Jane shrugs her shoulders. "Beats me. She paid upfront, so I did the job." Jane opens the trap door in the counter and walks through to the lobby area. She turns her "Open" sign to "Closed" and looks at me meaningfully.

I take the hint and say "thank you" before hightailing it out the door. I jaywalk across the street, dodging a cab along the way. I'm curious about the second dress, but I don't peek. Mostly because I need two hands to carry the garment bag.

The only person who could have dropped off a second dress is Willa. Why didn't she say something?

I smile. Willa and her surprises.

Chapter Two

Chloe

I'm snuggling with James on the couch when there's a knock on my suite door.

I pause our TV show. "Come in!"

Jessica walks in holding a giant garment bag. James jumps up to grab it from her.

"Thank you," she says with a breathless smile, "that was getting heavy."

James lays the garment bag on the bed. "What's in there? Bricks?"

Jessica laughs. "Sure felt like it."

James leans down to give me a kiss. "I'll be in the library."

I smile. "Okay."

"You ready to try your dress on?" Jess asks before unzipping the garment bag.

"Absolutely! I hope it still fits."

Jessica rolls her eyes. "Whatever."

I take off my yoga pants and t-shirt while Jess pulls out my dress. To avoid wrinkles, she stands on my bed and lowers it over my head. She hops down, adjusts the dress, and then zips the back.

I let out a sigh of relief. It fits! I walk over to the full-length mirror and check myself out.

"You look beautiful!" Jess gushes from behind me. "The dress fits like a glove."

I'm not having the same reaction as Jessica. Something feels off. I examine my reflection closely. I adore the material – sea green satin with a hint of sparkle that will shine under the ballroom lights.

It's not the fit – like Jess said, it fits like a glove. I turn around and look over my shoulder. My hawk tattoo is framed perfectly by the scooped back.

What is it? Why don't I love it?

And then it hits me.

"This won't work Jess."

She gapes at my reflection. "What are you talking about? You look great!"

My blonde hair and ice blue eyes paired with the sea green dress make me feel like a certain Disney princess.

"I look like Elsa from *Frozen*."

"No you don't!"

"Oh yeah?" I take a deep breath, belt out my favorite lyrics from "Let it Go" and shoot icicles from my fingertips.

Jessica cracks up. "Okay, I see it now."

I flop down on my bed. "What am I going to do? It's too late to get a new dress."

"No one will think you look like Princess Elsa. I didn't notice it until you pointed it out."

Another knock sounds on my door. "Chloe! It's Whitney!"

I yell "Come in" and Whitney whirls in.

"Ohhh, you're in your dress! Stand up! Let me see!"

Jessica and I exchange a glance. I do a 360 degree turn for Whitney.

"It's so pretty!" Whitney walks over and examines the seams. "The tailor did a fantastic job."

"Do I remind you of anyone?"

Whitney steps back and stares at me for a moment. "No, I don't think so."

Without saying anything, I produce ice from my fingertips again.

Confusion crosses Whitney's face, then understanding flickers in her eyes. "Oh…ohhhh…"

I nod. "Exactly."

I stand in front of the mirror again. The dress is beautiful, but I can't unsee Elsa. I sigh.

"Let me grab my laptop," Whitney suggests, "we can have a dress overnighted."

"Even if we find something Whit, there's no time to have it tailored."

Whitney frowns. "Right."

Jessica's eyes light up. "There may be another option."

"What do you mean?" I turn around to see Jessica taking another dress from the garment bag.

"What is that?" Whitney asks.

Jessica shrugs. "I don't know. The tailor said an older woman dropped off a second dress. They used Chloe's measurements from the first dress to alter this one."

"An older woman?" I ask. "Ah…Willa."

She nods. "Has to be, right?"

Jessica pulls the second dress out of the garment bag and we all gasp. It's gorgeous. The floor-length gown is made of intricate golden beads and sequence. It is sleeveless and fastens around the neck.

I unzip myself from the Elsa dress and step into the new one. A short zipper in the back stops just under my rib cage, leaving my tattoo exposed. The dress flows down from my hips and has a small train. The gold in the dress matches the gold in my hawk tattoo perfectly.

"Wow," is all I can manage to say as the three of us huddle in front of the mirror.

Jessica smiles. "Go Willa!"

"It's perfect!" Whitney claps her hands, giddy. She stops her celebration. "I almost forgot! I'll be right back!" she says before running out of my room.

"What is that about?"

Jessica looks as confused as I do. "No idea."

I return my attention to the mirror. "How should I wear my hair?"

Jessica twists my hair in her hand and holds it against the back of my head. "A French twist will look amazing."

"Agreed. Makeup?"

"I don't think you need anything more than some mascara and lip gloss. You have a nice tan from laying out."

"It's a miracle I got any color at all with the layer of suntan lotion you made me wear."

Jessica smiles. "See? You got a tan *and* you were safe."

I'm out of the dress and putting on my yoga pants and t-shirt when Whitney comes back into the room.

She hands me a small, white box. "I can't believe I forgot to bring this with me!"

I examine the box. "What is it?"

"Your birthday gift."

"Really?"

Whitney nods. "It's from me and Jessica."

I glance over at Jess and she smiles. I open the box and inhale sharply. "Oh my gosh…"

Sitting on top of white tissue paper is a beautiful hawk made of crystals and gold. Jessica picks up the hawk and turns it over. On the backside is a small golden band.

"It's a ring," she explains.

I hold out my hand and Jessica slides the golden band onto my middle finger. The hawk is two inches long and its wings stretch from my pointer finger to my ring finger.

I'm speechless. "It's perfect. Just perfect." Tears well in my eyes. I pull Whitney and Jess in for a hug.

"Thank you so much. I love it."

"We didn't know what to get you," Whitney says when we break apart. "After we went shopping for your dress, we realized you need accessories. Jessica came up with the idea for a hawk ring and I drew it. We found a jeweler to custom make it for you."

I admire the ring again. "It's beautiful you guys."

"It will look great with your new dress," Jess points out.

"I need to thank Willa. She really came through for me."

Jessica and Whitney head for their rooms and I take the steps to Willa's floor. Despite the late hour, I find her sitting in her office. She has a stack of documents in front of her.

I knock on the door lightly to get her attention. "Willa?"

She looks up and smiles. "Chloe! This is a nice surprise."

"I'm not interrupting anything, am I?'

"Heavens no. I'm reading the status reports from the Massachusetts covens. I could use a break."

I take a seat on the white leather couch across from her desk. "Anything exciting?"

Willa's smile falters. "Exciting, no. Worrisome, yes."

"Uh oh."

Willa sighs. "The Boston coven is notorious for being testy, but this is the worst I've ever seen them."

"They're *still* fighting?"

"Sadly, yes."

The Boston coven has been sketchy since the day I got here. They elected a new Coven Leader, but quickly learned she isn't what they expected. Half of the coven is for her, and the other half wants her to step down.

Willa's attempts to stay out of it are failing. She hoped the coven members would resolve their issues on their own, but it's not looking good. We continue to receive emails and calls from concerned coven members detailing their new leader's transgressions.

"This isn't going away on its own, is it?" I ask.

"Doesn't look like it."

"What are you going to do?"

Willa smirks. "You mean, what are *we* going to do?"

Willa is doing this a lot lately - asking for my opinion about how matters should be handled. Most of the time I have no idea. Battles I can handle. Diplomacy, not so much.

Willa sits patiently as she awaits a response.

"We should meet with the coven in person," I answer finally.

Willa nods. "I agree. You'll go next week."

My jaw drops. "Me? You want me to go to Boston?"

"Yes. You," Willa confirms.

I hesitate. "Willa, I'm not sure that's a good idea. I have no clue what I'm doing."

Willa leans over her desk. "Let me tell you a secret Chloe," she lowers her voice to a whisper, "neither do I."

"Yes you do! You're great at this. You have an answer for everything."

Willa laughs. "What is it the kids say these days?" She taps her fingers on her desk. "Oh yes - you have to fake it to make it."

I raise my eyebrow.

"All you can do," Willa continues, "is make the decision that feels right to you. It's not always easy. In fact, most of the time it's really hard. But you have to project knowledge and confidence at all times. People depend on you when they are in trouble or in need. They have to believe in you."

I sigh. "Okay, fine. I'll go to Boston."

"Excellent!"

"You sure you don't want to go with me?" I ask hopefully.

"I'm sure."

"Keep your phone handy - just in case."

Willa smiles. "Understood. Now, is there something you want to talk to me about?"

The dress! I forgot all about it.

"Willa, the dress you gave me is amazing. It fits perfectly."

Her face lights up. "Figured me out, huh? Do you like it?"

"Like it? I love it!

"I'm so glad. I hope you don't mind my dropping it off at the tailor."

"Not at all! In fact, I'm wearing it tomorrow night."

Willa beams. "You'll look fantastic, I'm sure of it."

"Where did you find it?"

"In my closet."

"Your closet?" I ask confused.

"It's mine. I wore it to my coronation ceremony."

My mouth falls open. "You did?"

Willa laughs. "Seems impossible now, but yes, I did. I loved that dress. I felt so powerful in it. It was the first time I felt like I could handle this job."

"Willa, that dress is too important to you. I can't wear it."

"Nonsense. It's hung in my closet for almost sixty years. Plus, it's tailored to your body now," she reasons. "All the spanx in the world won't get me into that dress."

I giggle. "Do you have any pictures of your coronation?"

"Not handy, but I'm sure they're floating around somewhere."

"How old were you when you took the oath?"

"Twenty-six."

Yikes. That's only five years older than me. Will I be ready at that age?

I shake my nerves and focus on the now. "The dress is awesome. I can't wait to wear it. I'll give it back after I have it cleaned."

"Keep the dress," Willa says, "I want you to have it."

I walk around Willa's desk and give her a hug. "Thank you so much."

"You're welcome sweetheart. Make good memories in it."

"Wake up birthday girl," James whispers into my ear.

I smile and open my eyes. Today is the big day. James is standing next to the bed holding a silver tray. I stretch and sit up.

"What is this?"

"I brought your favorite – blueberry pancakes." He rests the tray on my lap. "I hope you're hungry."

In addition to blueberry pancakes, my plate is filled with hash browns and strawberries. There's also a glass of orange juice to wash it all down. Much better than my usual oatmeal, yogurt and banana.

"Looks yummy." I inhale deeply. "Smells yummy too." I lean over and give James a kiss. "Thanks babe! This is so sweet."

He smiles. "You have to thank Jessica too. She made everything, I'm just the delivery guy."

"Want any?" I ask as I pour maple syrup on my pancakes.

"No, I'm good."

"How long have you been up? I didn't hear you get out of bed this morning."

"I snuck out an hour ago. I ate breakfast with Jessica and Willa. Willa is nervous about tonight."

"She is? Why?"

"She's afraid something major will go wrong."

I finish chewing a bite of hash browns. "Not gonna happen. Jessica and I have triple-checked everything. All we have to do is show up."

"How about you? Nervous?"

"A little," I admit. "I haven't done a lot of public speaking. I took a speech class in high school, but I didn't take it seriously."

James raises an eyebrow. "You? Not take something seriously?"

I chuck a piece of pancake at him. He picks it off his shirt and wings it back at me. We both laugh when it sticks in my hair. Just as I'm about to launch a spoonful of hash browns his way, my bedside phone rings.

James leans over and picks it up. "Yes?" After a few seconds, he nods and says, "We'll be there in fifteen minutes."

"We'll be where?" I mumble, blueberry pancake crammed in my mouth.

He laughs. "That's hot." Then he makes a face. "Don't kill the messenger, but you don't get birthdays off."

"What?"

"Frank wants us in the training center in fifteen minutes."

"No way! Why?"

25

James shrugs his shoulders. "Don't know. He said it's important."

I groan. I move the tray off my lap and put it on the bed. "He thinks everything is important."

"True."

I grumble as I search my closet for workout clothes. Can't Frank let me have one day of peace? It's my freaking birthday! I reluctantly put on yoga pants, a sports bra and a tank top.

Before leaving the room, I grab a pancake off the top of the stack and cover it in hash browns. I roll it up, dip it in maple syrup and take a huge bite.

James snickers.

"What? I can't waste pancakes!" I say before I bite off another huge chunk of my homemade breakfast wrap.

I immediately regret all the food I ate when I walk into the gym. Working out on a full stomach is never a good idea and it doesn't look like Frank plans to take it easy on me. There are three dummies set up on one end of the gym, small circular targets drawn around the areas where their hearts should be. Frank walks over and drops a bag at my feet.

"What's this?"

He grins. "Vampire training."

I roll my eyes. "Seriously? We have to do this today?"

Frank opens the bag and pulls out wooden stakes. "Two vampires are coming to your party tonight. Don't you want to be prepared?"

I grab one of the stakes and roll it in my hand. It's a smooth, light colored wood with one end carved into a sharp point.

"Where did you get these?"

"Stakes R Us."

I stare back at Frank unamused.

He clears his throat. "We made them."

"Is this really the only way to kill a vampire?"

"Yes," Frank and James answer simultaneously.

"Why do you think that is?"

Frank puts his hands on his hips. "Stop delaying the inevitable."

Dammit. He's on to me.

I ask another question anyway. "Willa says the vampires are our friends. Why the combat training?"

"Better safe than sorry," he reasons. "The last time Willa saw these two, you weren't born yet. A lot can change in twenty-five years."

I can't argue with Frank's logic, even if he's making me train on my birthday. "What do you want me to do? Throw these at the targets?"

"Try throwing a few naturally, no magic," Frank instructs.

"Who needs magic?" I ask, flipping my stake in the air like a baton. I catch it behind my back, but Frank and James aren't impressed.

Tough crowd.

I step away from the guys and face the dummies. I was never a baseball or softball player, so I'm skeptical of my ability to hit the targets without magic. I hold the stake like a javelin and hear Frank laugh behind me.

I drop my stance. "What?"

"Hold it like this."

Frank walks over and takes the stake from my hand. He grabs the smooth end and holds it by his side with the sharp point facing the floor. Before I can ask him why he chose this position, he swiftly brings the stake over his head, then flings it like he's throwing an axe. The stake sails across the room, spinning end-over-end until the point hits the middle dummy in the stomach.

I nod with approval. "Not bad."

Frank stands tall, proud of himself. "Okay, you try."

I do my best to copy Frank's throwing technique, but my stake sails between the dummies, hits the wall, and clatters to the floor.

I shrug my shoulders. "Well, that was fun." I start to turn away, but no such luck.

James crosses his arms over his chest, all business. "Again."

Despite being my boyfriend, James doesn't go easy on me in the gym. He has my best interest at heart, but sometimes after a brutal training session I'd rather punch him than cuddle.

All couples who work together have those moments. It's a difficult rope to walk. You want your partner to push you and bring out your best, but their criticism is the hardest to take.

After several attempts, the best I can do is hit one of the dummies in the leg.

"Alright," Frank says after my tenth try, "do it with magic this time."

"If I hit a target, can I go? My arm is tired."

"When you hit all three targets, you can go."

"Promise?"

"Promise."

I grab three stakes and bundle them in my right hand. I get in my starting position and raise all three stakes over my head at the same time. I bring my right arm down as hard as I can and release the stakes with a grunt.

As the stakes travel toward the targets, I use one of my summoning spells to gain control over them. Once they are at my command, I easily send each one toward its own dummy. The stakes strike with enough force to slice all the way through and slam into the back wall. Their paths create three perfect, circular holes through the targets.

I turn to Frank. "Am I good to go now?"

He blinks his eyes a few times as he stares at my handiwork. "Yep. You're good."

"Can you help me with this?" I call out to James.

I'm standing in my closet getting ready for the party. I'm almost done, but I can't reach the clasps at the top of my dress.

James struts in the closet looking like James Bond in his fancy black tux. Seeing my struggles, he walks up behind me and hooks the clasps together. He leans down and kisses the back of my neck, fully exposed after Jessica put it up in a French twist.

"You are stunning," he whispers in my ear.

I giggle, his breath tickling my skin. "Thanks. You don't look so bad yourself."

We embrace, enjoying this moment of peace before our hectic night. James pulls away when my bedside phone rings.

"I'll get it," he tells me before giving me one last kiss on my cheek.

The only thing left to do is put on my heels. Whitney found them at a shop down the street this afternoon. They're an inch taller than I'd like, but the metallic gold straps match my dress perfectly.

I balance on one foot, then the other, as I put the heels on. I hear James hang up the phone. "Who was it?"

"Frank. The cars are ready."

I take one last look at myself in the mirror. The dress is gorgeous. My hair and makeup are flawless. Who is this woman? I hardly recognize her. Gone is the rebellious teenager looking for a good time, replaced by a young woman forced to grow up overnight.

I think back to my last birthday. At exactly this moment three hundred and sixty-five days ago, I was hiding under a quilt tent in my bedroom with Chelsea. I smile when I think of her attempts to console me. My heart yearns for her now. It's my first birthday without her.

"You ready?"

James's question interrupts my introspection. "Uh, yeah. I think so." I smile, remembering that this night is for celebration. "How about you? Are you ready?"

"Almost. One last thing to do."

I glance his way. "What's left to do?"

He takes a small jewelry box out of his pocket. "Give you this."

My stomach drops. It's a ring box. Oh God...he's going to propose!

But instead of getting on one knee, James steps in closer and opens the box. Relief floods my veins when I see a sparkly pair of diamond earrings.

"They're beautiful!" I hope my voice sounds grateful as opposed to relieved.

"They were my grandmother's. Whitney told me about the ring she and Jessica gave you, and I knew these would match."

I remove the gold hoops I have in, and replace them with the diamond post earrings. I turn to the mirror on my vanity. "I love them. Thank you."

James smiles at my reflection. "Good."

I grab the faux fur wrap Jessica let me borrow for the night and cover my shoulders. "We better go before Frank has a coronary."

As we wait for the elevator, anticipation sets in. I'm tingling with excitement. This will be my first time in front of a crowd of high ranking witches and other supernatural beings. The first time they look at me as their future leader. It's scary and thrilling at the same time.

James takes my hand. "You're going to be wonderful."

I smile at him. "Thank you."

A group of Guard members is waiting for us in the lobby. They're all dressed in black suits and matching black ties. Frank stands at the edge of the group and steps forward.

"We're using our usual caravan," he explains as we head for the exit. "Two Escalades in front, and two Escalades in back. Willa, Ivan and Jessica are already at the venue. Whitney will ride with us." Frank turns to the group. "Let's roll."

As the Guard members disperse, Whitney becomes visible in the crowd.

She walks over and pulls me in for a hug. "You look fabulous!"

"So do you!"

Whitney is wearing a tight, full-length maroon dress. Its design is simple and sleek. The color of her dress plays beautifully off her tan skin. Her dark hair flows elegantly behind her.

She beams. "I found this on the clearance rack at Saks! It was only four hundred dollars!"

James and I exchange a glance.

"*Only* four hundred dollars," I whisper to James on the way to the car.

"What can I say? My grandfather spoils her rotten."

Note to self: make Whitney volunteer at a soup kitchen.

A few minutes later, we're seated in the Escalade and driving toward the venue. The butterflies in my stomach are going wild. I practice my speech in my head for the hundredth time today. I already regret not bringing notecards.

"When we get there," Frank says, "James and Whitney will proceed into the ballroom and take their seats. You and I will stay behind until Willa announces you to the crowd."

"I have to walk in by myself?" Oy, I don't like the sound of this.

"Yes. Willa wants all eyes on you."

Great. I start silently praying I won't trip as I walk into the ballroom. How embarrassing would that be? When we arrive at the hotel, I tense up. James gives my hand another squeeze.

"Hey," he whispers.

I look over at him.

"It's going to be okay."

"Easy for you to say," I mumble.

Somehow he knows my biggest fear. "If you fall, I'll tell everyone you did it on purpose."

"Gee, thanks."

"No problem." I stick my tongue out at him and he laughs. "You're not going to fall."

"Have you seen these heels?"

James extends his hand to help me out of the car. The Guard stopped all pedestrian traffic to allow us to get into the building. I walk to the hotel entrance as quickly as I can. I don't want to hold them up for too long. Willa and Jessica scouted the location, wanting it to be a surprise for me. It takes my breath away when I walk inside.

I marvel at the spectacular lobby. "Wow," I say with a smile.

The intricate woodworking and gold-leaf paint are awe inspiring. A massive crystal chandelier hangs from the ceiling and the traditional staircase with white marble steps and golden banisters is gorgeous. I must get a picture on those steps before I leave tonight.

The patrons in the lobby watch our entourage walk toward the ballroom. We come to a set of white double doors with gold trim. A sign outside the door announces, "Private Party" in gold script.

We have arrived.

Whitney takes my wrap from me. "Break a leg!"

I grimace. "That's exactly what I'm afraid of."

Whitney chuckles. "You have nothing to worry about. You look beautiful and your speech will be fantastic."

James gives me a quick kiss on the cheek. "You've got this."

I'm glad everyone else is confident.

I catch a glimpse inside the ballroom when James and Whitney walk in. Every seat is taken.

I groan as the door closes. "Why did Willa do this to me Frank? I don't want to walk in by myself."

"Because I told her to," he says with a smile.

I narrow my eyes at him. "You didn't."

"Oh yeah, I told her you looooove being the center of attention."

"I hate you."

He laughs. "Do you honestly think Willa listens to a thing I say?"

I smile. "No, probably not."

"Willa wants you to shine. She wants this night to be special for you."

He's right, but the moment I hear Willa's voice from the other side of the double doors, I panic. She's introducing me to the crowd.

"I can't do this."

I turn to walk away, but Frank grabs my arm. "You can do this. More importantly, you *have* to do this."

I start taking deep breaths. I sound like a woman in a Lamaze class. I've never had a fear of crowds before, but this is different. This is huge.

Frank puts his hands on my shoulders and looks me in the eyes. "You have stared down werewolves. You have relentlessly and fearlessly hunted your enemies. This is nothing."

I calm down a little. I think back to what Willa told me yesterday - I have to fake it to make it. I straighten up and roll my shoulders back. I do my best to exude poise and confidence.

Frank steps back and makes a face. "Why are you doing that?"

"Doing what?" I ask stoically.

"Sticking your chest and neck out like that."

I deflate. "I'm trying to look confident."

"Well, you look like an idiot."

"Thanks a lot! You're really helping me out here!"

He laughs. "I'm messing with you." After a pause he adds, "Seriously though, stop standing like that. You look like an ostrich."

I glare at him. Just as I'm about to tell him to f-off, he pushes a finger to his earpiece.

He nods my way. "It's go time."

He pulls the door open and everyone in the room turns to look at me. I take a deep breath and say one last prayer.

Chapter Three

Jessica

"Everything looks wonderful," Ivan tells Willa as we confirm the ballroom is set up per our specifications.

She nods. "It does. Hopefully the food is as good as it was during our taste testing."

"It will be," I assure her.

Willa's nerves are obvious. She hasn't hosted an event of this size in ten years. "Let's go over the list again."

Ivan puts his hand on her shoulder. "We've been over it three times. Why don't we test the bartender's skills instead?"

Willa smiles. "Point taken. A white wine does sound nice."

The pair walk toward the bar and I scan the room one last time. Fifty tables with ten seats each surround a wooden dance floor, making it the centerpiece of the room. White linens adorn the tables, gold plates and silverware are ready and waiting for tonight's meal. White roses in sparkly, golden vases sit in the center of each table. The atmosphere is classic Willa. Sophisticated and elegant, yet inviting.

I catch glimpses of Chloe here and there – the dance floor, the photo booth, and a chocolate fondue tower. It is her twenty-first birthday, there has to be some fun involved.

As guests arrive, the hotel staff shows them to their seats. I take my own seat and watch everyone walking in. I don't know any of them. In fact, the only people I recognize are the Guard members standing sentry, Willa and Ivan.

The room is nearly full when Ivan and Willa join me at the table.

"Chloe should be here any minute," Willa says as she takes her seat. "Do you think she'll like it?" she asks for the hundredth time.

Ivan and I both say "yes" in unison.

My phone buzzes with a text message from Whitney. "They're here."

A Guard member walks over, leans down and whispers something in Willa's ear.

She stands with a smile. "You are correct my dear. They are here."

A couple minutes later, Whitney and James walk into the ballroom. With the help of a Guard member, Willa ascends the stage steps and stands behind the podium and microphone. Any second now, the Guard will give her the signal that Chloe is ready.

Whitney takes the seat next to mine. "Hey Jess!"

Per her usual, Whitney looks amazing. Whitney is the kind of woman other women love to hate. She is thin, pretty and wealthy. But she is so nice, it's impossible to dislike her.

I self-consciously look at my own outfit and wonder if I'm underdressed. I put on a simple LBD – little black dress – with high-heel booties that stop just over my ankle. I borrowed a diamond tennis bracelet and a pretty pair of dangling earrings from Whitney. I put hair gel in my short pixie to give it spunky spikes, but that was the extent of my preparations.

All chatter in the room ceases when Willa clears her throat. "Good evening everyone."

I glance around the room. Every seat is taken. I'm not surprised. No one turns down an invitation from the Verhena.

Willa smiles. "Thank you so much for joining us tonight. A year ago today, a young woman was given the brand of the Verhena. This young woman faced a lot of challenges in her first year of training, but she handled those challenges with intellect and poise. She is powerful, yet compassionate. She is both street smart and book smart. She is fearless, but not reckless. She is everything our people need in a leader."

Willa pauses as the audience applauds.

"Years from now, she will be remembered for defeating a group of rogue werewolves, but she has so much more to offer us. It is my pleasure, and my honor, to introduce you to your next Verhena...Chloe!"

Everyone stands as we wait for Chloe to make her entrance. The door opens and Chloe steps inside. Despite already seeing her dress, Chloe takes my breath away. She exudes confidence and grace. Strong, yet feminine. As she makes her way across the dance floor toward the stage, people stare with awe at her golden hawk tattoo. Any nerves she had coming into this evening are not showing. Chloe climbs the stage steps and smiles as she turns to the crowd.

"She made it without tripping," James whispers to me. "She's good to go now."

Willa gives Chloe a kiss on the cheek, then steps back. She discreetly exits the stage and joins us at our table.

Chloe walks up to the podium and gives the crowd another dazzling smile. "Please, take your seats."

Everyone does as told.

Chloe scans the crowd with her eyes. "I know everyone wants to hear the story of the rogue werewolves and how my team and I were able to defeat them. I will tell you that story, but first, I want to talk about the girl who shared my birthday for twenty wonderful years. Her name was Chelsea and I miss her every day."

Chloe tears up and takes a moment to gather herself. My own eyes water. I never met Chelsea, but I know how much she meant to Chloe.

"From the very first day of my life, I was blessed with a caring and compassionate best friend. She was my rock, a shoulder to cry on and my constant companion. I'd say she was my partner in crime, but I was usually the only one causing trouble."

The audience laughs.

"Like every other girl, we were excited about our Branding Day. Our whole lives people wondered who would get the hawk and who would get the dove, although most of us would have bet the house Chelsea was getting the dove."

More laughter.

Chloe's smile fades. "I never guessed Branding Day would be our last birthday together."

I grab my napkin and dab my eyes as a tear rolls down my cheek. This must be so hard for Chloe, but she's getting through it like a champ.

"On our twenty-first birthday, I can't help but look back. Chelsea's final act was one of love – she bravely gave her life for mine. And now it's my job to make sure I live the best life possible for the both of us. Her legacy lives within me and because of that, I will be a better woman, witch, and leader."

I glance around the room. Everyone is caught up in Chloe's passionate speech.

"Tonight, please remember my sister and the sacrifice she made for me and for all of you."

Chloe steps back from the microphone for a second and the crowd erupts in applause. I watch her wipe a tear from her eye.

After allowing the applause to continue for a moment, Chloe smiles as she comes back to the microphone. "Now, about those werewolves…"

I've heard this story a dozen times, but I'm as intrigued by it as everyone else. I have no idea why Chloe was worried about giving this speech, the crowd is captivated by her.

When she concludes the story, she extends her hand toward Ivan, James and Whitney. "With us today are the leaders of the werewolf pack. Please give them a hand."

The hall explodes. People are standing, clapping, and yelling out, "Thank you!"

Chloe motions to quiet the crowd again. People take a second to continue clapping, then sit.

"I've read that every good speech is shorter than twenty minutes, and I think I'm at nineteen."

The crowd laughs.

"Thank you so much for coming tonight. You've made this a very special birthday. Dinner will be served shortly and there are plenty of drinks and yummy desserts. Please enjoy yourselves."

Chloe steps away from the microphone and gets another standing ovation. She blushes and mouths, "Thank you!" to the crowd. She walks off the stage and heads for our table.

Willa stands and gives her a hug. "Marvelous honey! Just marvelous."

Everyone at the table voices their agreement.

Chloe sits next to James and he rubs her back. She smiles as he whispers something in her ear.

"I'm just relieved it's over," I hear her say.

Dinner arrives five minutes later. I opt for the salmon, but almost everyone else at my table went with the filet mignon. My fish, purple potatoes and asparagus are delicious. I eat every bite and see that most of the other plates are empty as well. I wink at Willa when she glances my way. She smiles and nods slightly, her silent approval of how the evening is going.

I watch with anticipation as Chloe cuts her giant birthday cake. It is three tiers high and covered in white roses with gold tips. When we were planning her party, Chloe told me she loves confetti birthday cake.

"My mom made a confetti cake every year for me and Chelsea until we turned thirteen. She thought we were too old for confetti cake and started making chocolate cake instead."

After Chloe told me that story, I couldn't help myself. Chloe pulls out the first piece of cake and smiles when she sees the rainbow dots inside the vanilla cake.

She points the knife at me. "You did this, didn't you?"

I laugh and nod my head.

"I love it!"

The deejay goes to work after everyone is served cake. We told him to play fun party music, but to keep it tasteful. Our request eliminated more than half of the music Chloe listens to, but he put together a good mix. Soon, the dance floor is full and the bar has a healthy line. I laugh from my seat as I watch Chloe and Whitney dance like nutcases. They bust out the robot, the lawnmower and the cabbage patch.

In the midst of my giggles, I hear someone take the seat next to me. I turn, expecting to see Ivan or Willa. I'm surprised to find that I don't know my new tablemate.

He's my age, cute with blond hair and brown eyes. Like most of the men here, he is dressed in a black suit. His undone bowtie hangs around his neck.

He smiles at me. "I've been sitting at my table for the last twenty minutes thinking of a good pick up line."

I chuckle. "What did you come up with?"

He leans forward. "What's a human like you, doing in a place like this?"

His simple question shocks me. I usually mingle with the witch crowd without anyone suspecting I'm not one of them. I purposely kept my back covered tonight so no one can see I don't have a tattoo on my right shoulder.

I try to sound nonchalant as I ask, "How do you know I'm human?"

"I have a nose for those kind of things." He smiles at me again, his white teeth dazzling.

"Well, I'd appreciate it if you don't broadcast my humanity."

"Your secret is safe with me." He pretends to lock his mouth shut and throw away the key.

I giggle. "Thank you." I extend my hand. "I'm Jessica."

He returns my shake. "Baxter. It's nice to meet you." Unlike some men, he doesn't purposely squeeze my hand too hard.

His name doesn't ring a bell. "Have you met Chloe before?"

"I have not, but she seems like a nice girl."

"Oh, she is. You'll really like her."

"How do you know her?"

"I'm her assistant."

Baxter raises an eyebrow. "How does a human become the assistant of the most powerful witch in the world?"

I've asked myself this question a million times.

"By default," I tell him.

He looks at me with a face that says, "Go on…"

"I've lived with Willa since I was a little girl," I explain. "My mother is her personal chef. When Chloe came to live with us, Willa asked me to take the position."

"Do you get along with Chloe?"

I nod. "Absolutely. She's my best friend."

Baxter leans back in his chair. "Is it weird for you? Being around all of these people with supernatural abilities?"

I shrug. "Not really. I've been around witches my entire life."

"Hmmm," Baxter considers this. "You must be a very special person Jessica."

I laugh. "I'm probably the least special person in this room."

He frowns. "I'm sorry to hear you feel that way."

Before I can tell him I was joking, he tilts his head toward the dance floor. "You're being summoned."

I turn to look in the direction of his gaze and see Chloe waving me over. "I better go."

Baxter stands with me, and after scooting in my chair, leans in to whisper, "I just wanted to let you know that I love your haircut. It's incredibly sexy."

I blush.

"Not many women can pull off a short haircut. Your face and neckline are perfect for it."

My face is beet red now.

Baxter smirks. "Later," he says casually before walking away.

I gather my wits before turning toward Chloe. I look over my shoulder, wondering which coven Baxter is from, but he is lost in the crowd already.

Chloe meets me on the edge of the dance floor. "I wasn't interrupting something, was I?"

"No, not at all. What's up?"

She hesitates then says, "I have an idea. It's probably a crazy idea, but I want to talk to you about it before I act on it."

"Okay..."

"Elliott is here." She points to a tall man standing a few tables away.

"Your ex?"

She nods. "I told you he's a Reader, right?"

"Yes, you did." Where is she going with this?

"I want to ask him if he'll read you."

My jaw drops. "What?"

"You told me you wonder if you should have a brand," Chloe explains. "Elliott can solve that mystery for you."

I glance over at Elliott again. He can answer questions I've had since I was a little girl.

I suddenly feel like I might throw up.

Chloe

Jessica pales. Maybe this was a bad idea.

"I'm sorry Jess. I hope I'm not overstepping." When she doesn't respond right away, I continue explaining my thought process. "I saw him and it hit me – Elliott can help you. But if you don't want him to read your skin, I completely understand."

"What about Frank?" she asks.

I asked Frank months ago if he would read Jessica for me, but he declined. He said he doesn't want to be involved. Frank's fear is if he gives Jessica bad news, she will resent him for it.

"I already asked Frank," I confess. "He's uneasy about it. You guys are too close."

She nods. "Makes sense."

"I'm not sure when Elliott will be in town again. I don't want to pressure you, but now is the time to ask him if he'll do it."

Jessica stares at the dance floor. "Okay." She says it so softly I barely hear her.

"Are you sure? Don't let me bully you into it."

She straightens her back and meets my eyes. "Yes, I'm sure."

"Alright. I'll talk to him. How's our schedule for tomorrow?"

"Typical day for us."

"So…crazy?"

Jessica cracks a smile. "Pretty much."

"Well, I'm sure we can squeeze Elliott in." I put my hand on her shoulder. "If he says 'yes', it doesn't mean you have to go through with it. You can back out at any time. Okay?"

She nods again.

I turn away from Jess and walk toward Elliott. I haven't spoken to him since my phone call breaking up with him. He looks the same, except his brown hair is longer. He's not wearing his usual baseball hat given the setting. I laugh internally when I realize he's wearing a navy blue suit, always has to be a little different than everyone else.

I weave through the crowd and say "hello" to the people I pass. Many hold up their glasses to me as I go by.

The pretty brunette sitting next to Elliott sees me approaching before he does. She isn't what I was expecting. I was imagining a beefy woman, someone I wouldn't want to meet in a dark alley. To the contrary, her fierceness must only be in her attitude. She is petite with a mousy appearance. Her brown hair flows loose over her shoulders, a tight black dress accentuating her thin frame.

She frowns for a second, then plasters a smile on her face. Elliott turns to see what she's looking at, his eyes widening when he sees me heading his way. Unlike his wife, a genuine smile crosses his lips. It's strange to think that the last time I saw him, we shared a New Year's Eve kiss.

"Hello everyone," I say to his table.

They all smile and say, "hello" back.

I talk to the group for a few minutes and answer some of their questions about my training and how I'm doing. After I've spent enough time with them, I turn to Elliott.

"Can I speak with you privately for a moment?"

Shocked by my question, Elliott turns to his wife, then back to me. "Sure."

"I won't keep him long," I promise Elliott's wife.

Lips pursed, she shifts her weight in her seat. "No problem."

As much as she may despise me, she has to play nice. A part of me would love to make her grovel at my feet, but I resist the temptation.

44

I extend my hand to her. "We've never been formally introduced."

She takes my hand apprehensively. "Veronica. Nice to meet you."

"Likewise," I respond with a catty grin.

Elliott can no longer bear the awkwardness. He clears his throat. "Where should we talk?"

I point to a secluded area of the room. "Over there looks good."

Elliott follows me to our private spot. Out of the corner of my eye, I see Frank trailing slightly behind us. He's probably worried I'll deep fry his brother.

"I have a favor to ask you," I tell Elliott when we've reached the corner.

He raises an eyebrow. "Oh yeah?"

"Yes." I find Jessica in the crowd and point her out. "You see the woman with the dark pixie haircut?"

He follows my gaze. "Yes, I see her. Who is she?"

"She's my assistant Jessica, and she's human."

"She's not a witch?"

"No, but her mom is. One of those witch/human relationships that ended badly."

"Ah, gotcha."

"I want you to read her."

"Read her?" he asks surprised.

"Yes."

He contemplates my question. "What about Frank? Can't he do it?"

I sigh. "He won't. He doesn't want to be the bearer of bad news."

"What do you think a reading will do for her?"

"She'll finally know one way or the other if any part of her is a witch, and whether that part is strong enough for a brand."

"She's never been read before?"

I shake my head. "No. She wasn't read on her twentieth birthday. She never exhibited any signs of magic, so she and her mother never asked for it."

"How is it possible she escaped having to be read? Isn't she on a list or something?" Elliott asks. "I've read women of mixed descent before. I didn't think it was optional."

"Jessica may be on a list, but she lives with Willa. She didn't want a reading at the time, and Willa didn't force it."

"Why didn't she want a reading?"

I shrug. "I don't know. I just know she wants one now." I give him a second to think about it, then ask, "Can you do this favor for me?"

"I can. Let me know when and where."

I clap my hands together. "Thank you! How long are you staying in town?"

"We planned to leave tonight."

"Oh…"

"But I'll stay if the Verhena-to-be asks me to," he says with a grin.

I laugh. "Excellent. Does tomorrow morning work for you?"

"Sure."

"I'll have Frank text you the address for the building. I don't think I need to tell you it's top secret."

"Understood." His brow furrows. "I just remembered - I don't have my equipment with me. I'll have to come back to give her a brand. If her reading is strong enough for one."

46

"No problem. That's fine." I surprise Elliott when I give him a hug. "Thanks again. It means so much to her, and to me."

He hesitates for a moment, then hugs me back. When we separate, his face is solemn. "Are you doing okay?"

My smile widens. "I'm more than okay. I'm great. How about you? Are you and Veronica doing well?"

Elliott runs his hand through his hair. "We're good. Working out some issues, but good."

I glance over to see Veronica glaring at us.

"Wonderful." Although I'm not entirely sure he is, I add, "I'm glad you're happy."

"I'm glad you're happy too."

We stand awkwardly for a second, neither of us knowing what to say.

I break the silence. "Well, I have to get back."

"Of course. It was nice to see you again."

"Likewise." I turn away from him and head for the dance floor.

James intercepts me before I get there. "You alright?"

"Yes, why?"

James glances over at Elliott's table. "I saw you talking to Elliott."

"I had a favor to ask him."

"A favor? What kind of favor?"

I wiggle my eyebrows. "Something only he can do for me."

I'm being playful, but James's eyes darken. Whoa. Apparently it is too soon for jokes about my ex.

"I asked him to read Jessica for me," I explain.

He softens. "Oh, okay."

A slow song starts playing overhead. I take James's hand. "Dance with me."

He holds me close as we sway to the music. "I didn't know Jessica wants her skin read."

"I wasn't sure she did. I talked to her first before asking Elliott to come to the building tomorrow."

James's body stiffens. "He's coming to the building?"

Is it cute or annoying that James is worried about Elliott? We were a done deal a long time ago. But I suppose I'd be less than thrilled if James's ex showed up at my house.

I put my hand behind James's neck and look him in the eyes. "Are you a little jealous? Is that what this is?"

"No," he says with zero conviction.

"Are you sure?"

He sighs. "Why can't Frank read Jessica?"

Good grief. I feel like I'm trapped in that movie "*What about Bob?*" except the anxiety ridden goofball has been replaced with my bulky security guard.

"I asked Frank. He won't do it."

"Can Elliott read her now?"

"Now? At the party?"

James doesn't respond. Instead, he scans the room. Looking everywhere but at me.

I touch his face softly with my fingertips, turning his gaze toward mine. "Hey, you have nothing to worry about."

He presses his forehead against mine. "I know that, I do. But it was hard to see you guys together. You almost burnt down the building because of him."

I giggle when I think back to the day I found out Elliott got married. I unleashed my fury in the fireproof room. I was so upset, I also ripped into Whitney. It wasn't my best day.

"Ancient history," I say with a smile. Then more seriously I add, "I see no one but you."

James kisses my lips and whispers in my ear, "My mate. Forever."

Just as I'm thinking it doesn't get any better than this, our moment is interrupted by Whitney.

"Get a room!" she yells from behind us.

We both laugh and pull apart. Whitney is right, this isn't the time for me and James to pack on the PDA. As much as I'd love to spend the rest of the evening on the dance floor, I mingle with my guests. I shake hands, take selfies with those who ask, and interact with everyone as much as possible.

After I'm done schmoozing, I sit down and catch up with my parents.

"When are you coming home for a visit?" Mom asks.

"Soon. Maybe after my trip to Boston."

Dad raises an eyebrow. "Boston? What's going on in Boston?"

Mom elbows him in the ribcage. "None of your business."

I laugh. "Work stuff. Nothing too exciting." I change the subject. "Are you staying the night with me tonight?"

Mom shakes her head. "We can't. I'm covering a shift at the hospital tomorrow."

Dad checks his watch. "In fact, we should get going. It's a long drive home."

I'm disappointed they're leaving so soon. "Oh, okay."

I give each of them a kiss and a hug good-bye. I smile when they make a point to say good-night to James before they leave. My parents adore him. Maybe more than me.

I survey the crowd, it's thinned significantly. I take a seat at my table and give my tired feet a break. They're not used to being in heels. I'm not seated long before a woman approaches the table.

She is tall and very thin. Her royal blue dress hangs loosely on her frame and her graying brown hair hangs behind her in a braid.

She extends her hand and smiles. "Hi Chloe. I wanted to introduce myself. I'm Nina Dolan."

I recognize her name immediately. She is the new Coven Leader in Boston. "Nice to meet you, Nina. I'm glad we've had the chance to meet before my trip to Boston."

Nina's smile slips, then returns. "Yes, I received Willa's email about your visit. The coven members will be very excited. Can I tell them you're coming?"

"Absolutely. I'd like to meet with you privately before I address the entire group. Get your perspective on things."

"Of course! Let me know what day and time works best for you, and I'll make it happen."

"Sounds good. I'll give you as much notice as possible."

She glances down at the floor, then back at me. "Are you meeting with anyone else?"

I hesitate before responding. Willa and I swore complete confidentiality to the dissenters and I don't want to give too much away. I'm also well aware of the fact that we're at a public event and being watched.

"Nothing is set in stone. But as you know, a few members of your coven reached out to us. I will likely meet with them so they can air their grievances."

She purses her lips. "Indeed."

I've struck a nerve. The letters we received from her opposition describe Nina as a cold and maniacal woman. For a second, I see that potential in her eyes.

Realizing I'm assessing her, Nina stands tall. "I look forward to your visit."

"I'm sure you do," I say under my breath as she walks away.

"Ready to go?" James asks from behind me.

I forget about Nina and turn to him with a smile. "Yes, I'm exhausted."

I thank the few remaining guests for coming and drag Whitney off the dance floor. It's after 1 a.m. by the time we get home and I'm ready to collapse. I flop down on the bed and kick off my heels. I'd sleep in my dress if I wasn't afraid of ruining it. I lay on my stomach with my chin on my hands watching the stars twinkling in the sky through my wall of glass.

"I think the night went well."

"Definitely," James agrees. "Couldn't have gone better."

He climbs on the bed, one knee on each side of my hips, and unclasps the neck of my dress. He scoots down and unzips the short zipper in the back.

I look over my shoulder at him with a raised eyebrow.

"Just helping out," he says with a grin.

"Sure…no ulterior motives at all."

He leans down and whispers in my ear, "A man always has ulterior motives."

I shiver when he kisses the back of my neck. I'm suddenly wide awake.

Chapter Four

The next morning at breakfast, Jessica fills me in on my schedule. It's a relatively light day until Willa throws something into the mix.

"Elias and Baxter would like to meet with us today."

"Elias and Baxter? Who are they?" Whitney asks.

"The vampires," I tell her before taking a bite of my banana.

Jessica drops her fork and it clanks off the table. "Baxter is a vampire?"

"Yes," Willa says. "Didn't he tell you that last night?"

Oh yeah...I did see Jess talking to Baxter last night.

Jessica shakes her head. "No, he didn't mention it."

Whitney stares at Jess, eyes wide. "You talked to a vampire?"

"Apparently."

"See Whit? The vampires aren't so bad," I say. "Jessica's neck is still intact." I turn to Willa. "Why do they want to meet with us?"

"I don't know. Elias called this morning and said it's urgent."

I groan. "Great. That's never good."

"Can I sit in on the meeting?" James asks Willa between bites of scrambled eggs.

"Absolutely. As one of Chloe's advisors, and the future Pack Leader, you should be there. Never too soon for you to start building alliances with other supernatural leaders."

"If it's all the same to you, I'll hang back a little. I don't want to step on your, or Chloe's, toes."

Willa nods. "Whatever you think is best."

"I'm glad I'm leaving today." Whitney shivers. "Vampires give me the heebee geebees."

"What time is your flight?" I ask.

Ivan responds from across the table. "We're leaving for the airport after breakfast."

I'll miss Whitney. The girl drives me nuts sometimes, but she is also a breath of fresh air. She is always down for some girl talk and shopping.

James, Jessica and I make the trek down to the garage with Ivan and Whitney when everyone is done eating. An SUV is parked and waiting to take them to the airport.

I give Whitney a big hug. "Be careful."

"I will."

"Call me and let me know how things go with Brandon."

Whitney grimaces. "It's going to be awful. He sent me a text this morning saying how excited he is to see me." She rolls her eyes. "He probably just wants to get laid."

I laugh and everyone looks over at us. "Girl talk," I explain. "Do what you think is right Whit," I say after everyone turns away.

She smiles sadly. "I know he's not good for me, but I love him."

If I had a nickel for every time someone has said that...

A few minutes later, Whitney and Ivan are in the car and waving good-bye as the SUV pulls off.

"I hope she comes back soon," Jessica says.

I sigh. "Me too."

James pushes the button for the elevator. "When are you leaving for Boston?"

"I haven't finalized my plans yet. Why?"

"I think I'll head out west when you leave for Boston. My grandpa and uncle need help catching up on things."

I frown. "I was hoping you'd come with me."

The elevator doors open and the three of us step inside. "I'd love to Chloe, but I need to check-in back home."

I'm tempted to argue that he was just home, but I don't. Instead I say, "Makes sense."

"How long will you be gone?"

Jessica and I exchange a glance. "We're not sure about that yet either. I'll be in Boston a few days, but I might visit more covens while I'm away."

James nods. "Sounds like a good idea. Your people want to meet you."

"It's going to be awfully quiet around here Jess. Sure you don't want to go with me?" I ask her for the tenth time.

I'm not surprised when she says, "Nah. I'll stay here and hold down the fort. I need to cook for Willa while my mom is gone."

The elevator stops on Jessica's floor and she steps out. "By the way, I forgot to tell you – Elliott will be here around 10:30 a.m. We'll be in one of the guest rooms on Willa's floor if you need me."

I smile. "Excellent. Good luck!"

"Good luck to you too. Say 'hi' to the vampires for me." She winks before walking off.

I groan. I'd like to skip the meeting with the vampires. Something tells me they want a favor.

When the elevator doors close, James asks, "Think she's avoiding Frank?"

"Yep."

"Did you tell her you know about them?"

"Nope."

55

James laughs. "You ever going to tell her you know?"

I shrug my shoulders. "If she wants to tell me, she'll tell me. I'm not going to push it."

"Has Frank brought it up to you?"

"Negative. They both think I'm in the dark."

He shakes his head. "Oh well, what's done is done."

I frown. I knew Frank and Jessica wouldn't end well. He's too invested in the Guard. It was still sad when I heard they split up though. They may have been outside the Guard's camera range when Frank ended it, but our microphones picked up the entire conversation. The gossips in the Guard called me right away.

I want to comfort Jess, but I can't. I have to respect her privacy. What little of it she has.

James changes the subject. "What do you think Elias and Baxter want?"

"No clue."

Jessica

My hands shake as I wait for Elliott. I sit on the edge of the bed in Willa's guest room.

Like the other rooms on her floor, the guest suite is animal themed. The walls are painted a relaxing tan, with photographs of lions scattered across them. The linens are a clean, crisp white, and a stuffed lion sits on top of the pillows. The guest bathroom holds a claw foot tub and safari wallpaper. Every once in a while Willa sleeps in this room for a change of scenery.

I browse Instagram while I wait, but I can't focus. I've wondered my entire life how much witch runs through my blood, if any. When I was a little girl, I secretly tried different spells I saw my mom using. None of them worked.

Despite my failures, I always had a glimmer of hope that someday I will find my witch skills. There are so many spells out

56

there, so many different potential talents, maybe one of them is mine. Elliott will definitively tell me if I don't have a trace of witch in me. All of my small hopes will be extinguished. Do I really want to know?

I stand when I hear male voices in the hallway talking and laughing. I immediately recognize Frank's voice. A moment later, Frank and Elliott walk into the room.

Frank stiffens a bit when he sees me. "Hey Jess," he says, "this is my brother Elliott."

Elliott and Frank look nothing alike. Frank is bulky and combat ready. Elliott is tall and lean with a laid back, tattoo artist vibe.

I shake Elliott's hand. "Thank you for doing this on such short notice."

"No problem," he responds with a smile. Dimples appear in his cheeks. There's a cuteness underlying his edgy attitude. It's easy to see why Chloe was once smitten with him.

Frank claps his brother on the back. "I'll leave you to it. Call the Guard Operations Center if you need anything. I'll be in a meeting with Chloe for the rest of the morning."

Elliott pulls his brother in for a man hug. "It was good to see you bro."

"Good luck," Franks says before showing himself out.

Elliott turns to me. "I typically have a massage table for my clients to lay on, but I don't have it with me. Are you comfortable laying on the bed?"

"Sure."

I take a deep breath and unbutton my cardigan. Per Chloe's advice, I wore a tube top under my sweater. I lay on my stomach and turn my head to the side facing Elliott.

He stretches his fingers, a few of his knuckles cracking. "Chloe has a big meeting today, huh?"

"Yes. She wanted to be here for moral support, but something came up."

"Busy lady."

"You have no idea."

Elliott stands over me. "Okay, take a deep breath and relax. I'll do the rest."

I close my eyes and try to calm my heart rate. I take slow breaths and pretend I'm at a masseuse waiting to get a massage. Elliott's fingers run slowly down my back from top to bottom. He begins massage-like motions over my back with a bit more pressure. I'm getting a bit hazy when his movements stop.

"All done," he says softly.

After helping me sit upright, he sits down in a brown leather chair near the bed. He runs his hand through his hair, then leans forward with his elbows on his knees. His expression reveals nothing.

"Well?" I ask.

"I was able to read you."

"And?" The suspense is killing me! My heart is pounding.

He hesitates. "I'm not sure what you want to hear."

I myself am not sure what I want to hear. "Whatever it is, just tell me."

"I sense the presence of power, but it's a small amount. It wasn't strong enough for me to feel a brand."

"What does that mean?"

"It means there is a trace amount of magic in your blood, which is common for children of a witch/human relationship."

"But not enough for a brand?"

He nods. "Exactly."

I deflate.

"You definitely have some power in there," Elliott continues, "but you won't be able to practice magic."

"So I'm not really a witch," I conclude.

Elliott frowns and confirms what I've suspected all along. "Technically, no. You're not."

I inhale deeply, then let the air out slowly. "Okay."

I hide my devastation by fussing with my cardigan. I struggle with its tiny buttons, my fingers refusing to cooperate. Deep in my heart I knew this would be the outcome, and maybe that's why I put off a reading for so long. Hearing the truth hammers the nail into the coffin.

Elliott senses my unhappiness. "I'm sorry."

"No need to apologize. You answered a lot of questions for me."

"I wish I had better news."

I fight to keep my composure. I don't want to cry in front of him. "It's okay." I finish buttoning my cardigan and force a smile. "Thanks again. I appreciate your time."

"Sure, no problem."

Elliott walks with me toward the elevator. Desperate to lighten the mood, I ask, "Are you staying in the city long?"

"No. My wife and I are heading back to Vermont this afternoon."

I have zero doubt in my mind Elliott's wife wants him out of here as soon as possible. She was shooting daggers at Chloe last night.

"That's a shame, I'm sure Frank would love to spend time with you."

Elliott laughs. "No he wouldn't. He's too busy working to spend time with me."

I know the feeling.

Chloe

James and I walk into the conference room together, heads held high. In the hallway we were James and Chloe; in the conference room we are the future leaders of our people.

Willa, Bane and our vampire guests are already sitting at the conference room table. The scene reminds me of when I met James and his family for the first time.

Willa stands and the vampires follow her lead. I walk toward the vampires' side of the table. I recognize the younger, or younger-looking, vampire. He's cute with his spiky, blond hair and brown eyes. He puts off the appearance of a young, college-age guy who likes to skateboard on the weekends. I know this is all a ruse, but it's pretty convincing.

"Chloe, this is Baxter," Willa says as I extend my hand to him.

"Nice to meet you," he says with a smile.

"Likewise."

I turn my attention to the older-looking gentleman. He appears to be in his late fifties, his salt and pepper hair receding. He has piercing blue eyes that rival my own. He's dressed in a gray blazer over a pinstriped shirt and black dress pants. He is very nicely put together and reeks of money.

He extends his hand to me. "Elias, your grace. Pleased to meet you."

"Thank you for coming to my party last night."

The mental image of a shark floods my mind when he smiles and says, "The pleasure is all mine."

"And this is James," Willa interjects, "Ivan's grandson."

James exchanges handshakes with our guests.

"How is Ivan?" Elias asks. "He must be what – sixty? Seventy by now?"

"He's seventy-one."

60

"Ah, how the years fly." Elias turns to Willa. "I've seen a lot of things during my existence, but I must say, sharing the same table with the leadership of both the werewolf and witch clans was not something I anticipated."

Willa smiles. "It is a nice turnabout, isn't it?"

"Indeed. I hope this trend continues."

"Why wouldn't it?" Baxter asks as we take our seats. "We've got the supernatural Brad and Angelina right here."

I narrow my eyes at him. "You know they broke up, right?"

He puts his hand to his chest. "I had not heard! I'm shocked!"

I can't help it, I giggle.

"Enough Baxter," Elias says in his deep voice. "What he means to say is we were pleased when word of your union reached us. We feared another war was imminent."

"Our union?" I ask.

"Yes. Your marriage."

I feel compelled to correct him. "James and I aren't married."

"Living in sin, eh?" Baxter asks with a smirk.

"It's the best way."

He laughs. "I like this girl."

"Alright kids," Willa says authoritatively, but with a bit of amusement. "Elias, you said you have business to discuss."

"I do Verhena. Rather gruesome business I am afraid." Elias reaches into his blazer and pulls out a piece of newspaper. He unfolds it and hands it to Willa. She scans the page, then slides the article across the table so James and I can see it.

It is the front page of today's *New York Daily Report*. The headline screams:

YOUNG WOMAN FOUND MURDERED
OUTSIDE HER APARTMENT BUILDING

A photograph of a pretty redhead sits under the caption. Next to her picture is a shot of the crime scene – a blood covered sidewalk blocked off by caution tape.

James looks up from the paper. "Do you know this woman?"

"We do not, but we may know who killed her." Elias says it with no emotion or sense of urgency.

Willa frowns. "Was it a vampire?"

Before Elias can answer, the conference room door swings open. It's Frank.

"Sorry I'm late to the party."

When he reaches my chair, I ask, "Everything okay up there?"

He nods. "Elliott is upstairs with her now."

"Good." I turn my attention to Elias. "You were saying?"

He waves his hand toward Baxter. "Baxter can fill you in on the details."

My eyes shift to Baxter. The goofy grin on his face is gone.

"We believe Gregory Morrow is responsible for this."

"Who is Gregory Morrow?" I ask.

"A vampire who lives close to our home base in France."

James examines the crime scene photo with the intensity of a detective. "Why do you think Gregory is responsible for this?"

"Do you see the symbol painted in blood on the door?" Baxter asks.

I glance at the photo again. Upon closer inspection, I spot a small "B" written in blood in the lower, left-hand corner of the door. It is surrounded by a symbol similar to a circular sawblade.

I point the "B" out to James and he nods. He looks up at Baxter. "You think the 'B' refers to you?"

Without saying a word, Baxter lifts his t-shirt. On his right pectoral is a tattoo of the symbol in black ink.

"I see," James says.

Baxter pulls his shirt down. "Can you help us?"

Willa and I exchange a glance. I wait for her to take the lead, but she doesn't. She's giving me the reigns on this one.

I sit quietly for a moment, debating the best way to approach their request. I need more information before I can give him an answer. "It depends."

"On?"

"What did you do to piss Gregory off?"

"I killed his lover," he responds without hesitation.

Good grief. No wonder the guy has a vendetta against Baxter. I cross my arms, my voice dripping with sarcasm. "Is that all?"

Baxter squares his jaw. "My actions were justified."

"Justified in whose eyes?"

Before Baxter goes on the offensive, Elias steps in. "Gregory's lover had an addiction problem."

"An addiction problem? Can you elaborate?" Willa asks.

"Deanna had a taste for small children."

I grimace. Yuck.

"She climbed in their bedroom windows at night while they slept," Elias continues, oblivious to my disgust. "Her preference was little girls. She would..."

I wave my hands. "Stop! Stop! Stop! We get it."

"I warned her Chloe. I swear I did," Baxter says flustered. "She promised me she would stop. And she did for a few months, or at least I thought she did. Last month I found out she broke into another home. She drank from a little girl."

I cringe again.

"When the little girl died, I snapped. I hunted Deanna down and I killed her. It was impulsive and stupid, but I don't regret it."

63

I can't fault Baxter. I probably would have done the same.

"It was a reckless act," Elias says, still unemotional. "Baxter should have waited until the Council tried Deanna. The end result would have been the same."

Ah yes, the Vampire Council. I read about it as I prepared for Baxter's and Elias's visit. It is comprised of four vampires, one from each district in Europe. They are the judge, jury and executioner of the vampire world.

"Aren't you on the Council, Elias?" I ask.

He tilts his head in a single nod. "I am."

I turn to Baxter. "Well, his motive is clear, but why would Gregory kill someone in New York City? Especially someone with no connection to you?"

"It's common knowledge Elias and I were coming to New York for your party. Plus, it's easier for him to seek his vengeance in the States."

James rubs his chin. "Why is that?"

"All my allies are overseas," Baxter explains. "This is strange territory for me. I am much more vulnerable here than I am at home."

Willa asks the million dollar question. "What do you want from us?"

"Shelter. Use of your intel," Elias replies.

Willa sits quietly for a moment, pondering what she wants to do. After a minute she gives her answer. "You can stay with us. We'll prepare rooms for you."

"They can stay on the 13th floor," James offers.

I gape at him. "That's your floor."

He shrugs. "Whitney and my grandpa are gone, and I spend most of my time with you. I don't really need my room anymore, let alone an entire floor."

I start to speak, but close my mouth. I'm not sure what to say. I wish James had asked me before moving into my suite, but it's too late for that now.

Pushing my personal issues aside, I focus on the task at hand. "From an intel perspective, what do you need?"

We talk for another hour about different ways to track down Gregory. Baxter shows us a picture of Gregory on his cellphone. He is short with black hair and beady eyes. If he was thicker, he'd look like the Penguin.

"Can you send me that picture?" Frank asks. "I'll download it to our system to see if he's been within our boundaries. I'll also run a facial recognition scan through the police database."

"Certainly."

"Let's powwow on the 8th floor tonight," I suggest. "We'll find out if he's been anywhere near us, and if he has, any clues he left behind."

Everyone agrees to this.

Before we leave, Willa has one more thing to say. "To be clear, we will help you if we can, but this is your project. Chloe and I have our own matters to attend to."

Willa isn't directing this statement to just Elias and Baxter. She is putting me on notice to not get wrapped up in the manhunt for Gregory. Fine by me.

"We understand," Baxter says. "This is our deal."

This appeases Willa. "Good. I'll have the Guard show you to your rooms. I'll also make sure our kitchen is stocked with sustenance for you."

I'd almost forgotten Baxter and Elias are bloodsuckers. I make a face. "You aren't going to eat with us, are you?"

Baxter laughs. "I think you meant to ask - you aren't going to eat us, are you?"

I smile. "I'd love to see you try."

When Willa, Bane and the vampires leave, I stay behind with Frank and James. "I like Baxter."

Frank rolls his eyes. "Of course you do."

"What does that mean?"

Frank and James exchange a glance.

"What?"

James smiles. "You don't see it, do you?"

"See what?" I ask confused.

Frank smiles. "Baxter and Elias are the vampire equivalent of you and Willa. You and Baxter could be the same person."

"What?!" I turn to James. "You don't think that too, do you?"

James wipes the grin off his face. "Maybe just a little…"

Jessica

Chloe comes to see me in the apartment I share with my mom. Unlike Chloe's suite, our suite takes up an entire half of the 14th floor. We each have our own bedroom and full bathroom separated by a large common area. With Mom out of town, I have the place to myself.

I shut my book. "How were the vampires?"

She waves her hand. "We'll discuss them later. How did it go with Elliott?"

"He said I have a little witch in me, but not enough."

Chloe frowns. "I'm sorry Jess. I know how badly you wanted a brand."

I could tell her it was about more than just the brand, but I don't want to get upset again. So I change the subject. "I'm fine. Now tell me, how did the meeting go?"

Chloe gives me a rundown. I wince when she tells me about a little girl who was murdered by a vampire.

"So Baxter killed Gregory's lover, and now Gregory is seeking revenge?"

Chloe nods.

"But why an innocent woman?"

"That's the tricky part. If the symbol wasn't at the crime scene, I'd question whether Gregory is even involved."

"It seems like a big risk on Gregory's part. What if Baxter didn't care Gregory killed this woman?"

Chloe shrugs. "Gregory must know Baxter well enough to know Baxter will come after him."

"Sounds like something we should help with."

"Yes, but Willa made it clear we're not going to be involved in the manhunt."

"You don't get to be Buffy, huh?"

She laughs. "No dammit! And I was really looking forward to it."

"Do they seem okay? The vampires?" I ask.

"I like Baxter. Elias, I'm not so sure. He's indifferent about the whole thing. I think this will be Baxter's show."

I remember what Baxter whispered to me last night and I blush.

Chloe sees my reaction. "What's up with you?"

I shake my head. "Nothing."

"C'mon Jess. Out with it."

"I was thinking about something Baxter said to me last night," I admit.

Her eyes widen. "Tell me."

I recount my conversation with Baxter.

Chloe's forehead creases. "Jess..."

"I know what you're going to say - he's a vampire. Don't get involved."

"I've read a lot about vampires this past week. At least two of the books say vampires are seducers and enjoy the game, but they don't really have feelings." She pauses. "I don't know if I'm explaining it very well."

"I get it, I do. He's flirty and fun, but not boyfriend material."

"Exactly!"

I make a shocking confession, something I never thought I'd hear myself say. "Maybe I want a little fun."

Chloe gasps. "Jess-i-ca! I didn't think you had it in you!"

"I'm not sure that I do."

We both laugh.

"If you're in it for fun, Baxter is an excellent choice," Chloe tells me.

"Why?"

She smiles. "Vampires are supposed to be fantastic lovers."

"What floor did you say he's staying on?" I ask with a grin.

"Lucky number thirteen."

"James's floor?"

Chloe sighs. "Don't ask."

"Uh oh. Why the sigh?"

"James gave up his room. Which means he'll be staying with me."

"And you're not happy with that?" I surmise, a little surprised. James and Chloe are attached at the hip, what's the big deal?

"I don't know if I am or not. He kinda sprung it on me, no discussion."

I pat her hand. "It will be fine. You'll see."

She smiles half-heartedly. "I'm sure you're right." She stands. "On that note, I'm going to the gym for a while. I'll see you at dinner, okay?"

"Sounds good."

Chloe stops halfway to the door. "Oh…and Jess…"

"Yes?"

She grimaces. "You need to order some cow hearts."

Chapter Five

Jessica

I give up on my book. I'm distracted by thoughts of Elliott's visit and my new shopping list. Where can I get my hands on cow hearts?

I grab my purse and walk to the butcher a few blocks over. It's my quickest option and I don't want to leave the vampires hungry for long.

The butcher gives me an odd look when I tell him to add a dozen cow hearts to my order. I have no idea how many hearts a vampire eats in a day, but I'm hoping a dozen will hold them over for a while.

Thankfully, the butcher wraps the hearts in white paper before he puts them in my bag. "What are you doing with these?"

"I'm trying a new slow cooker recipe," I lie.

He raises an eyebrow. "Whatcha makin'?"

"Uh…chili. I read online that cow's heart adds a lot of iron."

The butcher shakes his head. "Whatever floats your boat honey. Let me know how it turns out."

I cringe when I put the hearts in the fridge. The thought of what's inside the white paper turns my stomach. I like to cook and I've used organ meat before, but never heart. With that gross task out of the way, I focus on dinner for my human housemates.

I open the freezer and smile when I see the meals Mom prepared before she left. She didn't leave enough for every meal, but they'll come in handy on days when I don't have the time or energy to make dinner from scratch. Willa offered to hire temporary help while Mom is out town, but I don't really need it. Whitney and Ivan are already gone, and James, Chloe and Frank will be leaving shortly. No sense in hiring someone to cook for just me and Willa.

I rummage through the freezer and find a vegetable lasagna Mom prepared. While it's baking, I slice fresh Italian bread and chop veggies to make a salad. I question whether a salad with vegetable lasagna is veggie overkill, but I roll with it.

It's weird making dinner without Mom. I turn on the satellite radio to keep me company. It's tuned to the '60s station – Mom's favorite. The Mamas and the Papas are singing one of my favorite songs and I find myself humming along.

I'm chopping carrots when a deep, melodic voice belts out the chorus. I nearly cut my finger off. I turn to find Baxter smiling in the doorway.

"You scared me to death!" I scold him.

"Sorry." The grin on his face tells me he's not sorry at all. He opens the refrigerator door and peers inside.

"They're in the white paper packages," I say, knowing exactly what he's looking for.

"Excellent!" He grabs a package from the fridge and lays it on the counter.

He doesn't plan to eat that in here, does he?

"I bought a dozen. How long will that last?"

"A day or two."

I frown. "Sorry, I should have bought more."

He smiles. "No worries. Thank you for getting them."

"You're welcome. The butcher is a short walk from here. We shouldn't have any problem getting more for you."

"Don't worry about it. I'll get them from now on. Just let me know the butcher's address and I'll take care of it."

"Are you sure? It's not a hassle."

72

"I've got it, but thanks."

I return to my veggie cutting when he peels back the white paper. Oh God... Don't look Jess, don't look.

"I'm surprised you know this song," he says, "seems too old for you."

"My mom loves it. When I was young, she played it on cold days and told me how much she wanted to see California."

"Has she ever been?"

"She's there now actually."

"I've never been to California."

"Really?"

"Nope. I've only been on the east coast of the United States."

"Same. Mom couldn't travel to California because the treaty between the werewolves and witches prevented it. She booked her flight as soon as Willa and Ivan amended the treaty." I laugh thinking about it. "She couldn't reserve her seat fast enough."

"You should do that more often."

I look up at him. "Do what more often?"

"Laugh. You have a nice laugh."

I blush when our eyes meet. I drop my gaze first. "Thanks."

I finish with the carrots and reach for the tomatoes. When I do, I can't help but see Baxter eyeing the two reddish-purple lumps in front of him. He is ogling the hearts with the same adoration I have for red velvet cupcakes.

In a flash, he picks up one of the hearts and plunges his teeth into the skin. The sound of his teeth ripping through the meat turns my stomach. When Baxter pulls away, his lips are covered in blood. I clasp my hand over my mouth as more blood oozes out of the heart.

Seeing my reaction, Baxter puts the heart down and wipes his mouth with a paper towel. "Sorry, I wasn't thinking."

I look down at the countertop and focus on my breathing. I really don't want to throw up in front of Baxter. "It's okay. I just wasn't prepared for that."

The paper crinkles as Baxter wraps the hearts. "You can look now." When I glance over at him, his face is solemn. "I thought being a cook, it wouldn't bother you."

I wave my hand and begin cutting tomatoes. "No biggie. I'm fine."

"I'll take these to my room." Baxter turns away, the hearts in tow.

"Wait, there's something I want to ask you before you go."

He stops and glances back at me. "What's that?"

"Why didn't you tell me last night who you are?"

"You mean, why didn't I tell you I'm a vampire?"

Bingo. "Yes."

"Didn't seem relevant."

I smirk. "Really?"

"Do you know how many women I would chase off if I opened with - Hi, I'm Baxter. I may or may not want to suck your blood later. Call me."

I chuckle. "I see your point."

"You didn't suspect it, not even a little?"

I shake my head. "No. In retrospect, I should have. But in my mind, all vampires are like Dracula. Older men with thick accents. Dark and brooding. You don't match that description in the slightest and you have no discernible accent. You sound like a New Yorker."

"I sound like I'm from whatever area of the world I'm in. I am fluent in a countless number of languages. As for my appearance," he says, glancing down at himself and then back up at me, "this is how I looked when I turned. I update my haircut and clothes, but I'm stuck with this age and this body."

74

"Nothing wrong with the body you're in." As soon as I say it, I blush again. I am so awkward when it comes to flirting. "How old are you?" I blurt out, hoping he doesn't notice my embarrassment.

"My age as in how many years I've been on this Earth, or my age at the time I turned?"

I dump the tomatoes into the salad. "Both." I grab a block of cheese and slide it against the grater.

"I was twenty-six when I turned in 1908."

My quick math tells me Baxter was born in 1882.

I stop grating the cheese and meet his eyes. "You've seen two turn-of-the-centuries…"

Baxter frowns. "Pretty weird, huh?"

"I think it's amazing," I say with awe. "The stories you must have."

He narrows his eyes for a second, analyzing me. Did I say something wrong?

"Baxter, I'm sorry if I'm being nosey."

His expression clears. "Not at all." He turns on his heels and heads for exit. "Thanks again for dinner."

Before I can respond, he's gone. Apparently I'm bad with males of both the human and supernatural persuasion.

Chloe

Deep breaths Chloe, deep breaths.

I stare at James's clothes in my closet. Out of the corner of my eye I spot his cologne bottle sitting on my vanity next to my perfume collection. There's plenty of space in here for his things, so why are the walls closing in on me?

I jump when James walks up behind me. "You ready for dinner?"

"Um, yeah."

I'm quiet in the elevator. James checks messages on his phone and doesn't seem to notice. I can't explain my uneasiness at seeing his Adidas next to my Chuck Taylors. It's not like I'm new to cohabitation. I shared space with Chelsea my entire childhood and teenage years. But something about this feels different. I love him. I want to be with him all the time. Why do I feel like he's intruding on my space?

"It's about time," Frank grumbles when we join the group at the dinner table.

Willa smacks his arm. "Enough of that. You just got here two seconds ago."

Frank smirks. He's in a good mood. Must have something terrible planned for me in training tomorrow.

"Hey Jess," I say before taking my seat. "Dinner looks great."

She smiles. "Thank you."

We pass around the food and dig in.

"The vampires are set up on the 13th floor," Willa informs us. "Thank you again James for giving up your room."

"No problem," he says between bites. Unlike me, James is completely unfazed by our new living arrangement.

I try to cover my mood with a joke. "We're like a supernatural Holiday Inn now. Who's checking in next? Swamp Thing?"

James smirks. "We do have a pool."

Frank clearly didn't get my memo on avoiding the topic of James's relocation. "Aww, isn't this cute? You guys are moving in together!" He bats his eyelashes with exaggerated enthusiasm.

If my foot could reach, I would kick him under the table. Glaring at Frank only eggs him on.

"Pretty soon you'll be shacked up and popping out babies. What will we call them?" He rubs his chin. "Oh, I know," he says, his eyes lighting up, "werewitches!"

76

"Shut up Frank," I warn through clinched teeth.

Frank's eyes get even bigger. "Oh God! Don't tell me - you're already knocked up!"

My hand tightens around my fork. I consider flinging it across the table and nailing him in the middle of his forehead. "I just turned twenty-one yesterday. Can we hold off on the baby jokes?"

Frank lets out a sigh of relief. "Thank God! We'd have Guard members chasing around hairy toddlers all day."

Jessica giggles, then looks at me apologetically when I narrow my eyes at her.

James gives Frank a hard stare. "Enough."

We all eat in silence for a few minutes.

Willa breaks the ice. "This is excellent Jessica. Your mom would be proud."

Jessica blushes. "I have a confession to make. Mom made this before she left and put it in the freezer. All I had to do was heat it up."

"Well, that's more than I did." Willa puts her fork and napkin on her empty plate. "Chloe, when are you leaving for Boston?"

"The day after tomorrow."

"How about you James?" Willa asks. "When are you heading west?"

"Same day," he responds, his tone still hard.

Frank must have pissed James off too. Probably the comment about hairy kids.

"It's going to be just us Jessica," Willa says.

"Plus the forty Guard members who live here," Frank points out.

"And a pair of vampires," I add.

"Speaking of vampires, are we still meeting this evening?" James asks.

Frank nods. "We have additional information to share."

Willa turns to me. "I meant what I said earlier. We will help Baxter and Elias, but don't get caught up in this. You have other things to take care of."

"I know."

Willa pats my hand. "Good. I don't want to harp on you, but Boston and the other covens come before the vampires. If it was a witch issue, it would be a different story."

I smile. "No worries Willa. I get it."

Willa stands. "I need a nap, especially if you youngsters plan on keeping me up late with talk of vampires and murder mysteries."

When everyone is finished eating, I help Jessica clean and load the dirty dishes in the dishwasher.

I lean on the kitchen island. "Frank is such an asshole sometimes."

"He's only teasing. We all know you and James aren't having kids any time soon."

"What if James wants to have kids soon?"

Jessica shrugs. "Maybe he does, maybe he doesn't. Ask him."

I frown. "I'm afraid to."

"Why?"

I run my fingers along the granite countertop and make little circles with my fingertips. "I don't want to mess it up."

"Which is exactly why you need to talk to him about it," Jessica urges. "Don't let things fester. It will only make it worse."

She's right, but I'm scared to death as I ride the elevator to my floor. I'm not ready for marriage and babies. I don't know what I'll do if James says he is.

I walk into the room and find James reading on the couch. It's another new addition to my suite. I'm slowly but surely putting my mark on my new home. Unlike Willa's furniture, I opted for comfy brown micro-suede instead of leather.

I take a seat beside him. "Reading a good one?"

"Eh, it's alright." He shows me the book cover.

"*The History of Vampires*," I read aloud. "I read that one. Kinda slow in the beginning, but it picks up."

James smiles. "Since when do you hit the books before me?"

"Don't be jealous of my mad research skills."

He puts the book down on the side table. "You want to talk about what's bothering you? Or should we just have sex?"

I laugh.

"I'd really like to skip to the sex," he says, "but I think we should talk first."

I look down at my hands. "What if you don't like what I have to say?"

"We'll have a huge fight, and then we can have make-up sex."

I smile, but don't laugh.

James scoots closer to me and raises my chin with his finger. "Whatever it is, we'll be fine."

I look into his eyes and do what I always do – I rip off the band-aid. "Do you want kids?"

James stammers, surprised by my question. "I don't know. I guess so."

"Do you want them now?"

"No." He tilts his head to the side. "Is that why you got so mad at Frank? You think I want kids right now?"

I nod. "Whitney told me you want kids. And now you're moving in, so I was thinking…"

James puts up his hand. "Stop. You're overthinking this."

"I am?"

79

"Yes. I should have talked to you before I invited myself to move in. I didn't think you would mind, but I should have asked. Once Baxter and Elias are gone, I'll move my things back to the 13th floor."

"No, don't do that." I tear up. "I don't want you to do that."

"Are you sure?"

"Yes, I'm sure."

He doesn't look convinced.

"I don't want you to move back downstairs. You're right – you're here most of the time anyway. I can't even remember the last time you slept down there." I pause, still searching for the right words. "When you said you were moving in, my mind started churning. Next it will be marriage, then it will be babies. I totally overreacted."

James pulls me in tight against his chest. "We have plenty of time for those things. I'm in no hurry."

"What if I never want kids?"

James kisses the top of my head. "I want you. If you don't want children, I'm fine with that."

"And if I *do* want children?"

James laughs. "I'll prepare myself for the craziest kids on the planet."

What will our kids be like, if we have them? Will they have powers like me? Will they shift into werewolves like James? Will they have the benefit of both?

"I've never come across a story about a werewolf and witch procreating, have you?" I ask.

He shakes his head. "No, but I haven't been on the lookout for it. We're the first witch/wolf couple to go public since before the war."

"Which means it's possible there haven't been any children of a couple like us for over a century."

80

"None that we know of. I can do some digging if you want me to."

I smile up at him. "Let's put that on the backburner for a while."

He grins. "Duly noted."

Our evening meeting is brief.

Frank gets right to it. "We reviewed our video surveillance. Gregory has not crossed our boundaries. Willa put up new wards this afternoon to keep him out. We can safely say he will not cross into our territory."

Elias steeples his bony fingers. "Very good."

"We also ran a search of the local media outlets and police reports," Frank continues. "This is the first and only murder where the 'B' symbol was left at the crime scene."

"What do you know about the victim?" Willa asks.

"She was twenty-two. An engineering student at NYU. She was originally from Texas and is survived by her parents and two sisters. No criminal history, no evidence of drug or alcohol abuse. From all accounts, an innocent young woman."

I consider this. "She was definitely a random target?"

"It's hard to say," Frank concedes, "but we can't find any connection between her and Gregory."

"Do we have any idea where Gregory is?" I ask next.

He shakes his head. "No, we don't."

Baxter sits up from his slouching position. "I'll start patrolling the city tonight."

"It's possible you won't find him," Elias notes grimly.

Baxter frowns. "I know, but I have to try. I can't allow Gregory to run around killing innocent people."

"What if you do find him? Do you need backup?" I ask.

"No. I'll have a stake with me."

"You're confident you can take him down?"

"Absolutely. Besides, none of your guys can keep up with me," he says with a grin.

I roll my eyes. "Whatever. Does Gregory have any friends here he could be staying with?"

"None that I'm aware of."

Frank rubs his chin. "I've heard that a vampire who turns a human has a special connection with that new vampire for the rest of their lives. Is that true?"

"Yes, we refer to it as the blood connection." Baxter pauses for a second. "Some say it's like a mother/child bond, but there's a little more to it. The connection is so strong, we can sense each other."

"What do you mean you can sense each other?" James asks. He must not have gotten that far in his reading yet.

"If you drop Elias somewhere in the city and tell me to find him, I'll be able to easily. It's akin to sonar. We can also temporarily sense someone we've drank from. But that only lasts a month or so."

Frank asks the obvious question. "Has Gregory turned anyone?"

Elias shakes his head. "No. If he has, he never registered the person with the Council."

This is news to me. "You have to register a vampire?"

"Yes. It's the Council's way of keeping track of our kind. As you can imagine, we want to maintain as low a profile as possible."

"Understandable," I agree. "What about his creator?"

"He was killed long ago."

Another dead end. We're quiet for a moment.

Baxter pushes back from the table. "Well, no time like the present."

In the blink of an eye, he's gone.

When I walk into the gym the next morning, Baxter and Frank are talking in the middle of the mats.

"Any luck last night?" I call out.

They both turn to look at me.

Baxter shakes his head. "None. I went to the crime scene, nothing helpful there. I ran through the city for a few hours, but it's a needle in a haystack situation."

"Did Gregory appear on any of our cameras?"

"No," Frank responds. "No sign of him."

"Will you go out again tonight?" I ask Baxter.

He shrugs. "I guess so. I don't know what else to do at this point. Gregory could be anywhere, but I can't sit here and hope he comes to me. He's too smart to show up at your front door."

"He can't even if he wants to," I point out. "He'll never get through Willa's wards."

"True."

Frank crosses his arms over his chest. "Enough chitchat. It's time to train."

The perpetual drill sergeant. "What's on the agenda today?"

Frank surprises me when he says, "Baxter is training with us."

"Oh really?"

"I was looking forward to it, but those dummies over there," Baxter points to our test dummies with perfect holes through their hearts, "are making me nervous."

"I'll go easy on you," I tease.

"No she won't," Frank interjects.

83

I grin. "He's right, I won't. You sure you want a piece of this?"

Baxter's eyes shine with excitement. "Bring it!"

I'm about to accept Baxter's challenge, but Frank stops me. "Hang on a second, tiger. Let's discuss some ground rules."

I frown. "Ground rules?"

"Yes, no fires or explosions,"

"Aww, man."

"And you," he turns to Baxter, "no biting."

Baxter tsks. "He's no fun, is he?"

I shake my head. "Welcome to my world."

Frank completely ignores us. "Baxter, you're up first. Try to knock Chloe over."

Baxter rubs his hands together. "No problem."

I smirk at Frank and he winks at me. Baxter stomps his feet like a bull, ready to charge. I walk thirty feet away and wait.

"You ready?" Baxter yells to me.

"Are you?" I yell back.

"Coming at you in three...two...one..."

It's a good thing I had my protective bubble in place before he finished his countdown. Baxter is on me in a flash. He's moving so fast, that even with my shield in place, I'm jostled by the impact. I watch in wonder as Baxter sails backwards through the air. He hits the mats flat on his back near his starting position.

Ouch.

Frank howls with laughter. His plan worked.

Baxter sits up and shakes his head like a dog. "Damn!" Once his head clears, he smirks. "You set me up!"

Frank, who is still laughing, admits nothing.

I walk over to Baxter and extend my hand to help him get on his feet. "You alright?" I ask when he's standing upright.

"I think so, I'm not seeing stars anymore. What the hell happened?"

"You ran into my bubble."

"Your bubble? It felt like a brick wall."

"Alright," Frank says when he gathers his composure, "let's get down to real training now."

Baxter and I spend the next hour showing off. I'm amazed by his speed and strength, and he's fascinated with my magic. We even have an arm wrestling competition. I let him think he's winning before I finish him off.

I'm pleased when Baxter tells me, "I've never seen a witch with such a wide variety of skills at your age."

"Thanks. I'm still working on it, but I'm happy with where I'm at."

Near the end of our session, I show him my "Spidey-skills" and climb up the wall.

"Hey! I can do that too!" he exclaims.

I'm shocked when Baxter jumps up onto the wall and scrambles toward me. "I didn't know vampires are climbers."

Baxter puts a finger to his mouth. "Shh…it's one of our hidden talents."

I shiver when I think about Deanna, Gregory's lover, climbing into children's bedrooms at night. When I get past that gruesome thought, I ask Baxter if he has any other secret abilities.

He lowers his voice. "I can read your mind."

"No you can't!"

He smiles. "You're right, I can't."

"Watch this!" I do a backflip on the wall. I've been working on that one and I'm particularly proud of it.

"That's nothing. Watch this!" Baxter does a string of cartwheels. It looks so odd with him hanging sideways.

We laugh as we chase each other up the walls and across the ceiling.

"Stop messing around!" Frank scolds from down below.

"We're training! Stop distracting us!" I shout from the highest point in the gym.

He shakes his head. "I'm out of here. I have work to do."

Baxter and I run around some more, then drop down to the mats. I'm exhausted.

I grab a bottle of water from the fridge. "Want one?"

Baxter is amused. "Not unless it's infused with blood."

Duh Chloe! Vampire!

We sit on the mats and lean against the wall. I'm trying to catch my breath, but Baxter is just fine. I also notice he's not sweating. Must be nice.

"You up for another round tomorrow?" he asks.

"I can't. I'm leaving for Boston tomorrow."

"Right. James going with you?"

"No, he's heading west to be with his pack while I'm gone."

"Ah yes, an east meets west relationship means time apart, doesn't it?"

I nod. "Unfortunately."

We sit quietly for a minute as I drink my water.

"Can I ask you a question Chloe?"

"You just did."

Baxter groans. "Good point."

"What's up?"

He hesitates. "It's about Jessica."

86

I stiffen. "What about her?"

"Is she...single?"

"Yes. Why?"

"I'm interested in her."

"Interested, how?"

Eyes wide and using his best Transylvanian accent he says, "Because I want to suck her blood. Waahaahaahaahaa!"

Despite my intention to come across hard, I laugh. Baxter mentioning his diet makes me think of something. "Can I see your fangs?"

Baxter is taken aback. "Why?"

I shrug. "I'm curious."

Baxter opens his mouth. I watch in wonder as his normal-looking canine teeth grow half an inch in length and sharpen to points. He lets me stare at his fangs for a moment, then retracts them.

"Does it hurt when they grow?"

"No."

"Do they ever grow when you don't want them to?"

He rolls his eyes. "No."

"What if one of them breaks?"

"They don't break."

"Ever?"

Baxter shakes his head. "Nope. I've never seen one break."

"Interesting." I'm about to ask whether blood still tastes like blood or if it has a better flavor to him, but he beats me to the punch.

"Can we get back to my original question please?"

"Oh yeah, sure. Sorry."

"Is Jessica off limits?"

"Off limits?"

"Do I have your permission to ask her out?"

I raise an eyebrow. "My permission? Why would you need my permission?"

"She is your assistant."

"True, but she's also an adult. Jessica can date whoever she wants."

"You say that, but your tone tells me otherwise. I don't want to step on your toes. I want our relationship to be amicable."

I play with the label on my water bottle as I contemplate how to respond to Baxter. I'm in an odd position. I don't want my best friend involved with a vampire. They are playboys. Despite her claim of wanting fun, Jessica isn't really that kind of girl. Plus, her breakup with Frank is a fresh wound.

But it's not my place to make Jessica's decisions.

"Okay, here's the thing. Jessica is an amazing girl. She's my best friend, and a great person. Don't mess with her."

He frowns. "So it's a 'no' then."

I shake my head. "I didn't say you can't ask her out. I said – don't mess with her. Do you understand the difference?"

"I don't plan to mess with her. I want to get to know her better."

"That's fine and dandy, but don't lead her on. She's been hurt before, and she doesn't need to get hurt again."

"I'll try not to."

I look him dead in the eyes. "Not good enough. I've read all about you vampires and your dating techniques. Jessica is not a game. She is a person, someone I really care about. She deserves better than being used."

Baxter's face is serious. "I won't start something with her without full disclosure."

I stretch my legs out in front of me. "Jessica's a big girl, she can do what she wants. For all I know, she's into guys with pointy teeth."

Baxter smiles. "How can she resist this?" He waves his hand over his six pack.

"I hate to burst your bubble Casanova, but hot guys are a dime a dozen around here. You'll have to do more than flex your abs to impress Jessica."

Chapter Six

Saying good-bye to James the next morning sucks. He rides along with me and Frank to the airport. I lean my head on his shoulder, relishing the last few minutes of physical contact we have.

For the first time in my life, I'm flying on a private plane.

"It will be easier for the Guard this way," Frank explained. "Keeping track of every passenger on a commercial flight would be a bear."

Our Escalade pulls onto the tarmac. I'm relieved to see our plane is a standard passenger plane, not a prop plane. Metal stairs are pulled up next to the hatch so we can board.

Frank opens the car door. "I'll give you some privacy." He steps out and jogs toward the Escalade behind us.

"I wish I didn't have to go," I whisper, still leaning on James. I'm not ready to move yet.

James kisses the top of my head. "I know. Being apart isn't fun, but we'll be back together soon."

I groan as I sit up. "Time to be responsible and all that jazz."

He raises an eyebrow. "All that jazz?"

"I picked it up from Willa. She says it sometimes."

A plane flies low overhead as I step out of the SUV. To my right, another plane is touching down.

James watches the plane fly overhead with wonder. "I've never been out on a tarmac before, it's pretty cool."

"Definitely," I agree. "Now come here and give me one more kiss before I go."

He pulls me in for a tight hug and lowers his mouth to mine. I love how soft his lips are. I'm going to miss this. Mindful that the Guard is watching, we don't go too crazy.

"Be careful," he says as we pull apart.

"I will."

James looks past me. "Frank!"

Frank is making his way up the airplane steps, but stops. "Yeah?"

"Don't let her do anything stupid!"

Frank gives a thumbs up. "It's all good. I brought a straitjacket with me."

"Ha ha," I say dryly. "You guys are hilarious."

James gives me one last hug. "You better get going."

I inhale his scent as I squeeze him tight. "You be careful too, okay?"

"Always am," he says with a smile.

I watch him get back into the SUV. After the Escalade pulls away, I walk up to the plane and give it a good onceover. The engines aren't falling off and the wings look relatively straight. Works for me.

I ascend the six steps leading to the plane's door and duck my head inside. The interior is simple with blue carpet and padded chairs. An aisle divides three rows of seats, two on each side. The pilot and his co-pilot step out of their cabin for a quick "hello." They seem to know what they're doing. All in all, I'm feeling good about the flight.

Frank already crammed his body into one of the seats in the front row. I take the seat across the aisle from him and buckle myself in.

"How long are we in the air?"

"About an hour."

The shaky tone of his voice catches my attention. I notice that he is sitting ramrod straight, his hands clenching the armrests hard enough to turn his knuckles white.

"What's wrong with you?"

He stares straight ahead. "Nothing."

"Oh my God. Don't tell me you're afraid of flying!" Of all the things for him to be afraid of…

Frank turns to me. There's a line of sweat below his hairline and his skin is a tad green.

"Please don't throw up," I beg him. If Frank throws up, I'll throw up. I better find some barf bags, stat.

"I'll do my best," he mumbles.

"We haven't even left the ground yet. Take some deep breaths." I rummage around in my bag and find a bottle of water. "Here, take a sip."

Frank stubbornly shakes his head no.

"I don't know why you're worried. If something happens, I'll put a protective bubble around us. No big deal."

Frank visibly relaxes for a second, then his body goes rigid again. "What if you get knocked unconscious?"

"Well," I pause, "then you're screwed."

Jessica

Chloe's office is eerily quiet without her here. I check emails and post an away message saying she is out of the office and to reach out to Willa for urgent issues.

I offered to man Chloe's phone while she is away, but she insisted I take time off. Aside from preparing meals for Willa, there won't be much for me to do.

I wander around the library and skim the pile of books Chloe set aside on the table. Almost all of them are about vampires.

I pick one up and read the title - *The Misunderstood Modern Day Vampire*. I smile when I see it is written by someone named Countess Regina.

I flip the book open and review the chapter titles. I don't need to read *Chapter 1: Modern Diet*. Chapter 2 could be interesting: *The Ease of Adaptation in a Multi-Cultural World*. However, Chapter 3 catches my eye: *Relationships with Humans – an Increasingly Dangerous Proposition*.

I turn to page 98 and begin reading:

> *While not a common practice for obvious reasons, vampires do occasionally mate with humans. However, with the invention of the Internet, cellular telephones and the prevalent use of social media websites such as Facebook, Instagram and SnapChat, a relationship with a human is becoming a less than ideal situation. All it takes is one bad breakup to expose a vampire for what he or she is.*

The Countess continues the chapter by discussing the various ways social media can be used to expose vampire culture.

Her point makes sense to me. I rarely look at my Facebook page. Too many people give out details about their life I don't need, or want, to know. I've read several posts between former friends or lovers in which they lay out the dirty details of their relationship for the whole world to see.

My face reddens when I turn to the next page. *Chapter 4: Sex with Humans*. I snap the book shut and set it on the table. I quickly exit the library, hoping no one in the Guard Operations Center was keeping an eye on me.

Chloe

I don't know who's more relieved when we land at Logan International Airport – me or Frank. His anxiety gave me anxiety.

"I'm drugging you next time," I tell him while unfastening my seatbelt.

I don't get a smartass comeback. Frank is already standing and heading for the exit. He nearly throws the flight attendant out of the way when she opens the hatch.

"Have a nice..." she starts to say, but Frank is halfway down the stairs. I won't be surprised if he kisses the ground.

I gather my belongings and check to make sure I'm not forgetting anything. I better double-check Frank's seat too. The man ran out of here and never looked back.

I'm relieved to see there isn't a wet spot in Frank's seat, but my happiness is cut short when I see the armrests. They are decimated. Frank's fingers left permanent indents in the plastic and steel.

"Um...just add it to our bill," I tell the stewardess when she walks over and sees the damage.

Her brown eyes widen. "Wow, I've never seen that before."

"I'm sorry. Next time I'll bring him stress balls or something."

"Don't worry about it Ms. Chloe," she responds with a smile. "We'll take care of it."

Her energy is pure and positive. Her blonde hair is pulled back in a bun and her blue uniform is pressed perfectly.

"What is your name?" I ask.

"Shannon."

I shake her hand. "Nice to meet you Shannon. Are you staying here in Boston?"

"Yes. Our crew will wait in the area until you're ready to go."

"Be sure you go out and see the sights. We won't be leaving for several days."

She grins. "I know. I'm actually from this area, so I'll be staying with family."

"Excellent! Enjoy your time."

Shannon walks behind me as I exit the plane. I stand on the top step and survey the tarmac. There are several Guard members waiting for me. Five Escalades are running and ready to leave. Frank stands outside the third vehicle holding the door for me.

I glance over my shoulder at Shannon. "It was nice meeting you. I'll see you again soon."

"We'll be here," she assures me.

I walk down the steps and climb into the Escalade. Unlike my SUV at home, the back rows of this vehicle are individual pilot seats. I climb all the way over so Frank can get in without having to go around to the other side. Two Guard members occupy the front seats and our driver pulls away as soon as my seatbelt is on.

We ride silently for a few minutes. I'm gazing out my window and taking in the sights. This is my first time in Boston.

"Our first stop is the Boston Guard Headquarters," Frank says, attempting to resume business as usual.

I turn to him. "Nice try. You know I'm never going to let you live this down, right?"

He groans. "I'll make you a deal."

"Go on."

"If you forget this ever happened, I promise, no more baby jokes."

I purse my lips, pretending to be deep in thought. "Deal," I say finally.

Frank breathes a sigh of relief.

I smirk.

"What are you smiling about?" he asks, daring me to say something about his fear of flying.

"I was just thinking you better start figuring out what you'll offer me after our flight home."

96

"You promised," he hisses.

"I promised to forget about our flight today. You didn't say anything about future flights."

Frank scowls. He clearly needs to work on his negotiating skills.

Jessica

After a yummy grilled cheese sandwich and tomato soup lunch with Willa, I struggle to find something to occupy my free time. I could go for a walk, but the humidity today is crazy. I could find a movie to watch, but then I'm wasting a beautiful day.

The perfect solution to my conundrum is to do something outside that requires no physical effort. I grab a book and head for the roof. I'm fifty pages in when a shadow blocks the sun. I look up and see Baxter standing in front of my lounge chair.

"Reading anything good?"

"It's pretty good so far." I hand him the book.

He scans the cover. "I read this one. I like it better than *Gone Girl*."

"You read Gillian Flynn?" I ask surprised.

Baxter takes the seat next to me. "Who doesn't?"

I smile. "Do you like to read?"

"I have a lot of time on my hands. Books help fill it."

"What type of books do you like?"

He shrugs. "I'll read just about anything."

"Reading anything good right now?"

"I just finished the *Dark Tower* series."

I crinkle my nose. "I don't know that one."

"It's Stephen King's masterpiece, his most thorough and thought out work. A lot of people don't like the ending, but for true King fans, it makes perfect sense. I wonder how I didn't figure it out beforehand."

"I've read *Cujo* and *'Salems Lot*." I blush when I realize *'Salems Lot* is about vampires. Not very nice ones either.

Baxter grins. "I love when you do that."

"Do what?"

"Blush. Your cheeks turn the most beautiful shade of pink."

I blush even more.

Baxter takes pity on me and looks away. "I did another run around the city. Still no sign of Gregory."

"Is that a good thing or a bad thing?"

Baxter's brow furrows. "I'm not sure."

"Chloe told me about him, Gregory. He sounds like a pretty shady guy."

"He is. He's the worst kind of guy."

"Chloe said something about Gregory's lover being addicted to children's blood. Is that a real thing?"

Baxter nods. "Most vampires made the transition to animal blood before I turned, but a few prefer human blood."

My eyes widen. "They attack people?"

"Not usually. You may not believe this, but there are people who voluntarily give their blood to vampires."

"Really?"

"Yep."

"Why?"

Baxter shrugs. "Who knows? People get off on different things."

Having someone suck my blood isn't my cup of tea, but who am I to judge? "Why didn't Gregory's lover get blood from one of those people? Why go after innocent children?"

"For the same reason a man who can have consensual sex decides to commit rape instead," Baxter says darkly. "You can't explain insanity."

"Have you drank human blood?"

"I have," he admits, "but it was given to me willingly."

"How do you find a willing donor?"

Baxter laughs. "Are you in the market for one?"

I giggle. "No, just curious."

"Some vampires live in small communities where their neighbors know what they are. For instance, my friend Elijah has lived in the same small village in Romania for over one hundred and fifty years. Given that he has never aged, people put two and two together. Women show up at his front door on a regular basis."

"Isn't he afraid someone will try to kill him?"

"Nah. He knows everyone in town and they know he means them no harm. Elijah is incredibly wealthy. He funds all of the community's events, emergency services, medical facilities and school systems. In exchange, they keep his secret."

"I see."

I examine Baxter's face. He is an attractive man who will never age. He probably has no problem finding willing donors.

"What are you thinking?" he asks me.

I try not to blush again. "I bet you have women knocking on your door every night."

Baxter chuckles. "Hardly. I used to, but I turn them away. I'm not interested."

"Why not?"

"I'm satisfied with my daily cow hearts."

I'm confused. "You said you've had human blood before…"

"Yes."

"Don't you want it again?"

He shakes his head. "I don't have a craving for human blood like some vampires do. I think they enjoy being in control, knowing they can take a life if they want to."

I shiver. "That's creepy."

"It is," he agrees. "I don't want to be like them."

"When did you have human blood?"

Baxter raises an eyebrow. "You're very interested in this."

"I've never met a vampire before," I explain, "and who knows when I'll meet one again."

"Fair point. I only drink human blood when I'm being intimate with a woman. It heightens the experience."

"Oh." I'm all flushed again.

"Any more questions?" he asks with his trademark grin.

"Um...no," I manage to say.

He softens. "I'm sorry if I made you uncomfortable."

I wave off his apology. "I asked, you answered. It's not your fault I embarrass easily."

Baxter stands and stretches his arms to the sky. "Is there a movie theater nearby?"

"There's one a couple blocks over. Are you going to see a movie?"

"Depends."

"On?"

He smiles. "Whether you're going with me."

Chloe

The sun has set by the time we're done touring the Guard's Boston Headquarters. It's a lot like our headquarters in New York City,

100

except they are in a single-story brick building instead of a high rise.

My visit started with a briefing session. Nina's coven is a mess and the Boston Guard had a lot of intel to share. We went over my schedule while I'm in town and the list of coven members I'm meeting with. The Boston Guard thoroughly planned out all my meetings and the necessary security details.

"Excellent work," I say to the group, pleased with the time and effort they put in.

After that, I toured their headquarters and introduced myself to all of the Guard members on duty. Despite being the incumbent Verhena for a year now, I still don't have a grasp on how large the Guard is. I am not isolated to the building in New York, but I don't leave it often. This trip is already opening my eyes to the fact that I need to get out and meet more of my people.

"I want to learn more about the Guard," I tell Frank on our drive to the condo where we'll be staying.

"What do you want to know?"

"Everything."

He chuckles. "That will take a while."

"I know, and I didn't mean we have to do it right now. But it's definitely something I want to hear more about."

"I think that's an excellent idea," he says, pleased with my interest in his organization.

We ride in silence for a moment, the day catching up to the both of us. Tomorrow won't be any better.

"My meeting with Nina is going to be intense."

"Agreed. We're bringing two extra Guard members with us to her house."

"Is she that crazy?"

Frank sighs. "There's something you need to know."

Uh oh. I don't like his tone. "That doesn't sound good."

"During your tour, two Guard members pulled me aside and gave me more info. They asked me to wait until we left to share it with you."

"Why?"

"They didn't want to ruin your visit."

Seriously? I swear these Guard members are more sensitive than thirteen-year-old girls. "Alright, out with it."

"One of the Boston Guard members, Henry, has been a member of Nina's coven his entire life. Nina believes he is a close ally. Which he was, until a few months ago. Like many of the people who reached out to us, Henry is concerned about Nina's mental health."

"Ugh. Did you see the letter from Ted?"

"I did."

Ted is the most recent Boston Coven member to write us. He described an incident after a coven meeting last month that hit me hard. He claims Nina believes all werewolves should be eliminated and expressed an interest in creating an underground group of witches to fight them.

Ted's letter troubled Willa. "Ted isn't one to exaggerate," she told me with a frown.

I repeat her sentiments to Frank. "Did Henry witness Nina's tirade about the werewolves?"

"He did, he was there when she went off. She lost it in front of a small group of people, all of whom she thinks she can trust."

"In reality, the people closest to her are the most concerned."

Frank nods. "Right. They witness her breakdowns up close and personal."

I'm dreading my meeting with her tomorrow. "Did you see the way she looked at me at my party? She hates my face."

"The thing is," Frank pauses, "she does hate you."

"What?" I ask shocked. I was only kidding when I said Nina hates me. What did I ever do to her?

"Nina is a traditionalist. She thinks witches are superior beings. She openly calls for the destruction of all werewolves, rogue or not. She believes you are the witch equivalent to the anti-Christ."

I rub my temples. "Awesome."

I thought the witches would be happy we made amends with the werewolves. We can travel west now, and we can put our fears of the wolves to rest. I thought I did what was best for my people.

Apparently, not everyone agrees with me.

We pull up to the security post for a gated neighborhood. Our driver gives the security guard our information and a few minutes later we're pulling into a short driveway in front of a well-lit brick townhouse.

In addition to Frank and the guys in the car with us, Guard members will stay in the townhouses that share walls with mine. It's crazy to think I will spend the rest of my life completely surrounded by armed guards.

The Guard members next door order a pizza and bring it over for dinner. I find out that the guys who were in the Escalade with us are Pete and Richard. They are funny and keep me entertained as I eat. We go back and forth saying different phrases in our Boston and New York accents. We debate whether the Patriots are really that good (they are, but I won't admit it) and talk about the places I should visit while I'm in town.

After dinner, Pete and Richard hang around to watch a Red Sox game. The game is tied up and it's the bottom of the ninth. The guys are totally engrossed, but I'm exhausted.

I yawn. "I'm going to bed."

"Okay," Frank mumbles, eyes glued to the television screen.

"Nite guys," I say while walking out of the room.

They ignore me and cheer for a double-play instead.

Thank God they're on top of things. A dinosaur could charge through the living room and they wouldn't notice.

Once upstairs, I open my suitcase and dig out some pajamas. I also find the teddy bear I sprayed with James's cologne before I left New York. I hug the bear and get a whiff of my man. I miss him.

I pick out my outfit for tomorrow and brush my teeth. I finish getting ready for bed and lay down on top of the covers. I take my cellphone off of its charger and call James.

"Hey babe," he says when he answers the phone.

His voice makes me smile. "Did you make it home?"

"Yes. I got here about an hour ago. How was your flight?"

I consider telling him about Frank's "episode", but I don't. I made a promise and I won't break it.

"Uneventful. No turbulence."

We talk about our nights. I laugh when he tells me Whitney has resorted to asking a Magic 8 Ball if she should break up with Brandon.

"What's on the docket for tomorrow?" he asks.

I sigh. "My meeting with the crazy coven leader."

"Maybe it won't be so bad."

"No, I'm pretty sure it's going to be awful." I tell James the new information I have on Nina.

"Good grief. The woman is off her rocker."

I express my biggest fear to James. "What if everyone agrees with her? What if they all hate me?"

"No one hates you. Everyone was in awe of you at your party."

"Not Nina."

"Nina is bat-shit crazy. She doesn't count."

I giggle, then sigh. "I really don't want to go tomorrow."

"I understand," James says sympathetically. "Don't worry about it too much tonight. She'll play nice with you tomorrow. If she wants to keep her position, she has to be on your good side. She needs you as an ally."

"What if she loses it?"

"Let her. If she does, then she's definitely out as Coven Leader," James reasons.

"True."

James is so freaking smart. He's better equipped to handle things like this than I am.

"Get some rest," he tells me. "Sounds like you're going to need it."

"I wish you were here. I wouldn't be so nervous if you were with me."

"I wish I was with you too, but I would be a distraction. Especially if the amendments to the treaty are a divisive issue. Your people need to see you for the woman you are, no drama attached."

I know he's right, but the self-centered piece of me is sick of making sacrifices. "Do you ever wish we were just a normal couple who could lead ordinary lives?"

"An extraordinary woman like you will never be satisfied with an ordinary life."

Jessica

What does a girl wear on a date with a vampire?

I stand in my closet and stare at my clothes. I'm waiting for the perfect outfit to jump out at me, but nothing happens. Then I remember a summer dress Whitney bought for me during one of her signature shopping trips. It's white lace over a white slip dress. It's dainty, cute and feminine. I put on a pale denim jacket and a pair of wedge sandals to complete my look.

I take a quick glance in the mirror. My days in the sun have given me a soft tan. I put a drop of gel in my hair and swipe clear gloss across my lips.

"This is as good as it's gonna get," I say to my reflection.

I dial Baxter's room extension.

"Ahoy hoy," he answers. Of course he doesn't answer the phone like a normal person.

"I'm ready to go."

"Cool. I'll come pick you up."

Before I can respond, the dial tone fills my ear. I put the phone on the cradle and walk toward my door, intending to meet Baxter in the hallway. I've taken two steps toward my door when I hear three sharp knocks.

Who is coming to see me now? Whoever it is, I need to get rid of them fast.

I pull my door open. It's Baxter.

"How did you…." I start to ask.

He grins. "Superfast. Remember?"

I gather my wits. "Right. I keep forgetting that."

"Shall we go?"

I smile. "Yes, we shall."

I check out Baxter's outfit as we head toward the elevator. He's dressed casually in khaki golf shorts and a long-sleeve blue t-shirt. His white tennis shoes look brand new and make his legs look incredibly tan. He is the opposite of the pale, undead vampires in movies and TV shows.

"What should we do tonight?" he asks as he pushes the down button for the elevator.

"Don't you want to go to the movies?"

106

"I'm good with the movies, but if there's something else you prefer, I'm game. My only stipulation is we stay inside Willa's wards. I don't want to take you outside the boundaries with Gregory running loose."

Baxter's caveat limits the things we can do. Willa's wards are half a mile wide. Even in a place like New York City, that doesn't give us a ton of options.

"There is a movie theater inside the wards," I tell Baxter. "It's an older, smaller one. They only have three screens."

"Fine with me. I don't need anything fancy."

"Okay, we'll start there and see what's playing tonight."

"What was the last great movie you saw?" he asks.

"Hmm, that's a tough one. Oh, I know, it was *The Curse of Grindelwald*."

Baxter smiles. "I saw that one. I liked it."

"It was nice to be in the world of Harry Potter again."

"Yeah, because you're not usually in a world with witches."

I laugh. "I've never thought of it that way."

We talk about movies and our favorite TV shows as we walk to the theater. Baxter's like me, he watches a little bit of everything.

When we reach the theater, we consider our options: a romantic comedy, an animated movie for kids, and an action thriller. I'm not quite sure which route we should go. Action films aren't my thing, but I'll feel silly suggesting the animated movie or the rom com.

Baxter makes the decision for me. "Well, I guess you're stuck watching a chick flick with me."

"Really? You don't want to watch *Hostage Situation*?"

My heart melts a little when he says, "Nah. I'd rather watch people fall in love than kill each other."

107

Baxter buys our tickets from the outside kiosk and we walk inside. The aroma of popcorn fills my nose.

"Smells yummy! Want some popcorn? I'll buy."

He raises an eyebrow.

And I'm blushing again. Will I ever get used to this vampire thing?

After Baxter buys me a small bag of popcorn and a soda (he insists), we find seats near the back of the theater. It's a week night and the theater is mostly empty. A few couples are scattered here and there, and a group of four women sits a few rows in front of us.

"Do you miss food?" I ask Baxter before shoveling a handful of popcorn into my mouth.

"I used to, but it's gotten easier over the years."

"What happens if you eat regular food?"

He hesitates. "You sure you want to know?"

"Yes."

"If I eat regular food, I throw it up. I throw up most of the cow heart after I eat it too."

I crinkle my nose. Yuck. "Why do you eat the whole heart then? Can you just suck the blood out of it?"

He nods. "I usually do, but there are times I want to bite into something. Chew it around."

"Um...okay."

Baxter laughs. "I know it sounds weird."

"Hey, whatever floats your boat."

The theater lights dim and the cute video asking people not to smoke or use their cellphones plays. As the third preview starts, Baxter drapes his arm over the back of my chair. I'm a little disappointed when he doesn't rest it on my shoulders.

The movie follows the typical romantic comedy formula, which is perfectly fine with me. It's keeping me entertained, but I periodically check on Baxter out of the corner of my eye to see how he's reacting. He laughs in the appropriate places and doesn't appear to be bored.

"I can't do this anymore. We're from two different worlds!" the lead female character exclaims one hour into the movie.

The man is crestfallen. "Dana, we can make this work. We're not that different."

Baxter whispers in my ear, "They have no idea, do they?"

I laugh. "Must be nice to only worry about what your country club friends will think of your auto mechanic boyfriend," I whisper back.

Baxter searches my eyes. "What would your friends think of me?"

"My friends already know you," I point out.

He doesn't drop his gaze. "What do *you* think of me?"

I have a sudden urge to kiss him, but making the first move is outside my comfort zone. I stare back at him and debate whether I should follow my impulse.

His brow furrows. "What is it?"

Screw it. I'm going for it.

I reach out my hand and run it through the back of Baxter's hair. Before he can say anything, I pull his mouth down on mine. He's surprised at first, but then he parts my lips with his tongue. My heart pounds as our kiss intensifies. Baxter's hands are strong and firm, holding me tight against him. It's a bit awkward kissing with the armrest separating us, but we make it work.

I'm not the type of person to indulge in public displays of affection, but I don't care if everyone in the theater turns around to watch us. I don't care if we get kicked out. The energy between us is like nothing I've felt before.

I'm not sure how long we're locked in our embrace when the theater lights come on.

Baxter pulls back. "Wow, great movie."

I hear the women from a few rows down whispering and chuckling. I smile as I catch my breath. "Best film I've seen in a while."

Baxter stands and extends his hand. "Come on, let's get out of here."

I take a deep breath when we step outside, the cool night air is refreshing. The sidewalk isn't nearly as busy as it was when we bought our tickets. The city lights twinkle, the dazzling skyline surrounding us.

"Where do you want to go now?" I ask Baxter.

"You tell me. This is your territory."

We walk around for a while. Typically I'd step inside a store or restaurant, but most of the stores are closed for the night and restaurants are out given that one of us doesn't eat food. We're walking in a giant circle, but neither of us minds.

"Pick a place to eat," Baxter insists after an hour of walking. "You must be hungry."

"No, that would be inconsiderate. I'll grab a bite when we get home."

"Are you sure?"

I nod. "Yes, I'm fine."

I stop at the edge of Willa's wards. We've been in this same spot a few times tonight. "If we go outside the wards, there's a few clubs not far from here."

Baxter shakes his head. "I'm not taking you outside the wards. Besides, you don't seem like a club person."

I smile. "I'm not, but I figured I would throw it out there." An idea pops into my head. "Do you like to swim?"

"Yeah. Why?"

110

"Have you been to our pool yet?"

He grins. "I haven't! I forgot Willa has a pool."

"It's been twenty-five years since your last visit, right?"

"Yep, something like that."

"Willa renovated the pool. You'll love it."

We turn back toward the building. I'm glad I came up with something to do. I'm not ready for the evening to come to an end.

"Do you and Elias live together?" I ask.

"No. We travel together to be on the safe side, but we live separately. Most of the time I'm in England, and he likes his home base in France."

"Did Elias turn you?"

"Yes."

"Why?"

Baxter smiles. "I feel like I'm on twenty questions."

I cringe. "Sorry! I'm just so curious about you."

His eyes sparkle. "I can relate."

Before I can ask another question, he suddenly grabs my hand and pulls me into a dark alley. He presses my back against a brick wall and leans into me.

"Baxter! What..."

He crushes his mouth against mine. The crazy energy I felt while kissing him in the theater courses through me again from head to toe. I get lost in him, completely oblivious to the world around me. The chatter of the people on the streets, the honking of taxi cabs, the sound of sirens – all gone.

Too soon, Baxter pulls away. "Sorry Jessica, I couldn't help myself."

"It's okay," I say breathlessly. "I deserved it after I jumped you in the movie theater."

He chuckles softly. "You can jump me anytime."

He stands straight and takes my hand. We step back onto the sidewalk and continue walking home.

"To answer your question – Elias turned me to save my life." I open my mouth, but he stops me. "Uh uh, my turn. How did you end up living with Willa?"

Ah, I see. It's my turn to be interrogated.

"It's kind of a long story."

"I've got time. I've got an infinite amount of time," he says with a smile.

I giggle. "True." I don't like to talk about my parents and their doomed relationship, but I trust Baxter. I feel like I can tell him anything.

"My mom met my dad at the first restaurant she worked at after she graduated from Leviston. She was a sous chef and he was the bartender."

"Your dad must not be a warlock," Baxter guesses, "or you'd be a witch."

I nod. "Exactly. My grandparents were not happy about it."

"I can imagine."

"Things were really good in the beginning. They got married, had me and talked about opening their own restaurant. But then my dad met someone new."

"Another woman?"

"Yes. A new waitress. Mom walked in on them together in the supply closet."

Baxter winces. "Ouch."

"It must have been awful for her. When she kicked my dad out, things went downhill for him. He started drinking heavily and doing drugs."

Baxter's eyes soften. "That's terrible."

112

"It was rough, but then Willa came in to the restaurant one night and asked to meet the person who cooked her meal. Things took off from there."

"Do you ever see your father?"

"Not anymore."

"When was the last time you saw him?"

"The summer after fifth grade. He got into some bad things and I didn't feel safe with him anymore."

"Do you know where he is now?"

I shake my head. "No. Last I checked, he was staying in a shelter in Minneapolis."

"I'm sorry Jessica."

I shrug. "It is what it is. I wish he was a better man and involved in my life, but he isn't. I'm not one of those girls who's going to have daddy issues because of it."

"What a shame. Girls with daddy issues really dig me," Baxter says with a grin.

I laugh. "I think most girls really dig you."

"I don't know about that. My fangs usually send them running."

Baxter and I walk into the building hand-in-hand. Rudy, the Guard member sitting at the reception desk, does a double take when we walk by.

"Hey Rudy!"

His eyes shift between me and Baxter. "Um, hi Jess. Everything okay?"

"Yes. Baxter and I are going to the pool. Can you guys turn off the cameras?"

"Uh…sure…"

The expression on Rudy's face says it all. He thinks I'm going to hook up with Baxter in the pool!

"I don't want you listening in on our conversation," I quickly explain.

"Right," Rudy says with a smirk.

Baxter laughs when we get in the elevator. "I do believe your reputation has been compromised."

"Whatever. Those guys are the biggest gossip queens I've ever met, and the girls at my private school were pretty bad."

Baxter turns to look at me. "I don't want to ruin things for you. Say the word and I'll back off."

I squeeze his hand. "I don't want you to back off."

He smiles, eyes sparkling. "Good."

The elevator stops on the 12th floor and we step out.

He scans the room. "Wow! This is amazing."

"Willa did a good job, huh?"

"Absolutely. I love the Spanish tile she picked." He walks over to the glass wall and admires the view of the city. "You're on top of the world."

I laugh. "It feels like it sometimes."

He turns from the glass and announces, "Time for a dip." In a flash, his shirt if off, giving me a glimpse of his toned midsection.

Wait a minute...is he getting naked?

Does anyone in this place wear a bathing suit anymore?

I make haste for the staircase. "I'm gonna grab my bathing suit and some towels. Be right back."

"Sure," Baxter says as he undoes his belt buckle.

I get out of there before he drops his shorts. I take the steps to my apartment, my heart pounding as I rummage through my dresser for my bathing suit.

Oh my God! There is a gorgeous man, I mean, vampire, downstairs completely naked. And he's waiting for me.

My hands shake as I put on my bathing suit. I don't know if I can do this! I'm not like Chloe. She is fearless and confident when it comes to men. My kiss with Baxter in the movie theater is the only time I've ever made the first move.

I'm in full-on panic mode. I don't know what to do. Then it hits me. I grab my cellphone and call Chloe.

"Hello?" she answers after the third ring. I look at my bedside clock and see it's 11:30 p.m. Chloe is usually a night owl, but it's obvious by her low and shaky voice that I disrupted her sleep.

"Hey Chloe, it's Jess. Sorry I woke you. Go back to sleep."

"No," she says with a yawn. "What's up?"

"I need your advice."

"Okay."

"It's about Baxter."

"What about Baxter?" Chloe asks, much more alert now. When I don't say anything, Chloe continues, "If that mother…"

"No!" I cut her off, "nothing like that. I'm fine."

Chloe lets out a sigh of relief. "Thank God. I'd hate to have to kill him."

I'd laugh if I thought she was joking. "I'm in a bit of a sticky situation."

"Like what?"

"We went on a date tonight."

"You did?! That's great!"

"It is?" I ask, less convinced.

"Did you have a good time?"

"A very good time."

"Then yes, it's great!"

"He's down in the pool now."

"You guys are going swimming?"

"Yes."

"So what's the problem?" Chloe asks confused.

"He's naked," I whisper into the phone.

Chloe breaks out into laughter.

"It's not funny!"

"Let me get this straight. Your problem is that you have a hot, naked man ready and waiting for you?"

When she says it like that…

"I don't know what to do."

"Don't overthink this Jess. If you don't want to go back down there, then don't. But if you like him, and you're having a good time, I say take the plunge!"

"I like him," I confess. "He's cute, funny and smart." I pause for a second. "We both know he's not boyfriend material. Maybe I should stop now before I get in too deep."

Chloe softens her tone. "I understand. Do what feels right. Baxter is a good-time guy, not a forever guy. Act accordingly."

"Okay. Thanks Chloe."

"Keep me posted," she says before we hang up.

I sit on my bed weighing my options. I should avoid Baxter. I will have no one to blame but myself if I fall for him. On the other hand, I'll be super pissed if I wuss out. I deserve a little fun, don't I?

"Yes you do!" I say out loud. "You do deserve some fun, dammit!"

With my newfound resolve, I stand up and walk out of the room. Three seconds later, I walk back in. I forgot the towels.

Chapter Seven

Chloe

Five minutes after I hang up with Jessica, there's a banging on my bedroom door.

For the love of God! Can a girl get some sleep around here?

"Come in!"

The door opens and Frank flips on the light.

"Hey!" I protest as my eyes struggle to adjust to the brightness.

Frank could care less about disrupting my sleep. "I need to speak with you."

"Now?"

"Yes, now."

I sit up in bed and lean against the headboard. "This better be important."

"It's about Jessica."

I roll my eyes. "She's fine Frank. Go to bed."

I start to lay back down when he exclaims, "She's with that leech!"

His anger amuses me. "A leech? Is that the politically correct term?"

His jaw tightens. "I'm not joking around."

I glare at him. "What did you think would happen? That she would just sit around and wait for you?"

His mouth drops open, stunned.

"Jessica is young, beautiful and smart. She's going to date other guys. And maybe, if she's lucky, she'll find one to love."

His eyes narrow. "She told you."

"No she didn't. Jessica keeps her word, you know that. It was your boys in the Guard. I went down there one day while you two were on a date. They were dying to tell me."

Frank crosses his arms. "Bastards."

"I don't know how things ended between you, but she was devastated. If you're not going to give her what she wants, leave her alone."

He stands silently, then sits on the edge of my bed. "I like her Chloe. I like her a lot."

Sigh. Doesn't look like I'm getting sleep any time soon. "Then do something about it."

He closes his eyes. "I can't."

"Why? Did she tell you to get lost?"

"No, I broke up with her."

"That was stupid."

He gives me a look.

"Well it was! Why did you break up with her if you like her?"

"She was interfering with my job."

"Interfering with your job? Are you serious? That's the most ridiculous thing I've ever heard."

"No it's not! My job means everything to me."

We sit quietly for a second. I can relate to Frank's dilemma. I broke up with Elliott to keep him safe. Would I pick being the Verhena over James? I hope I never have to find out.

I put my hand on his arm. "You made your choice. You chose the job," I say with more empathy than I had a moment ago.

"I'm wondering if it was the right choice."

"If she calls you right now and says she wants to give it another try, would you?"

"No," he admits.

"There are plenty of Guard members who have partners. Why do you think you can't?"

He looks at me. "I want to run the show Chloe. I can't have any distractions."

"I guess I don't understand. I mean, you're the personal security guard to the Verhena-to-be. What's higher than that?"

"Not to deflate your ego, but being your Kevin Costner wasn't my ultimate goal when I joined the Guard."

Oh... I've never asked Frank what his ambitions are. Self-centered me assumed he is satisfied with his position.

"Okay, fair enough. What was your ultimate goal?"

"Don't get me wrong Chloe, please. I love this job, but I want to be more than your right-hand man. I want to lead the Guard into a new era."

"And you don't feel like you can do that now?"

"That's not what I'm saying. Meeting you and becoming your security guard catapulted me into one of the highest positions in the Guard overnight. I loved sharing our new procedures with the Boston Guard members today. I feel like I'm making a big impact on our community, and I love it."

"Good. I want you to be happy."

"I am, but I've come to realize that my professional ambitions are all-consuming. I don't have time for a girlfriend."

"You found time to go on dates," I argue.

He nods. "True. A few hours every now and then isn't hard to come by. But she'll want more than that down the line, and I can't give it to her."

119

I pick at the blanket. "Seems to me you've already decided."

Frank sighs. "I have. It's a sucky choice though."

"Let her go Frank," I say softly. "If you're not going to commit to Jessica and give her the life she deserves, it would be cruel for you to interfere."

He gazes off into the distance. "She made me happy. Made me envision a different life for myself. A wife, kids, a happy home. Things I never wanted." He clears his throat. "But this is my calling. It's what I was born to do."

I crawl out from under the covers and give him a big hug. "I'm so sorry."

He squeezes me back. "Jessica deserves more than to be ignored. She needs a man who will give her all of his time and attention. She should be the center of someone's universe."

We sit in a silent embrace. I usually crack a joke to lighten the mood in moments like these, but humor eludes me.

Jessica

When I gather the nerve to return to the pool, Baxter is moving smoothly through the water. He looks like an Olympic swimmer, taking perfectly timed breaths as his arms and legs propel his body forward.

Baxter notices I'm back and stops mid-stroke. He slicks his wet hair back and smiles at me. "Hey! I was about to send out a search party."

I relax when I see Baxter is in his boxers and not his birthday suit. Thank goodness!

I throw our towels on a chaise lounge. "Do you need to take breaths when you swim?"

He shakes his head. "No, but old habits die hard."

"So I shouldn't challenge you to a 'who can stay under the water the longest' contest?"

"Not unless you like to lose."

I walk toward the pool, blushing as Baxter openly checks me out. "Do I make you nervous?" he asks.

I jump in the pool before I answer him. I swim a few strokes underwater before I pop up four feet away from him.

"A little," I admit.

"Why?"

"Not for the reason you think."

"My being a vampire doesn't make you nervous?"

"Not really."

Baxter laughs. "And here I thought I was a scary guy."

"I'm sure you can be scary when you want to be."

"Yes, I can," Baxter says without hesitation.

"Did you show Chloe your scary side in training?"

"Nah. We had fun in training, we didn't get too serious."

"Did she freeze you in place?"

Baxter's face lights up. "She did! Has she ever done it to you?"

I shake my head. "No way."

"There you are, going about your business, and the next thing you know, it's like you've been zapped through time. It was kinda cool actually."

"I'll take your word for it."

Baxter moves closer to me. "Why are you afraid of me?"

I look down at my feet treading water. "It's embarrassing."

He crosses his heart. "I promise I won't laugh."

I smile, but don't respond. I swim to the side of the pool and hold on to the wall. Baxter swims over next to me.

"Tell me," he presses gently. "Whatever it is, it's okay."

I meet his eyes. "I'm not good with men."

He wiggles his eyebrows. "Good thing I'm not a man."

I chuckle. "You know what I mean."

"You seem okay to me."

"I'm bad at flirting, dating, and everything that goes along with it."

Baxter reaches out and spikes my wet hair for me. "I haven't noticed any glaring deficiencies."

I laugh. "Thanks for the ringing endorsement."

"Why are you single?" He asks the question so bluntly. As if I will have a simple answer.

"I was seeing someone. We broke up recently."

"I'd say I'm sorry to hear that, but I'm not. His loss is my gain. What was your longest relationship?"

"My boyfriend in high school. We were together for two years."

Baxter whistles. "Two years is a long time. What happened?"

"He went off to college in Maine and I stayed here. We tried the long distance thing for a couple months, but it didn't work. He wanted to party and hook up with other girls."

"What about the most recent guy? What happened with him?"

"He wants to focus on his career. I was getting in the way of that." I frown. My love life sure does sound depressing.

Baxter touches my shoulder. "Don't be ashamed of men making poor decisions. They'll regret their choices."

"I doubt it."

"I don't."

Baxter leans in and presses his soft lips against mine.

I have never, ever felt this way kissing a man. My skin is on fire. I run my hands up his muscular back and into his hair. I love the way it feels between my fingers. Most of the guys I've dated had short hair or buzz cuts. Baxter's is longer, enough for me to wrap my fingers in.

Baxter groans, then pulls away. "I think we should stop now."

"Why?" I ask, a little dazed.

"Because if we don't, I'll do things to you that you might regret in the morning."

Before I can protest his assumption, he pulls himself up on the edge of the wall and gets out of the pool. He grabs a towel and dries off.

What is happening? I completely put myself out there for him, and he walks away. I never get this guy stuff right!

I get out of the pool and grab the other towel. I dry off silently. I'm upset he's brushed me off and I want to get back to my room. I wrap the towel around my body and start to walk passed him.

"Good night," I say coolly.

He reaches out and gently grabs the back of my arm. "Don't be mad. I'm trying to do the right thing." He gives me his puppy dog eyes.

"It's okay Baxter. I understand."

"I don't think you do. I'd love to lay you down on a chaise lounge and slip that bikini off of you." He sighs. "But I won't. Not tonight anyway. I want you to be sure about me."

Baxter continues to surprise me. I figured he would take advantage of me in a second if I gave any inkling he had a shot. But he didn't. In fact, he stopped it well before I was ready to call it a night.

"I appreciate it. I do. I was just hurt when you pulled away."

Baxter smiles. "Does it make you feel better to know it was incredibly difficult and I'll be kicking myself for it later?"

I chuckle. "Yeah, a little."

Baxter grabs my hand. "C'mon, I'll walk you home."

Chloe

My cellphone alarm goes off at 7:30 a.m. I grunt as I grab my phone and choose the "snooze" button. All too soon, it starts yelling at me again. I swear the fastest five minutes in the world are the five minutes between my snooze alarms.

Why, oh why, did I set a 9:00 a.m. meeting? I hate getting up in the morning. What's worse is it's my meeting with Nina.

I roll myself out of bed and take a hot shower. I blow dry my hair as opposed to putting it up in a wet bun like I usually do. I put on a green wrap dress and a pair of nude heels.

Jessica and I picked out brand new outfits for me to wear while I'm on my trip. All I had at home were casual clothes. While I didn't go so far as to buy suits, I bought several business appropriate outfits.

I put on lip gloss and wear the earrings James gave me for my birthday. I check my reflection in the mirror and I'm shocked to see how grown up I look. Anyone who sees me will think I'm a full-fledged adult.

I go downstairs to grab a quick breakfast and smile when I see someone has dropped off bagels and coffee. That's a lot better than the Pop Tart I planned on having.

My phone buzzes. I look at the screen and see I have a text message from Jessica.

J: *You up?* ☼

C: *Yes ma'am. Dressed and ready to go.*

J: *Okay, just making sure. Sorry I called so late last night.*

C: *No worries. I hope all went well* ☺

J: *I took the plunge.*

I laugh. Go Jess!

> C: *You ho. I swim in that pool you know!*

> J: *LOL Nothing happened.*

> C: *Sure... I'm having them drain the water anyway.*

> J: *I'm serious, he was a gentleman.*

Baxter, a gentleman? Maybe he took what I said in the gym to heart.

> C: *Good. I gotta go. We'll chat later.*

> J: *Good luck with Nina today!*

I sigh as I put my phone in my purse. I need more than luck to deal with Nina.

Frank walks into the kitchen. "You ready?"

"Ready as I'll ever be."

He gives me a onceover. "You look nice."

"Thanks! So do you."

Frank looks down at his outfit – still khaki pants and an Under Armour polo shirt. "Can't go wrong with a timeless classic."

Once we're in the car, Frank and I go over everything we know about Nina.

"Has something catastrophic happened in her life?" I ask. "Everyone is saying the same thing – she flipped a switch. All of the sudden saying and doing things that went against her prior beliefs."

Frank shakes his head. "I wondered the same thing, but no. No deaths in her family. No bad breakup. No financial crisis. The only thing that's changed is becoming the Coven Leader."

"You think the stress drove her crazy?"

"It's possible."

I think about my current position and how stressed I get at times. I can see how it would drive someone nuts.

125

Our vehicle stops in front of a pale blue cape cod with black shutters. Bright flowers bloom in well-kept flower beds. Two rocking chairs and an antique table sit on the front porch. Nina is rocking in one of the chairs holding a coffee mug. She waves and smiles when we get out of the car.

"Let the games begin," I whisper to Frank as we walk up the driveway. Pete and Richard follow close behind us.

When I step onto the porch, a small dog runs over to greet me. I bend down and pet his head.

"Hi little guy!" I say with a grin. I love dogs.

Nina sips her coffee, a small smile on her face. "His name is Brewster."

"Is he a Frenchie?"

"Yes, he's a French bulldog."

Frank extends his hand to Nina. "I'm Frank, Chloe's personal security guard. This is Pete and Richard, members of the local Boston Guard."

Nina says "hi" to Pete and Richard. They nod silently to acknowledge her greeting.

"Why don't you come in? I have more coffee if you're interested."

Nina walks us through her home. Her décor is simple and clean. Nothing flashy. I don't see any photographs of friends or family members. Plants are scattered in various places throughout her house. I smile when I see a corner filled with a fluffy dog bed and chew toys. At least she treats her dog well.

Nina offers me a seat at the head of her dining room table. Frank stands behind my chair, and Pete and Richard stand at the opposite end of the table.

"I'm getting a fresh cup," Nina says as she pours herself more coffee. "Would you like some?"

"No thank you."

Nina walks over and takes the seat to my right. She looks uneasy, but I would too if my boss and three ginormous bodyguards were in my house.

She pours creamer in her cup. "Where would you like to start?"

No sense in wasting any time, I cut to the chase. "There's been unrest within your coven. Why do you think that is?"

Nina stirs her coffee, then taps the spoon on the side of the cup before placing it on the matching saucer. "Pretty simple really. Half of the coven doesn't like me."

"Why don't they like you? As best you can tell."

Nina sighs. "The younger generation is the group that doesn't like me. I told them to take down any Facebook posts about our meetings."

"They were posting information about your meetings?" I ask shocked.

"Not about the content of the meetings. They would say things like, 'Group meeting tonight. I hope it doesn't last long. Big party at Jeanie's.' Things of that nature."

"Did the posts say anything about the group meeting being a coven meeting or mention that they are witches?"

"No, but I felt they were walking a thin line."

I sigh, relieved. I created a secure internet site where witches can interact with each other and I've sent countless emails with directives about social media use. I'd be incredibly disappointed if someone made a silly mistake like discussing coven meetings on their Facebook page.

"Any other reason you can think of for the unhappiness within the coven?" I'm purposely asking open ended questions. I don't want her to have any clue about what I already know.

After a half hour of Nina giving me b.s. stories about the young members of her coven, I've heard enough. She never mentions anything about our pact with the werewolves or how she is unhappy with my "modern" take on being the Verhena. It's clear she has no idea the people who voiced their concerns are the witches in her age group, not the younger coven members.

"I think we've covered all the bases." I stand and Nina does the same. "Thank you for your hospitality."

As we're walking to her front door, she asks, "Who else are you meeting with?"

"I'm sorry Nina, I can't reveal that information. I promised everyone I would keep our discussions, and their identities, confidential."

Nina purses her lips, showing frustration for the first time. "I'd like to know the allegations leveraged against me and who is making them."

"If people want to speak openly tomorrow night at the coven meeting, so be it. But I'm not going back on my word."

Nina crosses her arms, but says nothing. What can she do?

I mimic her fake smile. "All leaders have their critics. Am I right?"

Something flashes in Nina's eyes. I don't know if it's anger, understanding, or a little of both. "Indeed they do."

I extend my hand. "Nice to see you again Nina."

She returns my shake with a cold hand. "Likewise. I'll see you tomorrow night."

Nina shows us out and returns to her seat on the front porch. She glares as we climb into the Escalade.

"Wow!" Frank says. "She does not like you!"

"No shit. We need to be prepared for anything tomorrow night. Hard to tell how crazy things will get."

Jessica

128

I start my day in Chloe's office. I check her emails and voicemails to ensure nothing is urgent. I forward anything important to Willa and everything else gets put on a to-do list for when Chloe comes home.

I consider looking for Baxter, but I don't want to seem desperate. Instead, I go back up to the roof with my book. Might as well enjoy the sunshine while I can. I'm hoping Baxter will find me, but when I've been outside for an hour and he doesn't make an appearance, I go back to my room.

What am I supposed to do now? It's way too early to start making Willa's lunch, it's only 10:30.

I wonder if Chloe's meeting with Nina is over. Even if it is, her schedule for the rest of the day is full. She has three meetings with unhappy coven members, and another one tomorrow morning. It's funny how Chloe is slammed and I have nothing to do.

I put on workout clothes and head to the training facility. My workouts are nothing like Chloe's. I like to jog on the treadmill while watching a cheesy reality TV show on the built-in television. I occasionally lift weights and do sit-ups, but that's the extent of my physical activity.

The training facility is empty when I walk in. Chloe, Frank and James are its most frequent users in the daytime. Most of the Guard members work out first thing in the morning or late at night.

After running on the treadmill for half an hour, I'm back to not knowing what to do with myself. I take a long shower and clean my apartment. I look at the clock. It's 11:45. It is finally a reasonable time to prepare Willa's lunch. Woo hoo! I have something to do!

I make Willa her favorite – salmon and wild rice – and have it ready for her promptly at 12:30.

"It's certainly different with everyone gone, isn't it?" she asks while we eat lunch.

"Yes. It's weird."

"How are you filling your time?"

I sigh. "I'm bored to tears."

"You know what they say Jessica, only boring people get bored."

"Well, I must be the most boring person on the planet!"

Willa laughs. "I'm teasing. It's understandable for you to be restless. Your mom, Chloe and Whitney all deserted you at the same time."

"Do you have filing or any other office tasks? I already cleaned and organized Chloe's office."

Willa shakes her head. "Not really. Sue is on top of things."

Sue, aka Bane, is not only Willa's security guard, he's also Willa's personal assistant. When her last assistant retired five years ago, Bane volunteered for the post and Willa gladly gave it to him.

"Why don't you find Baxter? I'm sure he's looking for some company," Willa suggests.

I'm a little embarrassed to tell Willa about my date with Baxter, but I do. "I just went out with Baxter last night. I don't want to annoy him."

"You did?" Willa asks surprised. "How lovely."

"We saw a movie, then went swimming."

Willa smiles. "Good for you dear! Baxter certainly knows how to have a good time."

"How well do you know him?"

She shrugs. "I've been in contact with him through the years. It's important for me to keep close ties with other supernatural beings and Baxter is the easiest vampire to talk to. He's not as stuffy as some of the others."

"Does he have a good reputation?"

Willa tilts her head. "In the supernatural world or in general?"

"Both, I guess."

"Baxter is well-received in the supernatural community. It's hard not to like him. If your real concern is his social endeavors, I can assure you, he's not a playboy."

I'm relieved to hear this. I don't want to be another notch in his belt.

"If you're interested," Willa continues, "there is an excellent book in the library by a Countess, I can't remember her name at the moment. She goes into detail about relationships between vampires and humans."

I refrain from telling Willa I've already found the book she's talking about. Instead, I say, "Let's not put the cart before the horse."

"Fair enough." She sets her napkin on her plate. "That was a very good meal."

"Thanks!"

"No, thank you." Willa stands. "If you change your mind about Baxter, he should be back from his run through the city by now. I suspect he's in his room."

I clean up our lunch and wash the dishes in the kitchen sink by hand. That's how desperate I am to fill my time.

Should I go see Baxter? Will I come on too strong?

I'm torn about what I should do. I want to see him, but every time I do, the hole gets deeper.

Chloe

I'm exhausted after my afternoon meetings.

I met with three members of Nina's coven. Two of them are members who reached out to us and asked for assistance. The third is a member we contacted to discuss his opinion. We purposely picked a Nina supporter so we could hear both sides of the story.

The first two members, one male and one female, told stories about Nina completely losing her cool. They confirmed Nina hates the werewolves and doesn't speak highly of me.

I'm shocked and disturbed when the male coven member tells me Nina once mentioned forming a group that would travel west to assassinate Ivan. Luckily, this idea has gone nowhere.

The third member of the coven admitted he isn't close with Nina. He attends coven meetings and hasn't seen anything that makes him uncomfortable. He mentioned Nina being dismayed about Facebook and other social media usage, but it's the only time he's seen her upset.

I have one more meeting with a coven member tomorrow morning. She is another random member we picked out of the bunch.

I kick off my heels when I get back to the condo and put on flip flops. I meet Frank downstairs in the kitchen.

"What are we doing for dinner?"

"The guys suggested ordering Chinese food. Sound good to you?"

"Yeah, that's fine."

Frank hands me the takeout menu and a pen. "How do you think it went today?"

"Okay. I'm pretty sure Nina is a maniac, but other than that, it's all good."

Frank smiles. "I agree. She puts on a good front for most of the coven, but she's up to something."

"I don't get it. Why does she hate the wolves so much? We took care of the rogue wolves. The others are fine."

"We all grew up with stories about the werewolves. We've been told since we were kids to avoid them at all costs. Julian and his group killing Barbara and Chelsea only confirmed those fears. People like Nina don't care if it was a rogue group. They blame all wolves."

132

I strum my fingers on the countertop. "Should I tell Nina what I know?"

"Depends."

"On?"

"Whether you want her to voluntarily step down, or if you want the coven to vote on it."

"I have to let them vote on it, right? I don't want to walk in and take over. It doesn't seem right."

Frank shrugs. "You are the Verhena-to-be, you can do whatever the hell you want."

"Just because I can, doesn't mean I should."

He smiles.

"What?"

"You're starting to figure this out."

"I am?" He's not the first person to tell me this, but I don't feel like I've changed at all. I feel like a lost child sometimes.

"You're different now. The way you carry yourself, the way you engage with other people," he pats my back, "you're doing great."

"Thanks man," I say sincerely.

"Enough warm and cuddly stuff." He snatches the takeout menu from my hand and scans my selections. "You sure you don't want an eggroll?"

Jessica

As it turns out, I don't have to decide whether to seek out Baxter. He shows up at my doorstep.

There's a low knocking on my door around 2:30 p.m.

"Hey!" I say when I open the door.

"What's going on?" He's wearing knee length khaki shorts with a green t-shirt and flip flops. No one would suspect a vampire is underneath his casual summer clothes.

"Nothing. Nothing at all. You want to come in?"

"Sure."

I give him a tour of my apartment. It doesn't take long, there's not much to see.

"What have you been up to today?" I ask as we take seats on the couch in the living room.

"Roaming the city. I showed Gregory's picture to a few people, but no one recognized him."

"There haven't been any more murders, have there?"

Baxter shakes his head. "No. I'm beginning to think Gregory moved on."

"You think he went back home?"

"Maybe."

"What does the Guard think?"

"They don't know what to make of it either. Gregory hasn't attempted to come anywhere near here, and he's not popping up on any of the cameras in the city the Guard is linked to."

"The Guard has cameras throughout the city?" Chloe mentioned something to me about new cameras, but I didn't realize they are already in use. The Guard doesn't waste any time.

"The cameras aren't necessarily the Guard's cameras. They have access to the cameras, but they don't control them. They also have facial recognition software uploaded into the system."

"Facial recognition software?"

Baxter nods. "They upload a picture and the cameras will alert the Guard if that person appears within their range."

"So if the Guard uploads my picture, any camera they have access to will let the Guard know I've gone by?"

"Exactly."

I shake my head. "They never cease to amaze me."

"I am blown away by the technology they have down there. It's impressive."

"What are your plans for the rest of the day?" I ask after we sit quietly for a minute.

"I don't know. How about you?"

"I've got nothing."

Baxter laughs. "It's pretty boring around this place."

"Not usually. Most days I'm busy working. And during my off time, I hang out with my mom or Whitney."

"Have you ever thought about leaving?"

"What do you mean?"

"Have you thought about college or culinary school, or traveling the world?"

I start to answer, "no", then pause. "I almost went to college after high school, but decided not to go."

"Why?"

"I didn't want to waste the money. Willa told me long ago I had a job here if I want it."

"And you wanted to stay?"

"Yes."

"Why?"

"I like it here. Everything I need is here. Family. Friends. My job. Why leave? Some people spend their entire lives looking for a place like this. I'm lucky to find it early in life."

Baxter considers this a moment before asking another question. "What about your personal life?"

"What about it?"

"Won't you have to leave eventually? To find a suitable partner?"

"I've thought about that. The right guy will understand my ties to this place. I don't have to live here to work for Chloe. I can move out and commute like everyone else."

Baxter nods. "True enough."

We fall silent, Baxter out of questions. For now anyway.

"Want to watch television?" I offer.

"No, not really."

"Want to go for a walk?"

Baxter shakes his head. "I've spent the entire morning running through the city."

I laugh. "Okay then, what do you want to do?"

He gives me a meaningful glance. "I have a few suggestions."

I squirm in my seat. "I thought you want to take things slow."

Baxter sighs. "I do and I don't. Know what I mean?"

"Yes," I answer, because I know exactly what he means.

"There is something you need to know about me," Baxter says.

"Okay…"

He takes my hands in his. "I like you Jessica, an awful lot."

I smile. "I like you too."

"It makes me happy to hear that, but a part of me knows it's not right for me to pursue you."

"You don't have to do this. I know what you're about to say."

"You have to hear it from me though," he insists. "You have to hear me say it."

I brace myself. "Alright."

"I'm never going to be anything more than a passing dalliance. We're not going to get married. We're definitely never having

136

kids. And I'm never going to love you, not in the way you will want me to."

His blunt warning stings despite knowing it was coming. I'm not in love with Baxter, but it's still hurtful to have someone tell you they'll never love you.

I turn away from him and gaze out my apartment window. Like Chloe, I have a giant wall of glass on one side. I pretend to look out at the city skyline when in reality I'm lost in my own mind.

What should I do?

Send him away, the logical part of my brain screams.

Unfortunately, the rest of my brain tells the logical part to get lost.

I smile at Baxter. "That's fine because I'm never going to be in love with you either."

Baxter shifts uneasily. "I've heard that before Jessica."

"I mean it. I know how you operate."

"Oh you do, huh?"

I nod. "I've done some reading."

"Let me guess - the Countess Regina."

"No," I try to lie.

Baxter laughs. "So you read Chapter Four?"

I cringe. "No, not yet."

"Good. Then everything will be a total surprise."

"A surprise?" Crap! I should have read Chapter Four!

Baxter laughs again. "I'm joking. The mechanics are the same. I'm not going to grow tentacles or anything."

I relax. Thank God!

Baxter's face turns serious again. "Are you sure we're on the same page?"

"Yes. We're on the same page."

Baxter doesn't look convinced.

"I'm a big girl Baxter. I know when something is for fun and when it's for real. We're for fun. Nothing more."

"You won't be upset with me when I leave?"

I shake my head no.

"And you promise you won't tell Chloe to kill me?"

I chuckle. "I won't. I promise."

Baxter smirks. "Well then, I guess we have our afternoon booked."

In a flash, Baxter scoops me up into his arms. The living room flies by in a whirl and the next thing I know, I'm lying on my bed. It takes a second for my brain to adjust.

Baxter hovers above me, his hands propping up his body weight. "Sorry. I move quickly when I'm excited."

"I sincerely hope that's not your bedroom technique."

Baxter roars with laughter. "I guess you'll find out."

He softly kisses my lips and my body responds immediately. I've never had a man in my bedroom after just one date, but this feels right.

My body tenses when Baxter moves his lips down my neck line.

"Relax Jessica. I'm not going to bite," he whispers.

I calm down as his lips and hands roam my body. Things are starting to get hot and heavy when I realize we have a big problem.

"Baxter, wait."

"I'm sorry, did I hurt you?"

I shake my head. "No, you're great. More than great. But I don't have any condoms."

"We don't need one."

I raise an eyebrow. "Yes we do."

"For what?"

I prop myself up on my elbows. "STDs. Ever heard of them?"

Baxter laughs. "Humans get STDs. I'm not a human, remember?"

Oh yeah. Funny how I keep forgetting that.

"So you can't get STDs?"

"No," Baxter confirms with a smile. "I can't get you pregnant either. The undead can't create life."

"You learn something new every day."

He kisses my neck again. "Any more questions?"

I shake my head. "Nope."

"You know, all of this is covered in Chapter Four. You really should have read it."

He's right - I should have. It would have warned me that I'm playing with fire.

Chapter 8

Chloe

I wake up to a phone call from James.

"Good morning sunshine," he says in a fake singsong voice.

I groan.

"Shouldn't you be up by now?"

"I take approximately thirty-five minutes to get ready. I plan my alarm accordingly."

He laughs. "Which means I get three minutes of your time."

"Use those minutes wisely," I mumble.

"What are you wearing?" he whispers into the phone.

I laugh out loud. "Pajama pants and a t-shirt."

"Sounds hot."

I rub the sleep from my eyes. "You're happy this morning."

"Eh, just trying to get motivated."

"Long day ahead?"

He groans. "My grandpa definitely takes advantage of me while I'm here."

"I'm sorry."

"It's okay. Comes with the territory. Enough about me though, big night tonight, right?"

"Ugh, don't remind me."

"Remember, if Nina starts going off the rails, let her. Let everyone see how crazy she is."

I couldn't agree more, but I don't want to talk about work. "You used up your three minutes."

"Already? Darn."

"I'll give you five more on one condition."

"Which is?"

"We stop talking about our crazy jobs and you tell me how much you wish you were in this bed with me."

"Mmm...I can handle that."

Jessica

I'm eating a bowl of cereal, listening to more '60s music when my cellphone rings.

"What's up Chloe?"

"Not much. Getting ready for my interview with the final coven member. Anything going on there?"

"No. I forwarded a few emails to Willa because they are time sensitive. Everything else can wait until you get back."

"Great, but that's not what I meant. How's your undead friend?"

I smile. "He's officially my undead friend with benefits."

"Shut up!" Chloe exclaims into the phone. "Tell me you're joking."

"No, not joking."

"Oh. My. God. You hooked up with Baxter!"

"Twice actually."

"Twice!"

"Yes, twice."

"And...?"

"It was good."

"Details please."

I knew Chloe wouldn't let me off the hook easily. "Okay, it wasn't just good. It was *so* good. Like, best ever good."

"It's true what the books said then, huh?"

I don't know how to begin explaining it to her. "It felt like an out of body experience."

She laughs. "Good for you! You going to do it again?"

"Probably," I admit.

"Go get it girl. I gotta run. Promise me you'll be careful, okay?"

"Oh, he can't get me pregnant."

Chloe clucks her tongue. "I know that. I meant don't get hurt."

Oh.

"I won't," I promise.

After I hang up, I clean my breakfast mess. Willa didn't come down for breakfast this morning. She called to say she was sleeping in, which is very unlike her.

"Are you feeling okay?" I asked her.

"Perfectly fine. Just tired."

I check the refrigerator and kitchen cabinets to see what I need to pick up from the market. Once a month we get a bulk food delivery, but I need to go out weekly for dairy items, bread, and produce. I should probably get more cow hearts while I'm out.

I make a shopping list, grab my bag and head to the market. I don't meet the eyes of the Guard members I walk past on the way out. I know they saw Baxter come in my suite last night and not leave again until this morning. I'm pretty sure they don't think we played Yahtzee.

Baxter is out on his tour of the city. He didn't go out last night like he usually does. Instead, he laid in bed with me. I woke up in the middle of the night and sat up. Baxter was lying with his eyes closed and body still.

"You alright?" he whispered, face peaceful.

I laid back down. "I'm fine." He rolled over and held me in his arms. I fell right back to sleep.

Baxter was sitting in the chair beside my bed reading the newspaper when I opened my eyes in the morning.

"Any news?" I asked, bedsheet pulled up over my bare chest.

He smiled. "No."

"That's good."

"Yes, it is."

Baxter closed the paper and climbed back into bed. Before I knew it, we were wrapped up in each other again.

As amazing as it is to roll in the sheets with Baxter, I should avoid him from here on out. I can feel myself getting attached. Aside from the mind blowing bedroom activities, I love talking to him. He makes me laugh and I'm in awe of how smart he is. He's read all the classic novels and all the modern day bestsellers. He knows a ton about music and is well versed in artists. Despite being a genius, he has a laid back attitude about life. He doesn't take himself too seriously.

It doesn't help that he's the only person in the building I can spend time with. Willa is nice and all, but she's in her eighties. There's only so much she and I can talk about. I know most of the Guard members, but I can't hang out with them while they're on duty. Plus, they'll tease me endlessly about Baxter.

I wander through the grocery store, taking my time. I randomly smile every once in a while thinking about my night with Baxter. When I get home, I unload the groceries and ponder what to do now. I really need to get a life.

I call Whitney to see how she's doing. She doesn't answer, so I leave her a voicemail.

I try my mom next.

"Hello dear!" Her voice is light and cheerful.

"Hey Mom! How's the trip?"

"Fantastic! I'm in La Jolla, it's the cutest town. They have cool shops and good food. And they have sea lions!"

I smile. "Sounds nice." It's good to hear her so happy.

"Oh Jess, it's wonderful. You should come out here! Catch a plane."

I laugh. "And leave Willa in the lurch? I'm the only one here right now."

"I forgot about that! What are you doing to keep yourself entertained?"

A vampire…

"Not much. A lot of reading."

She tells me about her trip and all the places she still needs to see. She's having a ball. This is the first vacation my mom has taken since we moved in with Willa. She's long overdue for some fun.

When we hang up, I go through a list of things I can do. Nothing sounds good. Well, one thing sounds pretty good…

After five minutes of internal debate, I give in and head to Baxter's room. He's leaving soon, I have to get it while the getting is good. Right?

One more time, I tell myself as I head for the 13th floor.

Chloe

My head hurts. Just as I close my eyes to rest my brain, my cellphone rings. It's Whitney.

I check the clock. I have ten minutes before I need to leave for the coven meeting. I've been reviewing notes since I got back from my appointment with the fourth coven member.

145

She didn't have much to add. She attends meetings regularly, but she isn't close with Nina. The only thing she said of interest is that Nina seems a bit more on edge lately, like she's wired all the time.

I debate whether to take Whitney's call. She is one of my besties, but do I really want to listen to Brandon drama right now?

I ultimately decide to answer. "Hey Whit!"

"Hey Chloe." Her voice is lifeless.

I frown. "What's up?"

"Not much. How about you?"

"I'm in Boston."

"Oh yeah. Big coven meeting tonight, right?"

"Yes." I wait for Whitney to say something, but she doesn't. "I'm actually getting ready to go, but I have a few minutes. Do you need to talk about something?"

"I called to tell you I broke up with Brandon yesterday." She starts crying.

Oh God...

I'm not good at consoling people, especially over the phone. I try my best. "I'm so sorry Whit."

"It's okay," she gets out between sobs.

"Where is James?" James would kill me if he knew I'm pawning Whitney off on him, but she is his sister.

"He and my grandfather are at a pack meeting."

"Why aren't you there?"

She sniffles. "I didn't feel like going."

"You should go. It will take your mind off things."

"Yeah, you're probably right."

"Find something fun to do. Don't sit around wallowing over Brandon. He is a Grade A douche bag."

Whitney giggles. "He really is, isn't he?"

I smile, pleased I made her laugh. "You can do way better than him."

"I know. I'm mad at myself for not ending it sooner. It bothers me that I let myself fall in love with someone like him."

"You're young. You're allowed to make some mistakes. Just don't dwell on them."

"Is it okay if I come back to New York with James?"

"Absolutely!"

"I accepted the scholarship at the New York School of Fashion and Design. I start in two weeks."

"That's so awesome!" I am truly excited. I want Whitney to stay in New York.

"I'll find a place in the city. A lot of the students room together to save money on rent."

"You're welcome stay with me."

"I know, but I want my own place. I need to build a life for myself."

"I completely understand. I am so proud of you!"

"Thanks."

I'm about to tell her everything will be alright when Frank pokes his head into my room. "Time to go."

I nod in his direction, then return my attention to Whitney. "I have to go Whit. We'll talk more later, okay?"

"Sure. Good luck tonight!"

I grab my bag and notes. The car ride to the coven meeting is relatively quiet. Frank and I have thoroughly discussed everything we know and there is nothing more to say.

While I watch Boston go by, I take steady breaths to calm my nerves. I can't shake the feeling that tonight is going to be a complete circus.

We pull up to an anonymous looking brick building on a quiet city street ten minutes later. Passersby probably assume it's an old union hall. Every space in the parking lot is taken, I'll have a full house tonight.

Frank glances over at me. "You ready to go in?"

"Yes."

As previously agreed, Pete and Richard go in the building first to scope it out. They wave us in after they scan the room. Frank puts his hand on the small of my back and stays close as I walk in the building. There is a small vestibule area, but I can see into the meeting hall. It is standing room only. People are packed in tight.

All chatter stops when we walk into the room. I really know how to make an entrance.

There are rows and rows of folding chairs. Two hundred people are here and all of their eyes are on me. Frank and I, followed closely by Pete and Richard, walk up the center aisle and approach the podium. A folding table with two chairs is sitting next to the podium. Nina occupies one of the seats.

Nina puts on her fake smile and stands to greet us. "She's here everyone! Let's give Chloe a warm, Boston welcome!"

The quiet crowd suddenly erupts with life. The coven members all stand and clap for me. I step behind the podium and motion for them to sit. After a few more claps, they are seated.

"Good evening," I say with a smile. "Thank you for coming. I know it was short notice and I appreciate that you've taken the time to be with us tonight."

I pause and glance over at Nina. She is staring out into the crowd with her deranged smile plastered on her face.

I turn my attention back to the group. "I wish we were meeting on better terms. I'm sorry to say the reason I'm here this evening is to discuss some issues that have been brought to the attention of the Verhena and myself. I've met with Nina and a few coven members to discuss your concerns."

I spot the people in the crowd I spoke with, but I'm careful not to spend too much time looking at them. I don't want to give them away.

"Based upon these conversations, and the wishes of Willa, I am asking that you hold a re-election."

The crowd tussles. Some are surprised, but most are unfazed. This is what they were expecting.

Nina makes me jump when she slams her fist on the table. She stands and approaches the podium. Frank takes a step closer to me.

"This is ridiculous!" she exclaims. "Utter nonsense."

"Nina, please. This wasn't an easy choice."

"Ha!" She points her finger at me. "You've been gunning for me all along!"

"Nina, I hardly know you. I'm being as unbiased as possible."

"Unbiased?! Holding a re-election basically telegraphs to everyone here that you want me out!"

I shake my head. "That's not true. I'm doing this because your coven is asking for it."

"Is that so?" Nina turns and glares at the attendees. "So this is it? You're turning your backs on me?"

I reach out and touch Nina's shoulder. "They haven't voted yet."

She brushes my hand away. "Don't touch me, you whore!"

There is a collective gasp. I want to lash out at her, but I remember James's advice and let Nina go off the rails.

"That's right!" Nina yells at the audience. "She's a disgusting whore! She is sleeping with one of those nasty werewolves. Did you know that? Did you?!" she shouts.

Everyone stares at her in stunned silence. Pete and Richard are on high alert, eyes boring into Nina. I glance at Frank and nod slightly. He and I agreed earlier to let Nina rant all she wants so long as the situation doesn't become dangerous.

"While she's sleeping around with the Pack Leader's grandson, they are infiltrating our world. Pretending to be on our side, ready and waiting to strike!"

"What evidence do you have of this?" I ask her.

She turns back to me, her eyes wild. "Evidence? Evidence? How about the fact that they've been our enemies since before anyone in this room was born? How about the fact that they killed the last woman who was supposed to be the Verhena? Or did your boyfriend do that for you? Did he kill poor Barbara so you could take her place?"

Frank can't help himself. "That is the most ridiculous thing I have ever heard Nina. How could any of us possibly know who would get the next Verhena brand? Why don't you just sit down, and take a breath."

"Oh go fuck yourself!" she snarls at Frank.

Frank takes a step toward her, his chest puffed. Nina glares up at him. The two stare each other down. After a few intense seconds, Nina gives in first. She's furious, but she knows she can't intimidate Frank.

Instead, she turns back to the crowd. "It would be easy to get the Verhena brand when you're sleeping with the Reader!"

Murmuring sparks in the crowd again.

Seeing this gives Nina newfound energy. "Oh…you didn't know that? She was screwing the Reader too!"

Frank, whose veins are popping out of his neck like I've never seen before, speaks again. "I am also a Reader. I have read her skin. She is the next Verhena."

Nina sneers. "Yeah, right. She's probably blowing you too."

Frank is about to go off, but I touch his arm.

"Don't," I say quietly.

He steps back into place next to me and crosses his arms over his chest. I'm about to offer to have Frank's sister read me if it's a genuine issue, but someone in the crowd stands.

He appears to be in his fifties. He is wearing a short-sleeve, button down shirt tucked into a pair of khakis. He is balding and wearing a pair of rimmed glasses. He reminds me of Mr. Simpkins, my history teacher in high school.

"How dare you Nina!?" he shouts from the audience. He looks as angry as I feel. "How dare you stand up there and speak about our Verhena that way! Are you truly questioning what the universe has directed us to do? Do you really think we should turn against the traditions of our people because you say so?"

There are a few "yeahs" from the audience. People are giving Nina nasty looks. They are no longer stunned into silence. They are pissed.

"I've heard the story of the rogue werewolves," the man continues. "I've talked to people who were there that day. Our own coven member, Henry, was there and saw the things Chloe did. He gave a speech about it in this very hall."

I look around for Henry and see him in the back corner. When he sees me looking at him, he nods in acknowledgement.

"Because of this young woman, I can travel to Seattle and watch a Seahawks game in person. Because of this woman, I can drive across the Golden Gate Bridge. And more importantly, because of this woman, I no longer have to worry about werewolves breaking into my home at night and attacking my family. She has shown us that most of our fears were unfounded. She took care of the threat. And for that, I'm with her."

The crowd erupts in applause. The gentleman sits down and I mouth to him, "Thank you."

I read his lips when he says, "You're welcome."

Nina is enraged. "This is what you want?" she says pointing at me.

Several yeses ring through the crowd.

I'm almost in tears. Having their support means everything.

"I can't believe this!" Nina throws up her arms. "You ungrateful bastards. You can't even fathom the sacrifices I've made for you!"

"Like what?" someone calls out from the audience.

"The time…the stress…and for what? So you could all turn on me for this cunt?"

There is a gasp from every single person in the room, myself included.

Did she really just call me the c-word? I don't even use the c-word and I curse like a sailor!

I'm about to call her every name in the book, but Frank returns the favor and stops me this time. He puts his hand on my back and says, "Don't."

Instead of saying, "This bitch right here…" like I want to, I say, "Nina, please calm down."

She does the opposite of calming down, she completely loses her shit.

Nina kicks over a chair and points her finger at me again. "You are the reason our people will fall apart! You are everything that is wrong with society!" She turns back to the crowd, "And you assholes…"

Before she can go any further, I freeze her in place. The room is suddenly still and quiet. Nina is stuck pointing her finger at the audience, her mouth open wide.

Everyone in the audience stares back at her, not quite sure what to do.

I collect myself and take a few calming breaths. I turn back to the crowd. "We've heard enough."

Everyone nods, relieved Nina's tirade is over.

"It's clear to me Nina has some mental health issues she needs to deal with. I'm not saying that in a critical or judgmental way.

I know how stressful it is to hold a leadership position, and I think the pressure got the best of her."

Someone in the crowd raises his hand.

"Yes, sir. Please stand up."

"First of all, thank you. Thank you for stopping her."

"You're welcome."

"Second, what happens now? What will happen to Nina?"

I consider my answer before I give it. "I want all of you to think about who you would like to take Nina's place. I'm not asking you to do that tonight. I will come back in a week, and we will hold an election at that time."

I turn to Nina, still in her beast mode.

"As for Nina, I will wait until you've all left the building, then I will unfreeze her. I'll explain to her what happened, and I will have the Guard check her in to a mental health facility so she can get the help she needs. Hopefully with some time and professional help, she'll return to her normal self."

There is some murmuring amongst the crowd, but everyone seems pleased with my plan.

"Are there any more questions?" I ask them.

A young woman raises her hand. She appears to be around my age.

"Yes, please stand."

She looks nervous. "Can you, um, tell us about what life is like for you now? What can we expect from you when you take over your position?"

I smile. "I'd be happy to."

I talk to the crowd for half an hour, then invite everyone to come up and shake my hand. The first few give Nina an uneasy look as they walk by her, afraid she'll suddenly spring to life.

"Don't worry," I assure them, "she's fine."

153

Given my current abilities, I can leave Nina frozen all night. But I won't. I remember how angry James was when I froze him in the gym and left. I don't want to take too much of Nina's time away from her.

Henry is the last person in line. "I'll stick around if you want me to."

"I think that's a great idea. It may help Nina to see a face she trusts when I unfreeze her."

He shifts his weight. "I'm not sure how much she trusts me anymore."

"I didn't tell her anything you said to us," I assure him. "She has no idea that you provided us with intel."

"Thank you," he says relieved. "I also wanted to let you know there's a mental health facility not far from here. The head doctor is a witch."

"Really?"

"Yes. I'm sure they'll accept Nina if you ask."

After we contact the facility and call in additional Guard members, it's time to unfreeze Nina.

I take a deep breath. "You guys ready?"

We're standing in a circle around Nina, each of the guys nodding when I look their way.

Frank nods. "Let's do this."

I steady myself. "Here we go…"

Chapter 9

Jessica

I spend the rest of my day in bed with Baxter. All day.

He was easy to find – he was in his room reading a Dean Koontz novel. Within minutes we were engaging in our favorite pastime. I wake up in his arms after a short nap.

"What was your life like before you were turned?"

"I don't know."

"That bad, huh?"

He chuckles. "No, I really don't know."

"You don't remember anything about it?"

"It's not that I forgot, it's just not there. No vampire remembers their prior life. They may learn about it from someone else or research it, but none of us have memories of who we used to be."

I run my fingertips up and down his chest. My head cradled just below his shoulder. "That's sad."

"I think it's better this way."

"Why?"

Baxter rubs my shoulder with his hand. "We don't know what we're missing. I don't have to worry about or miss my loved ones."

"Did Elias know anything about you when he turned you?"

"Just that I was a smartass."

I smile. "Elias probably figured that out pretty quickly."

"Elias found me in an alley late one night. I'd been beaten up pretty badly. The men who did it were gone. We don't know if they were stealing from me, or if I'd done something to piss them off. I'm guessing the latter."

"How did Elias know your name?"

"He didn't at first. A local paper eventually reported that I was missing."

"What did the article say?"

Baxter sighs. "Not much really. My name, my age, and a few details about my life."

"Have you read the article?"

"No. I told Elias not to tell me anything about my former life."

"You aren't at all curious?"

Baxter shakes his head. "No. At this point, so much time has passed, it doesn't matter anyway."

Before I can ask any more about Baxter's history as a human, he distracts me with his soft lips. Despite having a taste of him already today, my body heat rises. I get lost in him and the way he makes me feel.

I lay in his arms after, catching my breath. "You're trying to kill me."

He chuckles. "They call it 'the little death' for a reason."

"I don't ever want to get out of this bed."

"I, uh, hate to be bearer of bad news, but it's after one o'clock. Doesn't Willa eat at noon?"

I sit straight up. "Crap!" I jump out of bed and find my clothes. "Want me to get you anything from the kitchen while I'm down there? I bought more cow hearts for you."

He stretches his long limbs. "No, I'm good."

"How long can you go without eating?" I ask while putting my crumpled t-shirt back on.

"A long time. I tried once to see how long I could go without fresh blood and I gave in after two weeks."

"Two weeks!"

"Yep. I was tired and weak after the first couple days, but I was still getting around pretty good."

"Why did you go that long without eating?"

"I was preparing for a hike in the Himalayas. I needed to know how long I could go without blood. I could only pack so much raw meat before it spoiled."

"You hiked through the Himalayas?"

He nods. "Sure did. It was beautiful."

"Do you travel a lot?"

"I've seen most of the world. The only place I haven't been that I'd love to see is Antarctica. It's hard to find an expedition there."

"That's because it's so stinking cold! Why don't you go somewhere warm?"

Baxter laughs. "The cold doesn't bother me. I can walk across an iceberg naked and not feel a thing."

"You're so lucky. I hate the winter."

"So why do you live in New York City? Why don't you move somewhere near the equator?"

I shrug. "This is my home. This is where my family and friends are."

"Do you plan on traveling?"

"Absolutely! Once things with Chloe settle down, I'll go on a vacation."

"Where will you go?"

My eyes light up. "I want to go to Maui and swim with the sea turtles. I've read about it online and it would be so cool. They also have black sand beaches and a volcano."

"Not to mention warm temperatures," he adds.

"That's a definite perk! Maybe I'll even take surf lessons."

"Damn. I was hoping you'd say you want to come see me in England."

I'm shocked at him mentioning a future visit. "I'd love to see England."

Instead of exploring our future further, Baxter says, "You better get going. I don't want Willa to think I'm holding you captive in here."

I turn on my heels and get to the kitchen as quickly as I can. I can't believe Willa hasn't tried to call me. Then again, she probably knows where I am. Actually, the whole building probably knows where I am.

I feel guilty when I bring Willa her lunch of a tuna fish sandwich with sweet potato fries and applesauce.

"Thank you dear!" she says when I put her plate down.

"Sorry I'm so late."

"No problem. I've been plugging away in here. I lost track of time myself."

"How are you feeling? Did you get some rest this morning?"

Willa gives me her usual sunny smile. "I did. I feel fantastic."

"Good!" I need to get out of here before she can ask me what I've been up to today. "Well, enjoy your lunch!"

"Jessica," she calls out to me before I can leave.

"Yes?"

"I'm ordering carry out from that Mexican restaurant down the street later. I'm in the mood for chimichangas. So don't worry about dinner tonight."

I smile. "Okay."

"Have fun my dear," she says with a wink.

Yep, she knows exactly where I've been all day.

When I get back to Baxter's room, he's skimming through internet websites on the laptop the Guard let him borrow.

"Whatcha doing?" I ask.

"Looking to see if there are any new homicide cases. I'm not limiting myself to New York City anymore. Gregory could be anywhere."

"Find anything?"

Baxter shakes his head. "Nope." He closes the laptop. "Maybe I jumped the gun. Maybe that woman's murder had nothing to do with me."

"You and Elias checked to see if Gregory is at home, right? Didn't they tell you he's missing?"

"The Council reached out to vampires close to Gregory and asked them to check on him. Gregory was gone and it looked like he's been gone for a while." Baxter rubs his chin. "For all I know, he is on vacation somewhere."

"Maybe he's hiking in Antarctica."

Baxter snarls. "He better not be on my vacation!"

Without warning, Baxter pounces on me and we roll onto the bed together. Both laughing hysterically, we wrestle around. Baxter can get the best of me at any time when it comes to horseplay, but he lets me believe I have a fighting chance. I pin him to the bed, sit on his stomach and hold his arms above his head.

I do a quick three-count and proclaim, "I win!"

Baxter smirks. "I feel like I'm the winner." He glances down my shirt.

I giggle and roll off of him.

"Where are you going?" he fake pouts.

"Away from you."

I'm just teasing, but Baxter's face turns serious. "You should. You should run away from me."

What is it about a man saying you should leave him that makes you want to stay more? Is it pure dumb luck on their part, or is it a conspiracy?

Of course we end up kissing. Of course we have fantastic sex that I will probably miss for the rest of my life. And of course I fall asleep in his arms in total bliss.

It's official. I'm a masochist.

When I wake up from my latest mini-nap, Baxter is resting next to me with his eyes closed. I roll over and check my cellphone. It's 8:30 p.m. Where the hell has my day gone? Time flies when you're having fun.

I haven't missed any calls or messages from Chloe, so that's good. I send her a quick text.

Hey! Haven't heard from you. I hope everything is going okay. ☺

"Do you always add an emoji to the end of your messages?" Baxter asks me.

I smile. "Yes. It's corny, but I love it."

I set my phone down and cuddle with him. For someone who is technically dead, he's nice and warm.

I ask about his body temperature. "How are you warm? Aren't vampires supposed to be cold to the touch?"

He laughs. "It's another one of our survival techniques. Feeling cold to the touch or looking really pale would make us stand out. We need to blend in."

I hesitate before I ask, "How long did it take for you to turn?" He always responds to my questions about vampires, but sometimes I feel like I ask too many.

"After the exchange of blood, the person falls into a sleep-like state for a couple hours."

"Did it hurt?"

Baxter shakes his head. "No, I didn't feel any pain and the people I've seen change lay so still they look dead." He pauses then adds, "Which I guess they are."

"Have you ever changed anyone?" I've been dying to ask him this one.

Baxter stiffens.

I prop myself up on my elbow, looking down on his face. "I'm sorry. You don't have to talk about it."

Baxter gets out of bed and walks over to the window. The sun is dipping below the horizon, shooting pink and orange light across the city skyline.

"Why are you asking?"

I'm sitting completely upright now. "Just curious, I guess."

Baxter turns around and I'm shocked to see he's furious. "Do you want me to change you? Is that it? Well I won't!" he snarls.

I put up my hand. "No! That's not it at all."

Baxter moves so quickly I can hardly see him. When he stops, he's dressed in his shirt and shorts. I'm dumbfounded when I see he already has his sneakers on too.

"I'm going out to look for Gregory," he says curtly.

"Okay," I say, still stupefied by his rapid movements.

And then he's gone.

Chloe

I don't get back to my condo in Boston until 10:00 p.m.

When I unfroze Nina, she was not a happy camper.

She screamed and shouted, but with the crowd gone, she lost steam quickly. I told her about the plan to check her in to a local mental health facility. She tearfully agreed to the arrangement and left willingly with three Guard members.

I called Jessica on my way back to the condo and she sounded like shit. She insisted she was fine, but it sure seemed like she'd been crying. I'm too tired to try and pull anything out of her tonight. I'll call her in the morning to make sure everything is okay.

I take a long shower and want nothing more than to crawl into bed. After I'm in my pjs and cozy under my blanket, I call James.

I frown when I get his voicemail message. I don't usually leave him voicemails, but I'm too tired to text. "Hey babe, just calling to say 'hi' and to tell you about the coven meeting. It was just as bad as I thought it would be. But it's all good now. I'm going to fall asleep soon. I'll talk to you in the morning."

I put my phone on the charger and curl up with my James teddy bear. I'm out within a minute or two.

Jessica

It's 1 a.m. and I can't sleep.

After Baxter flew out of his room like a tornado, I got dressed and went to my apartment. My crying was interrupted by Chloe and a brief phone call. She told me about Nina and the coven meeting, but I was half-listening. I think I said, "yes", "no" and "wow" in the right places.

I knew my time with Baxter was coming to an end, but I didn't expect it to end like this. I thought I'd at least get a good-bye kiss and a "take care of yourself." Instead, I got yelled at and left behind.

There's no use lying in bed. I can't sleep. I'd love to go for a walk, but it's too late to do that now. My mom and Willa would kill me if I went walking the city streets at one o'clock in the morning.

I decide to go up to the roof, my new favorite place. I put on a sweater over my tank top. It may be August in New York City, but the nights can be crisp, especially when you're twenty stories up.

I say a quick "hello" to Marcus, our nighttime-rooftop watch, and pull a seat over to the ledge of the roof. I prop my feet on the brick wall, lean my head back and gaze at the stars.

When I was young, Mom brought me up here to show me the constellations. I loved the stories she told me about the stars and the characters they represent. I've forgotten most of those stories, but I can pick out the dippers and Orion's belt.

I watch the night sky until my eyelids are heavy. I fold my chair and lean it against the greenhouse before I walk back inside. Although my apartment is several flights down, I take the stairs. I'm hoping to burn more energy and make myself even more tired.

I walk into my dark apartment and traverse it with no lights. I don't want anything ruining the tired state I've finally reached. I nearly faint when I see a dark figure sitting on my bed. I flip the light switch with shaky fingers.

I let out a breath when I see it's Baxter. "Good grief Baxter! Don't do that!"

He frowns. "Sorry. I forgot you can't see in the dark."

"No, I can't." I take off my sweater. "Why are you here?"

"I want to apologize. To say sorry for yelling at you earlier."

Don't be that girl, I tell myself. Don't you dare be that girl who just falls back into his arms.

I keep my response curt. "No need to apologize."

"Why do I feel like that's a hollow sentiment?"

I cross my arms. "Gee, I don't know. Maybe because you yelled at me for no reason?"

Baxter stands. "I know, and I'm sorry." He tries to reach out to me, but I pull back.

He sighs. "Can we talk about this? I can explain."

"Sure." I walk back into the living room. I'm hoping to send him a clear signal. One that says, "I'm pissed and you're not welcome in my bedroom right now."

Baxter follows my lead and sits with me on the couch. I maintain a safe distance.

"There was a girl," he starts telling me. "A very pretty girl. She was tall and thin. She had beautiful brown eyes and blonde hair. I met her in the 1920s. She was exactly what movies and books say a flapper girl was. She wore her blonde hair in pin curls and loved to dance. She was the daughter of a wealthy man, a man who would lose it all during the Great Depression. Her name was Ruth, but she asked me to call her Ruthie."

He pauses to see if I am listening. When I give him a little smile, he moves on.

"I met her at a party thrown by her parents here in New York City. Elias and I were in the States for a meeting with the woman who was the Verhena at that time. I don't remember Elias's connection to Ruthie's family, but somehow he scored us an invite."

Baxter is lost in his story.

"She was out on the dance floor. Her silver and white dress flapping as she moved to the music. She had a shiny headband with feathers and white gloves up to her elbows. She was so full of life, she glowed. I couldn't take my eyes off of her.

I made Elias introduce me to her. I kissed her gloved hand and she smiled. She called me 'sir' and asked if I wanted to dance. From that night on, we were inseparable. Her father liked me, probably because he believed Elias was my father and Elias has a lot of money."

"Did she know about you?" I ask when Baxter pauses. "Did she know you are a vampire?

Baxter nods. "I had to tell her. You can only duck so many meals before someone becomes suspicious."

164

"What did she say?"

He smiles. "She thought it was neat." Then his face turns grim. "She became fascinated with it. Talked all the time about me turning her and how badly she wanted to be a vampire."

A light bulb turns on in my brain. This is why Baxter got so upset earlier. I was reminding him of Ruthie.

"That must have been really hard for you."

Baxter nods. "It was. I wouldn't do it. I refused to change her."

"Why?"

"I wouldn't wish this upon anyone. Let alone a woman I loved."

I smile sadly. He loved Ruthie – a human woman. Why not me? The thought flashes through my mind, but I quash it.

Baxter is oblivious to my momentary jealousy and moves on with his story. "We fought about it. It was impossible to go an evening without her bringing it up. Things got worse as her birthday approached. She didn't want to be older than me. Something about it freaked her out. I told her I didn't care about her age, that I would stay with her throughout her life, but nothing I said appeased her. She wanted us to be perpetually the same age."

Baxter falls silent.

"What happened to Ruthie?" I ask softly, pushing him to keep going. Not because I'm curious, but because it's something he needs to get off his chest.

Baxter shuts his eyes for a moment, then opens them. "The night before her birthday, she came to my hotel room. Everything seemed fine. We were supposed to have dinner with some of her friends. She told me she needed to use my powder room and I didn't suspect a thing.

After she was gone for several minutes, I got worried. I banged on the door, but she didn't respond. I broke down the door and found her lying in the tub. Both of her wrists were slashed and blood was pooling in the tub."

"Oh my God," I whisper.

"I grabbed towels and tried to stop the bleeding. When I picked her up out of the tub, she was semi-conscious. 'Change me Baxter' she said. So I did." Baxter looks at me, pained.

"It's okay Baxter." I move closer to him and rub his back. "Go on."

"I performed the blood exchange the way I'd seen it done in the past. I laid her down on my bed and waited. She didn't move for a long time, it felt like an eternity.

Finally, one of her fingers twitched. Then another, and then her hands. I watched as her body reanimated. I sat next to her on the bed and held her hand as she started waking up. I was so hopeful."

Baxter meets my eyes. "I had no idea what was coming."

Dread fills my stomach. Whatever happened to Ruthie, it changed Baxter forever. I sit quietly and wait until he's ready to talk again.

"When Ruthie opened her eyes, she looked up at me and smiled. Her face as beautiful and warm as always. For a moment, I saw the loving and energetic woman I fell in love with."

Baxter's smile fades. "But then, something changed. She snapped. She jumped up from the bed and ran through the room like a caged animal. She hissed and gnashed her teeth at me while knocking over furniture. She broke a window trying to escape."

"What?" I ask shocked.

"I held her down, fighting for control so she would relax. I'd heard stories of feral vampires before, but I'd never seen it in real life."

"Feral vampires?"

Baxter nods. "Yes. Whenever a human is turned, there's a chance they will lose their mind. They become crazy and destructive. They hunt and kill anything with a pulse. We don't know why it happens, but the change in their bodies is too much for them to handle. They go insane."

"I had no idea. That's awful!"

He frowns. "I had no choice Jessica, I had to kill her. I used the leg from a wooden chair and drove it through her heart."

I wince. I can't imagine having to kill someone you love. It's beyond horrific. I hug Baxter as tightly as I can. "Oh Baxter, I'm so sorry."

He's done telling his story and I'm done being angry. I completely understand why he got upset earlier. Should he have yelled at me? No. But he came to apologize and explained himself. I can't ask for more than that.

"I don't come back to the city often. It's hard for me to be here."

"I'm sure it is. How is it walking through the city now?"

Baxter shrugs. "It's okay. The house Ruthie used to live in is gone. All the places we used to go have been torn down or renovated to the point that they don't look the same. Which makes it easier for me."

I nod. "I'm sorry I asked so many questions. I was intruding."

Baxter takes my hand. "It wasn't your fault. It was mine. I shouldn't have reacted that way. I just... I just want you to know that you mean a lot to me, but I won't turn you. Please don't ask me to."

My eyes widen. "Baxter, I don't want that. I don't want you to change me."

He squeezes my hand. "Good."

Chapter Ten

Chloe

I wake up refreshed the next morning. I slept like a rock. I check my cellphone and see I missed a call from James.

"What are you doing up already?" he asks after the second ring.

I laugh. "I went to bed early last night. I'm like an old person now. I can't stay up past eleven."

"I tried calling you back, but you were asleep already Granny." He chuckles, then asks, "How was the coven meeting?"

I tell him about Nina and all of the awful things she said about me. Some of them true.

"She was hitting below the belt. She was desperate. I'm glad they didn't buy into it."

"Me too. I was worried there for a minute."

"What's your plan? Are you staying in Boston until the election?"

"No. I want to go home, but since I'm already out of the building, I'm going to visit more covens."

"Makes sense. Will you be back in New York City after the election?"

"Yep. I'm flying home that night."

"Can't wait to get back, huh?"

"As much as I whine about the building being stifling, I miss it. I'm ready to sleep in my own bed again. Do you know when you'll be back?"

"I can be there the same day as you, if that's what you want."

I smile. "Of course that's what I want."

"Okay. Confirm what day you'll be home, and I'll be there."

"With Whitney, right?"

James sighs. "Yes, if she doesn't change her mind before then."

"I think this decision will stick. She sounded pretty sure of herself yesterday."

"That was before Brandon sent her flowers."

"What? For real?"

"Yes. She threw them straight in the garbage can though. I'm taking that as a sign they're not reconciling."

I laugh. "Seems like a safe bet."

"I miss you," he tells me in his smooth voice.

"I miss you too. One more week."

"It will go fast."

"Not fast enough."

We talk for a few minutes about his schedule for the coming week. The pack doesn't have the drama the witches are having lately, but he's busy just the same.

When we hang up I can't help but wonder if this will be our life together. Long distance phone calls and meetings in different places. Shaking that grim thought from my mind, I call Jessica to see if she's feeling better.

"Hey lady," she says when she answers. Her voice is back to its normal, cheery self.

"What's up biotch?"

Jessica laughs. "Nothing. How about you?"

"I'm good. Are you feeling better this morning?"

170

"What do you mean?" she asks confused.

"You sounded awful last night."

"Oh, right. Last night was interesting."

"Everything okay?"

"It is now."

"Good. Anything going on?"

Jessica hesitates, then says, "I'm worried about Willa. Have you spoken to her?"

Willa? Why is Jessica worried about Willa? "I spoke with her last night after the coven meeting. She sounded okay to me. Why?"

"She didn't come down for breakfast yesterday and she called me earlier to say she isn't coming down this morning either."

My forehead creases. "That's not like her. Did she say why?"

"She said she wants to sleep in."

"Do me a favor Jess, will you go up there and check on her?"

"Absolutely. I'll go right now."

"Text me and let me know what's up, okay?"

"Will do. I'm sure she's fine and I'm overreacting."

"Let's hope so."

My stomach is in knots. Willa never sleeps in. Ever. She gets up with the sun, and in the winter, she's up before it.

I don't like this. I don't like this at all. I may be heading home sooner than planned.

Jessica

I'm a smidge panicked. As soon as I voiced my concern to Chloe, I realized I should have checked on Willa already. I should have gone up there right after she told me she was skipping breakfast.

171

I take the elevator up to the 17th floor. I rush out as soon as the doors open and almost walk smack dab into Elias. He steps out of the way just in time.

"Oh, sorry Elias."

Elias gives me a cold grin. "No worries my dear."

He gets in the elevator without another word. I stand and watch as the elevator doors close. His facial expression never changes.

Chills run up my spine. Why was Elias on Willa's floor?

A sickening revelation puts me in motion. He's been drinking from Willa! That's why she's so tired! That bastard!

I run down the hallway yelling Willa's name. "Willa! Willa!"

She doesn't respond. I look in her office, but she isn't in there. I knock on her suite door, wait ten seconds, then swing the door open so hard it bounces off the doorstopper.

"Willa!" I call out as I run into her room.

Her bed is empty. The sheets and blanket thrown back. Her bunny slippers sit beside her bed unused.

"Willa! Where are you?!" I'm scared as hell now. My heart pounding.

"Jessica?" Willa asks from behind me.

I turn around to see Willa standing in her bathrobe. Her long gray hair is wrapped in a towel on top of her head. Confusion is written all over her face.

"Jessica, is something wrong?"

"Willa! Thank God!" I run to her and give her a big hug. "I was so worried!"

She is too stunned to hug me back. "Worried about what?"

"You didn't come down for breakfast and then I saw Elias on your floor. Something is going on."

Willa smiles sheepishly. Her cheeks pink. "Why don't you wait for me in my office while I get dressed? I'll be over there in a few minutes."

"Um...sure."

I walk over to Willa's office with a mixed feeling of relief and confusion. What is going on? Why was Elias on Willa's floor? Was he going through her office? If so, why is he snooping around? What could he possibly want?

I sit in Willa's office waiting for her. Bane isn't around. Willa must have called him to let him know she was sleeping in too.

My mind is still spinning when Willa walks in the room. Her hair is pulled up in her usual bun and she's wearing white linen pants and a black linen shirt with white embroidery.

She takes a seat in her chair and folds her hands on the desk. "Jessica, I'm sorry if I scared you. I should have been more upfront."

I give Willa a onceover. She isn't pale and there are no obvious bite marks on her, although I'm not sure they would show.

"Elias is up to something Willa. He gave me a creepy smile." I shiver thinking about it.

Willa shifts her weight awkwardly. "He isn't up to anything nefarious Jessica."

Willa always sees the best in people. Of course she doesn't think Elias is up to no good. "How can you be sure? What was he doing up here?"

Willa blushes.

Oh...ohhhh...

"Oh my goodness," I say embarrassed. "I feel like an idiot."

"Don't. I should have told you. I should have known you would worry about me."

I don't know what to say. I'm absolutely speechless. Willa and Elias? Hooking up?

173

"Elias and I have been friends for a long time. We've kept in touch over the years. I was married, happily by the way, and I never looked at him romantically. But something happened this visit. We went out for a walk one night, and I felt a connection with him."

"Vampires can be charming."

Willa smiles. "Yes they can."

"Does everyone know but me? I'm always the last to know."

She shrugs. "I imagine the Guard knows. They've probably told Chloe."

I shake my head. "No, they haven't. Not yet anyway."

Willa laughs. "Well that's the first secret they've ever kept."

I laugh too. "They must be buzzing like bees with all we've given them to talk about the last few days."

"May I ask how things are with you and Baxter?"

How are things with me and Baxter? "Good, I guess."

Willa frowns. "You guess? What's wrong?"

I shrug. "He's fun. He's smart. He's cute. He's great in bed."

"Vampires are notoriously good lovers."

I try not to cringe when the mental image of Willa and Elias creeps into my mind.

"Chapter Four doesn't do them justice," I tease.

She smiles, then furrows her brow. "Help me understand Jessica, what's the problem? It sounds like you are having a wonderful time.'

"I am, but he's leaving soon. I'll miss him."

"He will be leaving soon," Willa agrees grimly. "As will Elias."

"Do you regret getting involved with Elias when you know he'll be leaving?"

174

"I'm eighty-four years old. I'm not looking for long term commitment."

I laugh.

"Besides," she says, "I had several great years with the love of my life. I've had marriage and a family. Those things are behind me, not in front of me."

Willa's right. She and I may both be involved with vampires, but we're in totally different places.

I frown. "I'm so stupid. Why do I set myself up?" It's a rhetorical question, one I'm sure I'll ask myself over and over again.

"You are not stupid. Don't say that again," Willa chastises me. "You like Baxter. He likes you. There's nothing stupid about acting on a connection."

"That's the thing Willa - I don't think he likes me the way I like him. I don't think he's capable of having feelings for me."

Willa looks out her window for a moment then back at me. "Why hasn't Baxter gone home yet?" she asks.

"Because he's looking for Gregory," I answer.

"Has there been any sign of Gregory in the last week?"

I shake my head.

"Did you know Elias offered to stay in the city with me for a while longer and keep an eye out for Gregory himself?"

"No."

"Elias told Baxter days ago to go home. Baxter can leave whenever he wants. Yet he's still here. Interesting..." Willa smirks.

I smile a little. It would be nice to believe I'm the reason Baxter is staying in New York, but I don't want to get my hopes up.

"I like him Willa. A lot. What am I going to do when he goes home and I never see him again?"

"My theory is, if he walks away, let him."

"I couldn't stop him if I tried. He's pretty fast," I joke.

Willa laughs. "Exactly the attitude to have. With all partners. If they're leaving you, let them. They'll come back if they smarten up. If they don't, their loss."

She makes it sound so easy.

I stand up to leave. "I'm supposed to give Chloe a reason for why you missed breakfast two days in a row. What should I tell her?"

"You tattled on me, huh?"

"Sorry. I was worried about you."

Willa grins. "It's okay. You can tell her."

I walk toward the door and stop when Willa says, "Jessica…"

"Yes?"

"How do you kill a vampire?"

I'm surprised by her question. "Stake through the heart."

She raises an eyebrow. "Which means they have one, right?"

I smile, getting her message loud and clear. "Thanks Willa."

I don't tell her Baxter closed his heart a long time ago. The 1920s to be exact.

Chloe

"Shut. The Front. Door," is all I can manage to say when Jessica tells me about Willa and Elias.

She giggles. "I know. It's crazy. I'm glad I didn't walk in on them. If I had shown up ten minutes earlier, I may have been scarred for life."

"Oh my God. Willa is getting freaky. I don't know how to handle this. Isn't she too old for sex?"

"She's old Chloe, not dead."

"And Elias?" she continues. "Really? He has the personality of a dead fish."

"I'm as shocked as you are. I haven't seen him the entire time he's been here. I guess I know where he's been…"

Images I never want to see flood my mind. "Yuck. Stop!" I beg her.

Jessica laughs again. "It's better than her being ill."

"Is it?" I ask. "Is the Guard pumping pheromones through the vents? I leave for a few days and the place turns into a brothel."

"It has been a lot more fun since you left."

"Are they staying? Baxter and Elias?"

Jessica sighs and I hate to hear it. "Baxter could be leaving any day now. The Guard and Baxter can't find any sign that Gregory is still around. "

"What about the symbol at the crime scene? Seems too specific to be a coincidence."

"I agree, but Baxter patrols the city every night, and the Guard hasn't seen Gregory on any of the cameras. He disappeared."

"Baxter will stick around for a while longer, to be on the safe side," I say, trying to cheer her up.

She doesn't sound convinced. "Yeah. Maybe."

I feel bad for Jessica. I have a sneaking suspicion she and I will be sharing a lot of Ben & Jerry's when I get home.

"Have you talked to Whitney?" I ask her, hoping my topic change won't be too obvious.

"I did!" Jessica's voice brightens. "I'm so excited she's coming back! And she's going to fashion school!"

"The gang will be back together."

"I can't wait. It's boring around here without you guys."

"Yeah right," I snort. "I think you've stayed occupied."

She laughs. "About that. You might want to go ahead and schedule a pool cleaning."

Gross!

I hang up with Jess and head downstairs for breakfast. Frank nearly chokes on his blueberry muffin when I tell him about Willa.

"You're joking!" he accuses me when he's done hacking a lung.

"Nope. Willa's banging Elias."

He pretends to gag. "Please don't ever use the words 'Willa' and 'banging' in the same sentence again unless a drum set is involved."

Jessica

"Did you know about Elias and Willa?" I ask Baxter when he comes to my room.

"Yes."

"Why didn't you tell me?"

He shrugs. "I don't know. Never came up."

Men. I mean, vampires.

Chapter Eleven

Jessica

The next few days fly by. Chloe is moving around a lot from coven to coven and I have to send her information about each one. Its members, its demographics, recent events in the coven's community, the coven's charitable organizations, and anything else she should be aware of.

I've spent a lot of time in Willa's office going through files and doing research online. Chloe thanks me over and over again for my hard work and it makes me feel good. I like contributing again, being a part of the team.

Next time Chloe goes out of town, I may go with her. I can't let my awkwardness with Frank hold me back. I have to be a big girl and do my job.

In my free time, I'm with Baxter. Like a moth to the flame...

I gave up on trying to stay away from him. No more internal debates, no more second guessing whether I'm doing the right thing. I'm enjoying it while it lasts. It will hurt when Baxter leaves whether I keep seeing him or not. I'm going to take advantage of the time I have.

We've fallen into an evening routine. We go for a walk, then sit on the roof to admire the stars. Baxter bought each of us a pair of binoculars for our nightly stargazing.

He points toward the sky. "That is where Andromeda should be. We can't see her because the city lights are too bright."

I laugh. This isn't the first time Baxter's complained about the city's light pollution.

"It's killing my constellation mojo," he whined the first night.

179

Mojo or not, he's filled me in on astrology, space and the stars. Some of his stories I remember my mom telling me when I was a little girl. Others are brand new. Either way, I'll listen to anything he has to say.

"They call Andromeda 'the chained lady'."

"Why?"

"She was chained to a rock as a human sacrifice to a sea monster."

"Yeesh. That's a little harsh."

Baxter smiles. "Mythology is pretty dark, isn't it? Anyway, it ended well for Andromeda. Perseus, after killing Medusa, freed Andromeda from her chains. Then he used the head of Medusa to turn the sea monster to stone."

I love watching Baxter's face as he tells me these stories. "Perseus was a busy guy, huh?"

"His flying shoes came in handy, that's for sure."

Baxter moves on to Aquila, an eagle and thunderbolt carrier for Zeus.

"Pretty demanding job," I quip.

"Definitely."

"I didn't realize there are so many characters in Greek mythology. I know the names of the main Gods and Goddesses, but I definitely didn't learn all of this in school."

"I wonder sometimes if they were real," Baxter says, eyes twinkling.

"The Greek Gods?"

He shrugs. "Sure, why not? Look at me. Look at Chloe and James. We're mythology, right? We don't really exist to most people, yet here we are."

He has a point.

180

Chloe

I'm in Delaware. It may be a tiny state, but its witch population is comparable to its sister states. The Guard has me staying in a small bed and breakfast outside Wilmington.

I've been in three different states in five days. I'm happy to report every coven has welcomed me with open arms. They are excited to meet me and they like my town hall meeting style. I let them ask me questions and I tell them about my future plans.

Many ask about Willa and how she's doing. They're concerned that my personal appearances mean Willa is unwell. To calm their nerves, I Skype with Willa during my meetings so they can see her for themselves.

Everything is going well, but I'm ready for the "Chloe World Tour" to come to an end. My James teddy bear is losing his scent. I'm sick of being on the road, and I miss my man.

I convey my sentiments to Frank over breakfast. "Only one more day until we're back in Boston. Then we're home."

He grunts. "Can't come soon enough. I've spent way too much time with you lately."

"Ditto."

We're quiet for a moment, then he asks, "Did you talk to Jessica this morning?"

"No. Why?"

Frank frowns. "She's probably upset. You should call her."

I put down my cereal spoon. "Upset? About what?"

"Sherman called me. There's been another murder."

"What?" I ask shocked. "Was there a 'B' at the scene?"

He nods. "It wasn't in the city this time. The victim was in England."

"England?"

"Yes. Which means Baxter will be leaving soon."

Which also means I will have a very upset best friend. Oy.

I pick up my phone. "I better call Jess."

Frank puts his hand on mine. "Don't."

"Why?"

"She may not know yet. Let Baxter tell her."

I bite my bottom lip. What should I do? If Jessica knew something about James, I would want her to tell me. Then again, Frank has a point, Baxter should be the one to tell Jessica, not me.

"I'll give him until tomorrow morning," I decide, "then I'm telling her."

Frank nods. "Fair enough.

Jessica

I roll over, the morning sun shining on my face. I smile and open my eyes, ready to say "good morning" to Baxter, but he's not in bed with me.

I take my cellphone off the charger and check the time - 7: 45 a.m. I notice I have a text from Baxter. It was from 5:30 this morning.

Something came up. I'll catch up with you later.

Hmmm…wonder what that's about…

I convince myself to get out of bed and take a quick shower. After I'm dressed, I head to the kitchen to make Willa's breakfast. She didn't cancel on me this morning, so I actually have to cook.

I make scrambled eggs with egg whites, turkey bacon and whole wheat toast. Willa joins me in the kitchen and we eat at the island. No sense in sitting at the huge dining room table when it's just the two of us.

She puts strawberry jam on her toast. "What are your plans for the day?"

"Don't know yet. I have to check Chloe's email and send her research for her last stop. After that, no clue. How about you?"

"My usual. Work and then a walk with Elias."

"You guys go out every day, don't you?"

"Yes. He walks with me while I strengthen the wards."

"Is Elias always quiet?"

Willa smiles. "Not with me. The man won't stop talking."

I laugh. "I'm sure he has a lot of stories to tell."

"He's been alive for three hundred years. He's a walking history book."

"Wow! That's amazing."

"It is. Never a dull moment with him." Willa's eyes sparkle. She's always a positive person, but she seems more content lately.

"What do you want for lunch today? I'm thinking salmon with wild rice."

"I'm glad you asked. Elias and I are going to the Italian place up the street."

"Really? Elias is going too?"

"Yes. He loves the smell of pasta. He says it's the meal he misses the most."

"I wonder which food I would miss the most if I couldn't eat," I ponder out loud.

"Too many good choices," Willa says with a wink.

I clean our dishes and put away the jam. I ride the elevator to Chloe's floor and take a seat behind her desk. She has a ton of emails, many from Boston Coven members asking questions about the upcoming election. I flag a few and pass them on to Willa.

Next, I sort through the stack of papers I printed out yesterday and scan the ones Chloe needs for her last coven visit. Baxter is still M.I.A., so I tackle a filing project Chloe and I have put off. I lose track of time and before I know it, my stomach is grumbling. Is it already time for lunch? I check my watch – 2:30 p.m.!

I'm uneasy about Baxter's absence. I consider texting him, but I don't want to bother him. We've been together almost every minute of every day for the last week, I should give the man some space.

I make a sandwich and hang around in my room. Daytime TV is the worst. I don't like judge shows and I don't want to get caught up in a soap opera. I settle on a *Love It or List It* rerun, but my mind wanders. In less than forty-eight hours everyone will be back except for my mom, but she won't be far behind them. It will be back to reality.

Wait a second, if Whitney is coming home, she'll be back in her suite on the 13th floor. I wonder how she'll feel about sharing a floor with Baxter and Elias. Before I can think too much about where to put her instead, there's a knock on my door.

"It's open!" I yell.

Baxter walks in. He's wearing his standard outfit of shorts and a t-shirt, but missing his usual smile.

"What's wrong?"

He plays it cool. "Nothing."

"Where have you been?"

He sits next to me on the couch. "With the Guard."

"Any progress?"

Baxter's eyes are conflicted. "I don't want to talk about it right now, if that's okay."

I want to know what's going on, but I don't push. "That's fine."

He smiles for the first time. "What have you been up to today?"

"Nothing too exciting. Same old, same old."

"Wanna go out tonight?"

184

It's clear he's looking to avoid whatever is bothering him and I want to help him feel better. In my merriest voice, I say, "Sure! Where do you want to go?"

"A museum downtown, then to a Broadway show."

I'm surprised. "That's outside the wards."

"I'm sick of worrying about Gregory. I want to take you out for a fun evening on the town."

"Okay," I say tentatively.

Baxter takes my hand. "Nothing will happen to you. I'll protect you. I promise."

I'm not worried about my safety. I know I'm safe with Baxter. I'm concerned about the elephant in the room he refuses to discuss.

Let it go Jess, the fun side of my brain warns.

I smile. "The museum and a Broadway show sounds wonderful. I'll get ready."

"Me too. I'll be back in a little while."

I rush through my closet searching for something to wear. I usually dress up for a show, but we're going to the museum first. I have to find something comfortable, yet nice enough for Broadway.

I pick a fitted, grey Calvin Klein dress with a thin, black belt at the waistline. I opt for black ballet flats because my feet will not survive a museum in heels.

I'm putting gel in my hair when Baxter comes back. His grey short-sleeved dress shirt is tucked into black suit pants. Instead of sneakers or flip flops, he's opted for black dress shoes.

"We're twins," he says when he sees my grey dress.

"Great minds..." Baxter comes up behind me as I finish my hair. "You have a reflection!" I say with a grin.

He rolls his eyes. "I don't know where people came up with that one."

I turn around to face him. "I'm ready to go."

He pulls me in close. "You look perfect."

I blush. "Thanks. You don't look so bad yourself."

Baxter leans down and kisses my neck. "You sure you don't want to stay in?" he whispers in my ear, his hands securely on my waist.

"You should have thought of that before I got dressed up," I tease.

Baxter grunts and steps back. "Okay. Let's go."

I take his hand as we walk down the hallway to the elevator. I love how my hand fits in his. I glance at him and see he's lost in thought.

"What's going on Baxter?"

He quickly smiles. "I was just thinking about which museum we should go to."

I'm not sure I believe him, but I drop it. I want to enjoy our evening out, even if my gut is telling me something isn't right.

We go to the Museum of Modern Art. I marvel at Andy Warhol, Van Gogh and Picasso. So many great artists in one place. Baxter holds my hand as we wade through the crowd and tells me what he knows about each masterpiece.

At times, people stop and listen to Baxter. They are shocked that a man who looks like he belongs on a surfboard knows so much about the artists and their work.

Baxter surprises me with his pick of Broadway shows.

"*Cats*?" I say when I see the sign. "We're seeing *Cats*?"

"Yes. Have you seen it?"

I shake my head, smiling. "I haven't, but I want to."

"Good," Baxter says with a grin.

We find seats in the third row, and read through the playbill while we wait for the show to start. Baxter and I exchange excited glances when the lights turn down in the theater. I watch in wonder as the music plays, actors dressed in intricate feline costumes prowling the stage.

I'm lost in the alleys of London as the characters sing and dance. An actress brings tears to my eyes when she sings her heart out, begging her lover to stay. The lyrics strike a chord, almost too reminiscent of my feelings for Baxter.

I stand and clap heartily as the actors take their bows and the curtain closes for the last time.

"Did you like it?" Baxter asks when we are out in the cool, summer night air.

"I loved it!" I gush. "It was amazing!"

"I'm glad you liked it."

"I can't believe I waited so long to see it."

Baxter pulls me to the side, out of the stream of people leaving the theater. He touches his hands to my face and kisses my lips.

I smile when he pulls away. "What was that for?"

He runs his thumb over my cheek. "No particular reason."

"Baxter...I..." I stop myself before telling Baxter I love him. Didn't I promise not to fall in love with him? Didn't I swear I wouldn't let myself feel this way?

His brow furrows. "What? What is it Jessica?"

I come up with something else to say. "Thank you for tonight."

He kisses me softly. "You're welcome."

We walk toward home. We talk about the show and the artwork we saw today, but something is missing from Baxter's normal banter. He's maintaining his end of the conversation, but it lacks his usual energy and wit.

I'm nervous and scared. As much fun as I had tonight, something is wrong. The other shoe is about to drop. I prepare myself for the worst when we get back to my room.

I sit on the couch and pat the cushion next to me. "Please, tell me what's wrong."

He sighs and sits beside me. "I didn't want to tell you earlier. I wanted one more good night with you."

One more good night? I gulp. "Okay…"

Here it comes, he's about to tell me he's leaving.

I'm shocked when he says, "There's been another murder."

"What? Oh my God!"

Baxter frowns. "It was in the paper this morning. Another young woman found dead on her doorstep yesterday. Seemingly no connection to me or Gregory, but the symbol was written on the door in blood."

"Where? Here in the city?"

"No. In London."

"London?" I ask surprised.

"Yes. I have to go. I have to find Gregory."

"Of course you do! You have to stop him."

"I leave tomorrow. My flight is at 7:00 p.m."

Something dawns on me. "That's why you're okay with going outside the wards. You know Gregory is gone."

Baxter nods. "He's not a threat to you anymore."

I sit quietly and process everything. Baxter is leaving for London. Tomorrow. He's understandably sad about another young woman being murdered. I get it. But why is he looking at me like that?

"You aren't coming back, are you?"

He avoids my eyes. "I don't think I should."

I take a deep breath. This is it - the moment I've been dreading since I decided to give in to this "passing whim." I don't say anything. I'm trying desperately to keep my composure.

"Please understand," he pleads, "you are human. You are fragile. Any number of random and infinitesimal things can take you from me. I can't feel pain like that again."

I focus on my hands, unable to meet his gaze. "You should go now."

"Now?" he asks stunned.

"Yes."

"You don't want me to stay with you tonight?"

I shake my head.

"Do you want me to come see you before I leave?" His request has a hint of desperation.

I close my eyes, holding the tears back. "No. Just go."

"Jessica, I'm sorry."

The pain in his voice causes me to meet his eyes. He doesn't look like an emotionless, supernatural being to me. He looks like a man struggling with rejection.

I drop my gaze. I can't let myself believe that. Regardless of appearances, Baxter will leave tomorrow and never give me a second thought.

"This isn't your fault. You told me upfront what this was." Despite my efforts, I start to cry. "You tried very hard not to hurt me, and I appreciate that. I did this to myself."

Baxter touches my arm, but I pull back.

"Don't. Please don't."

He sighs and stands. "I wish there was something I could say. I feel like a complete asshole."

I wipe my tears with the back of my hand. "You should go now," I say again.

He hesitates, then says, "Good-bye Jessica."

I stare out at the city through my glass wall. "Good-bye Baxter."

A light breeze crosses my skin. In a flash, Baxter is gone.

I crumble, my sadness crashing down on me. I sob with my head in my hands.

Chloe

I'm in the backseat of an Escalade heading back to Boston when I receive a text message from Jess.

> *FML* ☹

I sigh. "Well," I tell Frank, "Jessica knows about Baxter."

He raises an eyebrow. "Oh yeah?" I show him Jessica's text. He shakes his head. "That's not good."

I type out a response:

> *I'm so sorry Jess. I'm in the car now, but I can talk in an hour or so.*

Her response is quick:

> *Did you know?*

Oh man! I'm honest with her:

> *I did, but I just found out this morning. I was giving Baxter until tomorrow morning to tell you. Please don't be mad at me. I'll call you as soon as I get to my room in Boston.*

I pick at my nails as I wait for a response.

> *No worries. I understand. No need to call me later. I'll just cry in your ear.*

I frown.

> *Are you sure? I'm a decent listener when I try to be.*

"What is she saying?" Frank asks.

"She's upset."

He huffs. "Bastard."

I could point out that he hurt Jessica himself not too long ago, but I don't.

My phone buzzes again.

> *I'm sure. We can talk about it when you get home. Maybe by then I'll be cried out.*

I feel bad for Jess, but there's not a whole lot I can do. I'm stuck in a car with Frank sitting right beside me.

> *Call if you need me.*

I set my phone in my lap and lean my head on the headrest. I'm worn out from being on the road. I enjoyed meeting everyone, but I'm ready to be home.

"From now on Frank, let's limit our trips to four or five days. This is exhausting."

"I agree. This was a lot. Didn't help that Nina was our first stop."

I grimace. "No joke. Has the coven sent us a list of potential replacements?"

"They have." Frank pulls out his phone and scrolls through his messages. "June Mead and Karen Bar."

"What do we know about them?"

"Both are ideal candidates. June is a few years older than Karen, but Karen is a bit more active with the coven's outreach programs."

"Any concerns about either one?" I ask. I don't want another Nina to deal with.

Frank shakes his head. "No, but we didn't have concerns about Nina before her election."

"Well, it's in their hands. Hopefully they choose wisely this time."

I kick off my heels as soon as we get back to the townhouse in Boston. My feet praise me for it. I flop down on my bed and call James. I haven't had the chance to talk to him all day.

191

I smile when he answers. "Hey Chloe."

"Hey babe. How's it going?"

"Okay."

"You at home?"

"No," he says without further explanation.

"Where are you?"

"My grandfather's office." It doesn't sound like he's in a very good mood.

"What's wrong?" I ask.

"Nothing. Busy."

"Are you upset with me?"

He sighs. "Why would I be upset with you?"

"You're acting weird."

"I'm busy Chloe. This is what it sounds like when I'm busy."

Damn! Excuse me!

"Okay." I try to cheer him up. "I'm excited to see you."

"Yeah, me too." Except he doesn't sound excited at all, he sounds irritated.

"Did something happen today? You sound mad."

"No, just busy. I'll have to come back out here again next week."

"Oh really?" I say disappointed. "That stinks."

"I have a lot going on. You're not the only one with an important job."

"I'm just going to miss you, that's all."

"Have you ever thought about coming out here with me?" he asks, his tone icy.

I stammer. "I'd love to, but work is crazy."

His volume increases. "Have you considered for a second that you expect me to spend my life with you in New York when my pack is here?"

"Whoa, whoa, whoa. Where is this coming from?" I'm getting really pissed. I don't deserve this. He's never asked me to go to Colorado with him.

His rant continues. "You expect me to travel back and forth all the time because of your job, totally disregarding the fact that my job is here. Have you thought about that?"

"Of course I have!"

"Have you? Really?"

"Yes!"

"It doesn't seem like it."

That's it. I'm done. "What the hell are you talking about? When have I said or done anything that degrades your future position as Pack Leader? I've never acted like my job is more important than yours."

"It's been implied," he shoots back.

"This is bullshit," I hiss into the phone.

Silence fills the line for a minute, both of us trying to calm down.

James sighs. "What are we going to do?" he asks defeated. "I can't be in New York all the time. I have responsibilities here."

I rub my temples, a headache coming on. "I can't talk with you about this right now. We're both pissed and we won't accomplish anything this way."

"Fine, but you can't put this conversation off forever."

I hang up the phone and fall back onto my bed.

What just happened? Did James have a bad day and decide to take it out on me?

Worse, has he been holding this in for a while?

And what happened to, I just want you Chloe?
In the words of my dear friend, FML.

Chapter Twelve

Jessica

I manage to get out of bed and cook Willa her breakfast in the morning. My face is puffy and my eyes are bloodshot. She tries making small talk with me over our french toast, but I mumble responses.

She eventually cuts to the chase. "I'm sorry about Baxter. I know you're upset. Is there anything I can do?"

I shake my head. "No, not really."

"Chloe will be home tonight and Whitney will be back tomorrow. Are you excited?"

"Yes," I say with zero enthusiasm.

"Alright." Willa pushes her chair back from the table. "I'll leave you alone."

"Sorry I'm such poor company. I promise not to be miserable for too long."

Willa gives me a hug. "I wish I had some words of wisdom for you."

"You don't have a spell or potion for me?" I joke weakly.

Willa pats my shoulder. "If I did, I'd be rich. Only time heals a broken heart."

I trudge to Chloe's office and read emails. There's no research or documents to pass along today. It's not even noon and I don't have anything to do. I need to get out of the building, get some fresh air.

I call Willa's office.

"Yes dear?"

"I'm going out for a while. I'll be back for dinner."

"Have fun."

Yeah…right.

Before leaving, I change out of my pajamas and into shorts and a tank top. I put on tennis shoes in case I go for a long walk. Hard telling how far I'll venture out today. I put my cellphone and wallet in a red leather cross-body bag and head downstairs.

Leaving the building isn't just a reprieve, I'm also avoiding a potential visit from Baxter. I can't take another crushing good-bye. Who wants to be told repeatedly they're not worth coming back to?

I step outside and tilt my face toward the sky. The summer sun is warm and feels good on my skin. I put on my sunglasses and mentally prepare myself for a day walking around the city. There's something freeing about being lost in a crowd, your individual problems insignificant in comparison to the collective chaos.

I glance in store windows, even step into a few. Nothing catches my attention. After a little while, I stop at a street vendor for a pretzel and a bottle of iced tea.

I find a bench on the sidewalk and sit with my goodies. I watch people pass by as I munch on my pretzel. The school year hasn't started yet, so there are lots of parents out with their kids. Business people walk by on their cellphones talking a mile a minute and a small dog stops to smell my shoe before its owner pulls him along.

I'm not quite sure what happens next. One minute I'm on a bench taking a drink of iced tea, and the next, I'm not.

Chloe

The election is going well. Both candidates give strong, impassioned speeches. Frank is right - either one of these women

196

will be a good leader. I don't voice an opinion about which woman I like best when I give instructions for the vote.

"You were all given ballot forms when you came in tonight. Please put an 'x' on the line next to the candidate you want to see as your next Coven Leader and place it in the ballot box. We will count the votes as soon as every form is turned in."

One by one, members bring up their ballots. We're about halfway through when my phone rings. It's Willa.

I excuse myself from my seat and step away from the group. "Willa, what's up?"

"It's not Willa, it's Baxter."

"Baxter? What are you doing on Willa's phone?" My mind immediately jumps to the worst conclusion. "Is Willa okay?"

"She's fine. She's letting me borrow her phone. I figured you wouldn't answer a call from an unknown number."

He's right. I wouldn't. "I'm kinda in the middle of something. Can I call you back?"

He ignores my attempt to brush him off. "Have you heard from Jessica?"

"No. Why?"

After a pause, he says, "She's missing."

"Missing? What do you mean she's missing?"

Frank walks over on high alert. "Someone's missing?"

I put my hand up, shushing him. I'm trying to hear Baxter over the noise in the room. "She called Willa earlier to say she was going out and would be home for dinner. She hasn't come back."

I check my watch – 8:23 p.m. Way past dinnertime. "This isn't like her."

"I know. Willa is worried."

And now, so am I.

"Okay, let me think for a second." I take a deep breath and evaluate my options. "I'm hanging up so I can call her myself."

"She isn't answering her phone. We've tried several times."

"Not to be rude Baxter, but you're not her favorite person right now."

"Yes, I know. But she ignored Willa's calls too. Would she normally do that?"

"No," I concede. "Let me call her anyway. I'll call you back."

I hang up before Baxter can protest. Jessica always takes my calls. One time she even jumped out of the shower to answer my call.

"Please Jess, please answer your phone," I whisper under my breath as the phone rings. I hope we're overreacting, but I have a terrible feeling about this.

I get her voicemail. Shit. "This is Jessica. Leave a message!"

"Jess, it's Chloe. Please call or text me right away. Thanks."

I call Baxter.

"Any luck?" he asks.

I rub my temple. "No. She didn't answer."

"I'm worried. Willa is freaking out. She says Jessica never disappears like this."

"What did Jessica take with her when she left?"

"The Guard checked the footage and all she had was her purse. She wasn't planning on being gone long."

Frank taps my shoulder. "They're done."

I glance over my shoulder. Everyone is back in their seats waiting for the results of the election to be announced.

I turn my attention back to Baxter. "I'm leaving here in ten minutes. We're heading straight to the airport. Keep me posted until I get home."

"Will do."

I end the call and get myself together. Frank shows me the results of the election. I walk up to the podium and put on my best Verhena smile.

"Ladies and gentlemen, I'm pleased to announce that your new Coven Leader is Karen Bar!"

Everyone in the audience claps, including June Mead, the woman who lost. Karen walks to the podium beaming, and I shake her hand.

"I'm so sorry to cut this short," I tell the audience, "but something has come up and I must go. Before I turn the microphone over to Karen, I want you all to know I wish you the very best. Please feel free to reach out to me with your questions and concerns. Willa and I love hearing from you."

I step away from the podium and walk toward Frank. "We need to go, now!" I whisper to him.

He raises an eyebrow, but doesn't question me. I smile and wave at the crowd as I make a hasty exit.

When we're in the car, Frank lets me have it. "What the hell was that? A little rude, don't you think?"

"Jessica is missing."

His demeanor changes completely. "Missing?"

"No one knows where she is and she didn't answer my call." I check my phone. "She hasn't called back or sent a text either."

"That's not like her."

"I know. We need to get home and figure out what's going on."

I call James on the way to the airport. I ignored his calls earlier today because I wasn't ready to play nice after our argument last night. Now I feel like an immature fool.

"Chloe!" He sounds relieved. "I'm so glad you called back. About last night…"

I interrupt him. "Babe, I hate to do this to you, but not right now. We have a problem."

I tell him about Jessica being M.I.A.

"Something's not right," he says. "Whitney and I will get there as soon as we can. Hopefully we can be on a flight tonight."

"I'm worried about her," I admit to him.

"I am too. I'll be there soon."

"I love you."

"I love you too."

I hang up with James. My stomach is in knots. Jessica is in trouble. I just know it.

Our airplane is waiting for us on the tarmac. I say a quick "hi" to Shannon before buckling myself in my seat. I jump when Frank's phone rings, worried it will be bad news about Jess.

"Shit," Frank hisses into his phone.

Oh no… I calm a little when I see his face is filled with annoyance, not concern.

"Call me tomorrow morning with an update," he demands before ending the call.

"What is it?"

"Nina checked herself out of the hospital today."

"What? Already?"

Frank nods. "They thought she was stable, so they let her out."

"Where is she now?"

"At home."

"We're sure?"

"Yes. The Guard checked in on her."

I let out a deep breath. For a second, I was worried Nina had something to do with Jessica's sudden disappearance.

The Nina issue tabled, Frank and I debate the various places Jessica could be.

"The movies?" he throws out. "She loves going to the movies."

"She does, but she'd be home by now. She wouldn't skip out on making Willa's dinner for a movie."

"Any bands or singers in town this weekend she would see?" Frank suggests next.

We research the city venues, but there isn't a single performance that would appeal to Jess.

"Maybe she just needs a break before we all get home," I think out loud. "She had a rough couple of days."

Frank doesn't look convinced, but says, "Yeah, maybe."

We both know Jessica would never fall off the face of the Earth like this.

The rest of our flight and the drive home from the airport are quiet. I wait for my phone to ring with an update, or even better, with a call from Jess. But it remains silent. As soon as we arrive at the building, Frank and I immediately go to the Guard Operations Center. Willa is in the conference room with Baxter and Elias.

"Any news?" I ask.

Willa is a mess. Her eyes are bloodshot and the lines in her face are deeper than ever. "We have no idea where she is. We found her on a few cameras, but it was early in the day. Nothing in the last few hours."

"Show me," Frank says.

Willa slides him three pictures. I lean in and scan them for clues. In the first, Jessica is walking down the sidewalk outside our building. She's wearing a cute tank top with shorts and tennis sneakers. Jess loves flip flops, so her choice of footwear indicates she wasn't planning on a quick errand.

Frank flips to the second picture – Jessica walking out the front door of a boutique. Her hands are tucked in her pockets, no bags with purchases dangling from her arms.

"Where is this shop?" I ask.

"Four blocks from here," Baxter responds.

In the final picture, Jessica is buying a pretzel from a street vendor.

Frank hands me the photos, done with his analysis. "What time was the last picture taken?"

Baxter answer again. "Around 2:30."

I examine the pictures once more. Jessica appears to be perfectly fine as she walks nonchalantly with her favorite pair of black sunglasses on.

I put the pictures down on the table and turn to Baxter. "Are you sure Gregory isn't involved?"

"How can he be? He's in England."

"How do you know for sure?" I press. "He may have hired someone else to kill the woman in England."

"I thought of that, but we checked the flights. He boarded a plane four days ago, the day before the woman was murdered in England. His passport hasn't been used since."

"What if he used a fake?" Frank asks.

Baxter and Willa exchange glances. "We didn't think of that."

Frank charges out of the room and I'm hot on his heels. He stands behind a Guard member, Jeremy, who is watching the television screens. He nearly barks, "Run facial recognition on Gregory in the three major metropolitan airports for the last three days."

"Understood," Jeremy says. His fingers fly across the keyboard.

Within seconds, Gregory's face flashes on one of the screens. He is walking through the airport crowd holding a small duffel bag. He's wearing jeans and a polo shirt. He blends in perfectly with everyone around him.

"When is that from?" Frank asks.

"Yesterday at 4:30 p.m."

Frank slams his fist on the table. "Shit!"

My stomach lurches. Gregory has my best friend.

"Run his face again," I tell Jeremy. "This time on the city cameras we have access to."

"Will do Ms. Chloe."

Nothing comes up this time.

"How is that possible?" Frank asks flustered. "How does he just disappear?"

Suddenly, it clicks. "He's moving too fast," I whisper.

"What?"

"He's moving too fast," I explain. "That's how we keep missing him. I read in one of the books in the library that some vampires can move faster than a camera's image-capturing technology."

"She's right," Baxter says from behind me.

Frank's nostrils flare as he turns to Baxter. "You! This is your fault!" Frank charges toward Baxter and Baxter readies himself in his fighting stance.

I step in front of Frank and use a power spell to hold him back. "Frank! Stop!"

He is pushing so hard my feet slide backwards on the tile floor. "I should kill you! She could be dead because of you!" he yells at Baxter.

Baxter drops his defenses. "I know."

"Frank! Please! This isn't helping!" When he doesn't stop, I add, "Don't make me freeze you in place! I'll do it!"

Frank stops leaning against me. He crosses his arms over his chest and glares at Baxter. "You better hope we find her alive and unharmed. If we don't, I will hunt you down."

"Can we focus please?" I plead. "Jessica is in trouble. How are we going to find her?"

No one has an answer.

Jessica

I wake up on a cold floor.

What happened?

Where am I?

I sit up, my head pounding. I put my hand on my forehead and cringe with pain. My fingers are warm and sticky. A thick crust of blood has formed in my hairline. How long have I been unconscious?

I scan my surroundings, my eyes struggling to adjust to the darkness. I spot a window against the opposite wall. Unfortunately, the sun is down and the streetlight outside doesn't cast much light into the room.

"Hello?" I call out. "Is anyone here?"

A deep laugh fills the room. "Just me sweetheart."

I squint my eyes in the direction of the voice, but can't see anything.

"Let me get closer," the voice says and within a heartbeat whispers, "can you see me now?" in my ear.

I shriek and crawl away as quickly as I can. The hardwood scraps my hands and knees.

The voice laughs again. "No point in trying to get away. I'll catch you."

The dark shadow moves like a gray blur and comes to a stop in front of the window. The light it provides isn't much, but it allows me to see the figure more clearly. The dark hair...the beady eyes...

I gasp. "Gregory..."

He smiles. "Ding, ding, ding!"

I close my eyes tight, then open them again. "You weren't in England?"

"Oh, I was. For a very brief stay. Just long enough to kill another young woman. Sad too. She was pretty." He shrugs his shoulders. "Oh well."

"Why are you back here?"

Gregory is suddenly in my face. "For you my dear."

I pull back from him. "Me?"

He sneers, but moves away. "Yes, you. At first I planned to kill Elias. He is the only person Baxter cares about, but then I saw Baxter out with you. Always within the boundaries of course." He pauses. "Lucky for me I can see from great distances, so you two never suspected I was watching you."

He's right, I never suspected a thing.

"I realized Baxter wasn't going to let you outside the wards as long as he thought I was in the city," Gregory explains. "I'm impatient, an odd trait for an immortal, I know. So I flew to England, killed the young woman, and flew back using a phony passport. No biggie, as the kids say."

I frown. Baxter fell for it hook, line and sinker. He's probably on his way to England right now.

"He won't come looking for me," I tell Gregory. "He doesn't care about me."

Gregory balks at this. "Please. He spent the entire week with you. Showing you constellations, walking around the city streets. When he thought I was gone, he took you to the art museum and a musical. You two shared the sweetest little kiss outside the theater."

205

Goosebumps run up my arms, but I fake confidence. "Too bad you didn't see him break up with me. You might not be so convinced."

Gregory laughs. "Nice try. He cares about you, I've seen it with my own eyes. He'll come for you."

"How is he supposed to find me?"

"By your blood."

"My blood?"

Gregory rolls his eyes. "Don't play stupid with me. He drank from you, he'll be able to find you."

"No he didn't."

"Yes he did."

"No really, he didn't." I tilt my head, exposing my neck. "Look."

Gregory zooms over. "Show me your wrists." He grabs my hands and flips them over. He squeezes my wrists, fury on his face.

I wince in pain. I don't want to cry out, but his fingers feel like vice grips. "Please, you're hurting me…"

He drops my hands in disgust and returns to his spot in front of the window. "You mean to tell me you spent all that time together and he never drank from you?!"

I shake my head, rubbing my wrists. "No, he didn't."

Gregory paces back and forth, whispering to himself. "I thought for sure he'd drink from the girl. What to do now? I was moving too fast for anyone to see me. Do I call him? Do I show up outside the boundaries with her?"

"Why don't you let me go?" I suggest.

In a flash, Gregory has his hand on my throat. "You'd like that, wouldn't you?" His breath is hot against my face. "Never. Gonna. Happen."

206

I claw at his hand with my fingers, struggling to breath, but he doesn't let go.

His beady eyes bore into mine. "I'm going to rip your throat out in front of him. Let him feel the pain I felt when he killed Deanna."

Gregory lets go of my throat and I gasp for air. I cough painfully as my lungs start filling again.

"And then what?" I ask when I can speak. "Chloe will hunt you down and kill you."

Baxter may not care if I'm dead, but Chloe sure will.

Gregory shrugs his shoulders. "I want nothing more than to see the devastated look on Baxter's face when I kill you. I'm willing to pay the Verhena's price."

He means it. There's nothing I can say to convince him to let me go. All I can do is hope help gets here as soon as possible. Then I remember a conversation I had with Baxter.

"Walk outside with me," I say in a raspy voice.

"Beg your pardon?"

"The Guard has access to several cameras throughout the city. It's relatively new technology for them. If we walk around together outside, they may see us."

Gregory rubs his chin. "Do you think there are cameras around here?"

I shrug my shoulders. "I have no idea where the cameras are. Just a thought." Then I add, "You can use my cellphone too if you want."

Gregory shakes his head. "I ditched your purse."

"What?!" For some reason I find this the most infuriating thing of all. "My driver's license and bank card are in there!"

Gregory smiles. "Don't worry, you don't need them anymore."

I deflate.

He grabs me under the arms. "Get up. We're going for a stroll."

Chloe

I'm standing with my back to the television screens searching my brain for the next steps. Where do we start? The shops she visited? The pretzel vendor? What could they possibly have to say that will help us?

"Guys! Look at this!" Jeremy calls out from behind me.

I turn toward the TV screens. "Oh my God…"

Frank, Baxter, Jeremy and I stare at the center television. We watch as Gregory leads Jessica down a sidewalk. His hand is on the small of her back, his eyes darting from side-to-side. Anger boils inside me when I see clotted blood on Jessica's forehead.

"Willa!" I yell toward the conference room. "Get out here!"

"What are they doing?" Baxter asks.

Frank shakes his head. "I'm not sure."

"Looking for a camera," I say, my eyes glued to the television. "Why else would he move so slow? He wants us to see him."

My suspicions are confirmed when Gregory spots the camera. He rushes toward it, dragging Jessica along with him. He holds her in front of the lens, giving us a close-up of her bruised face. My fingers clench into tight fists.

"She's alive!" Baxter exclaims.

"No thanks to you," Frank mutters.

I glare at both of them. They shrink and avoid my stare. I turn back toward the television.

"You think they can see us?" Gregory asks Jessica.

"I don't know. This could be one of their cameras," she answers. Her voice is raw and ragged.

"We'll stand here a moment to be sure they see us."

208

Jessica says nothing as she stares down at her feet.

Suddenly, Gregory pulls Jessica's hair, making her cry out in pain. "Look into the camera my dear. They have to see your pretty face."

"Where is she Jeremy?" I ask through gritted teeth.

"The Brooklyn Naval Yard."

"The Naval Yard?" Frank asks shocked. "There should be a ton of people around. It looks deserted."

"They're re-developing this section of the Yard," Jeremy explains. "This camera is on a lamp post, one of the few in the area."

"Shh!" I hiss. "They're moving!"

We watch them walk down the street and into an old, dilapidated brick building.

Baxter moves for the elevator. "Let's go!"

Frank puts his hand up. "Hold on a second. We need to figure a few things out first."

"Like what? We know where she is! We know Gregory has her! We need to get there right now!"

Both men look to me for help.

I'm processing everything, not quite ready to take action. "Give me a second."

Gregory wanted us to see Jessica. He wants us to come after him. What if he has a trap set up for us?

"Jeremy, keep your eyes glued to that screen. Call me immediately if anything changes or looks suspicious."

He nods. "Understood."

I turn to Frank. "We have to go get her now. We can't wait for one of your grand plans."

"Chloe," he protests, "we can't barge in there. He's ready and waiting for us."

209

"Sometimes you just have to wing it Frank."

I turn to Baxter. "And you," Baxter looks at me like a man on the verge. "You need to calm down. We have to be smart."

He takes a deep breath, then nods.

Willa joins our group. "What's going on?"

"Show her," I tell Jeremy.

He nods and replays the video.

I watch Willa's face become even paler. "Oh no," she says when she sees Jessica. She takes the empty seat next to Jeremy. "This is awful."

I kneel down in front of Willa. "We're going to get Jessica."

"Now?"

"Yes, now."

She pats my hand. "Be careful."

"We will." I stand. "Frank, we need three SUVs."

"Three?"

"Yes. We split up. Gregory can't take out all three vehicles at the same time."

Frank nods. "Good point."

"Get the stakes ready. I need to change out of this dress. I'll meet you in the garage in five minutes."

I hit the button for the elevator and it opens instantly. I step inside, then turn back to Frank and Baxter. Just before the doors close I give a final instruction.

"Have the cars running. We're going to get our girl."

Chapter Thirteen

I hop in the backseat of an Escalade. Tobias, the best driver in the Guard, is at the wheel.

"What do you know about the Naval Yard?" I ask him.

"Not much to be honest."

"Me neither."

He glances at me in the rearview mirror. "I'm sure Frank is on top of it."

I stare out my window watching the city go by. Tobias puts on classical piano music.

"Let me know if this is bothering you. I'll turn it off."

"No, don't. I like it."

"I listen to classical music before competitions. I find it relaxing."

In addition to his navigation skills, Tobias is also a cross-fit competitor. Standing at 5'8", he's one of the shortest Guard members, but he wins their pull-up competition with ease.

I sit back and close my eyes for a few minutes. Mentally preparing myself for the battle to come. Gregory is luring Baxter in, practically begging for a fight. I'll let the two of them duke it out. I'm hoping Baxter distracts Gregory long enough for me to grab Jessica and get out of there.

"We'll arrive in five minutes," Tobias tells me from up front.

I call James, but get his voicemail. He's probably on an airplane by now.

"Hey babe, it's me. We had to go after Jess. Gregory has her. Just wanted to say 'I love you'. See you soon." I hang up wishing I could have heard his voice.

"Why not wait for James?" Willa asked before we left. "He would be incredibly helpful."

She's right, but we couldn't wait for him.

Elias also offered to come with us, but I made him stay behind with Willa. She is too distraught to be alone.

Tobias slows the vehicle. "I'm turning into the Naval Yard Ms. Chloe."

I lean forward and glance out the windows on high alert. The Brooklyn Naval Yard gets its name from the ships that used to be built here. Nowadays, commercial and residential contractors have bought up the property and are developing it for more modern uses. From the map Jeremy showed us, the section Gregory is hiding in has been purchased, but undeveloped.

We roll to a stop in front of the building Gregory and Jessica walked into earlier. As soon as I step out of the car, I put a protective shield around myself. Frank and Baxter exit their cars and stand next to me. We are all wearing utility belts with four stakes in holsters. Hopefully one of them will find its way through Gregory's heart.

I expand my protective shield to include Frank and Baxter. "If you stay close, I can keep the protective bubble around you," I explain to Baxter.

"Can you get it around Jessica?" he asks.

"Only if she's close. And if Gregory is touching her, there's no point. He'll be in the bubble with her."

Baxter nods. "Got it."

"We ready?" Frank asks, his eyes trained on the building.

It is only three stories tall. Bricks are crumbled and missing in places. Most of the windows are broken out and the foundation has several cracks.

"Gregory is mine," Baxter hisses.

"Fine," I say. I could give a shit about Gregory. I'm here for Jessica.

Frank nods in agreement.

We walk toward the entrance of the building, glancing over our shoulders and scanning our surroundings. Jeremy never called to say Jessica and Gregory moved, but with Gregory's superfast speed, I'm not confident he's still inside. For all I know, this building is filled with explosives.

A part of me wishes Baxter had drank Jessica's blood. He was proud to tell us he hadn't, but it would be helpful in this situation. He could tell us if Jessica is actually here.

We cross the threshold of the building tentatively. It's dark, the building's electricity turned off long ago. Frank uses the flashlight on his cellphone to guide us through the main floor. Someone has started renovations in here. All of the sheet rock is gone, the wooden beams exposed.

Baxter sniffs the air, then stiffens. "She's here."

"How do you know?" I whisper.

"I can smell her. She's here."

"Where do you think she is?" I ask, trying to be as quiet as possible.

"I can hear you," a deep voice says from above us.

I look up. There's nothing to see but the ceiling. "What the..."

Before I can finish my sentence, a cloud of dust surrounds the protective bubble. It's nearly impossible to see.

"It's Gregory," Baxter says. "His movements are kicking up dust."

Frank and I exchange weary glances. This isn't going to be easy.

Before we can discuss a plan, Baxter points to his left. "There they are."

213

When the dust settles, I spot Gregory and Jessica standing twenty feet away. A row of wooden beams where a wall used to be separates us. Gregory is holding Jessica's arms behind her, a menacing smile on his lips. Jessica is dirty, but she doesn't look any worse than she did earlier. Her eyes are wide and scared.

Baxter speaks first. "Let her go Gregory, this is between us."

I watch Gregory's hands carefully, hoping he'll let go of Jessica. But his grip is strong.

"You want the girl, Baxter?" Gregory sneers.

Before Baxter can say anything, I interrupt. "Give Jessica to me Gregory. We can make a deal. Just tell me what you want."

Gregory cocks his head to the side. "You are as beautiful as they say. I'm sorry you are involved in this Verhena. I mean you no disrespect. You will be a great and powerful leader."

"I appreciate your kind words, but please, let me have my friend. She is innocent in all of this."

Gregory frowns. "As were the others. But a debt is a debt Verhena. You of all people understand that. Didn't you burn the werewolves who killed your sister to a crisp?"

"I did, but Jessica didn't kill Deanna. Please let her go."

Gregory's eyes shift away from me. "Baxter, do you want the girl?"

Jessica squirms. "No! He doesn't," she insists, looking at us meaningfully.

Baxter plays it cool. "I'm only here because Chloe made me come."

Gregory grins. "I don't believe you."

In a flash, Gregory puts his hand on Jessica's head and tilts it toward her shoulder, her neck fully exposed.

He smirks. "Funny, isn't it Baxter? I'll taste her before you do."

"No, don't!" I shout.

214

Gregory ignores me. I watch in horror as he sinks his fangs into Jessica's neck and rips violently. Jessica screams out in pain, then falls to the ground. She leans on her hands as blood pours from her neck. Within seconds, her arms give out, and she's lying face down on the floor.

Without any hesitation, I run toward her on wobbly legs. The sight of the skin on Jessica's neck hanging loosely makes me queasy. Frank comes up behind me and puts his hands under my arm pits. He lifts me up and practically carries me to Jessica's limp body.

Meanwhile, Baxter is frozen in place, disbelief and devastation on his face as he stares at Jessica.

Gregory stands in the corner of the room, an amused grin on his face. "There it is - the look I've been waiting for."

"Get Gregory!" Frank shouts to Baxter. "We'll heal Jessica."

Something inside Baxter snaps. He bares his teeth. "You're dead!" he growls as he launches himself at Gregory.

Gregory charges forward and the two clash in the middle of the room. They begin fighting, gnarling and gnashing sounds filling my ears. The two vampires move so quickly, I can't keep track of where they are.

Frank and I fall to our knees next to Jessica, one of us on each side of her. I put my shield up around the three of us. Dirt and debris fly as Baxter and Gregory slam each other against the walls, the floor, and the wooden beams. They hit a beam so violently, the house shakes.

We roll Jessica onto her back. My jeans are soaked with the blood flowing from her wound. Frank takes the loose flap of skin on her neck and lays it in place where it should be. He puts his hand flat on the skin and starts repeating healing spells out loud.

At the same time, I take Jessica's hand and repeat different healing spells, hoping our combined power can help her.

Frank pulls his hand away from Jessica's neck and smiles. "The bleeding stopped."

As soon as the words are out of his mouth, a small trickle of blood oozes from the wound.

"Keep going!" I tell him desperately.

We repeat this cycle two more times. Just when we think we're getting somewhere, the blood starts pouring again.

"She's losing too much blood," Frank says, his jaw tight and eyes distraught.

"Keep trying," I urge him. I place my hand on Jessica's forehead. "I can't lose you Jess. Please! Please hold on!"

Meanwhile, Baxter and Gregory continue to go at each other. I thought Baxter would be able to handle Gregory easily, but that's not the case. They are destroying the framework of the house as they fight. The creaking noise coming from the floors above us makes me nervous.

"We have to get out of here!" I yell when Baxter and Gregory crash through two wood beams and break them in half.

"It's too dangerous to move her. We have to keep trying to heal her," Frank insists.

"Should we call 9-1-1?"

He shakes his head. "They won't make it in time. And I don't think we can get her to a hospital quick enough."

There is so much blood…

I check Jessica's pulse again, it's getting weaker. Baxter and Gregory crash onto the floor near us. It gives me an idea.

"What if Baxter runs her to the hospital? He can get her there superfast."

Frank considers it. "That might work, but he's a little preoccupied at the moment."

I look out beyond my protective bubble. It's hard to see anything.

"Fuck this," I mutter. "Enough."

I stand up and freeze the room. Frank is kneeling next to Jessica, frozen with his hand on her neck. Despite everything in the room coming to a standstill, blood seeps out of Jessica's wound.

"Magic cannot prevent death," Willa told me once. "You may be able delay it, but you cannot stop it."

I desperately search the bottom floor of the house for the vampires. We need to get Jessica medical help as quickly as possible. We are losing her.

I find Baxter and Gregory locked in a bear hug. Baxter has Gregory pinned against the wall. Both of their faces are contorted in snarls and their fangs are out. I cringe when I see the blood on Gregory's fangs, knowing it's Jessica's.

I take a stake out of my utility belt. I touch Baxter and he immediately falls back into fight mode. He stops when he realizes Gregory isn't moving.

"What the hell?" he asks perplexed, then turns to look at me. "Is he frozen?"

"Yes. Here." I hand Baxter a stake. "Hurry up and do the damn thing. Jessica needs us."

Baxter frowns. "I didn't need your help."

"Just do it or I will!"

Baxter grips the stake and plunges it deep into Gregory's chest. I watch as Gregory slowly melts away and turns to dust. What was once Gregory's body is now another dust pile in a dirty, old house.

I grab Baxter's arm. "C'mon!"

We run back to Frank and Jessica. I unfreeze them as Baxter and I kneel down on the floor. Baxter grabs Jessica's hand and touches her face.

"She's not going to make it," he whispers. "Her heart is about to stop."

"Can you run her to the hospital?" I ask. "You can get her there in no time."

He shakes his head. "It's too late Chloe. She's lost too much blood. Even if I get her there before she dies, she won't make it."

"Try!" I yell at him. "Try dammit!"

Baxter turns to me. "There's only one way I can help her now."

"What?" I ask confused. Then it sinks in. "You can't mean…" my voice trails off.

Baxter nods. "The only way she'll make it is if I turn her."

"No!" Frank roars. "Absolutely not! I will run her to the hospital myself before I sit here and let you change her!"

My mind races. I look down at my friend, her eyes closed and face pale. Her clothes and body covered in blood.

"What's the worst case scenario?" I ask Baxter.

Frank's jaw drops. "Chloe! Don't you dare!"

I glance at him a moment, then turn back to Baxter. "What is the worst case scenario?" I ask again.

"I change her and she wakes up feral. I will have to kill her."

I already knew this, but I needed to hear Baxter say it. I want him to confirm what I've read about blood transfers. "And the best case scenario?"

Baxter runs his hand through Jessica's hair. "She survives the change, but she won't be Jessica anymore."

"Meaning?"

"She won't remember her life, or any of you."

I consider the options quietly.

I look at Frank and he shakes his head. "No Chloe."

What would Jessica want? What would I want if the situation was reversed?

"Her heart has stopped," Baxter tells us quietly. "Chloe, I need you to tell me in the next thirty seconds what I should do. Of the three of us, you know her best. I will do whatever you feel is right."

The decision is all on me. I flip back and forth. No matter what I decide, my best friend as I know her is gone. Even if she survives the change, she won't be Jessica anymore. But she won't be dead either. At least she'll still be around.

I make what is probably the most selfish choice I've ever made in my life.

"Do it."

We ride back to the building in the same car. Frank is sitting next to me and Baxter sits across from us, Jessica in his arms.

The blood transfer didn't take long. Baxter sliced his wrist open with one of his fangs and held it over Jessica's neck wound. I watched in a haze as the skin around her neck started to heal. Then he let several drops of his blood fall into Jessica's open mouth.

"It's done," he told us before sweeping Jessica's lifeless body into his arms.

All we can do now is wait. We'll put Jessica and Baxter together in a room down in quarantine. If Jessica wakes up feral, she won't be able to harm anyone.

Frank is pissed. He won't even look at me.

Did I do the right thing?

Tears roll down my cheeks.

"Don't cry Chloe," Baxter says softly.

I wipe a tear away. "What if she hates me?"

"She won't know any different," Frank snarls, unsympathetic to my torment. "She won't even know who you are, let alone whether she should be pissed at you."

"I'll tell her it was my choice," Baxter offers.

I shake my head. "No, we'll tell her the truth."

Frank snorts, but says nothing.

The rest of the ride home is silent.

The Escalade pulls into the garage. We ride the elevator down to the quarantine level. It isn't as creepy as I thought it would be. I expected concrete walls and leaky pipes, but it's nothing like that. The rooms are more along the lines of what you would see in a mental health hospital. Padded walls with built-in beds and bathroom facilities.

All the rooms in quarantine are currently empty. The last person to stay here was Daniel, the rogue werewolf I swapped bodies with at Julian's farm.

The Guard members standing sentry watch solemnly as we walk by, many of them visibly shaken when they see Jessica's body. They adore Jessica and are as brokenhearted as I am.

We pick the first room on the left. Baxter lays Jessica down on the bed. She is still covered in blood.

"I'll get washcloths and clean clothes from her room," I say as I look down at her tiny body.

"Why bother?" Frank asks.

I glare at him. "Because she is our friend! She doesn't deserve to wake up covered in her own blood."

Frank storms over and gets in my face. "Wake up Chloe! She's not your friend anymore!"

I poke his chest with my finger. "She will always be my friend! She may wake up completely different, but I'm going to do all I can to make sure she has a good life. Whether it's as human Jessica or vampire Jessica, I will not let my friend wake up in dirty clothes!"

Frank softens, but doesn't apologize. "Fine. While you do that, I'll go upstairs and tell Willa and Elias we're home."

220

Frank is saving me from a very difficult conversation, his way of making amends.

I squeeze his shoulder. "Thank you."

As I'm walking to the elevator, the doors open. James comes rushing out.

My heart skips a beat. "James?!" I run toward him and crash into his arms.

He holds me tight. "Chloe! Thank God! You scared me to death."

Something about being in his arms and feeling the love makes me break down. I'm sobbing into his chest, finally letting out all the pain and anguish.

He strokes my hair. "It's going to be okay."

"Jessica's gone," I get out between sobs.

He pulls away from me. "What?"

I point down the hallway. "She's in there. She's a vampire."

"What?" he asks again. "How?"

I shake my head. "It's a long story. I have to get her washed up and in clean clothes."

"Okay, let me help you."

James keeps his arm around my waist as we ride up in the elevator. He doesn't ask any questions, just holds me tight.

I avoid looking at the personal items in Jessica's room, it will only make me sadder. Instead, I focus on finding her clothes. I also grab washcloths, a towel from her bathroom, and a comb.

I bring the items into the quarantine room and set them on the floor next to the bed. James takes a minute to stand over Jessica and surveys the damage.

"Jesus," he mutters.

I struggle to take off Jessica's shirt. It's matted in blood and sticking to her skin. Tears spill from my eyes as I clean the blood

221

from her forehead. My beautiful friend will open her eyes soon. Who, or what, will she be?

Baxter comes over and takes the washcloth from my hand. "I'll do this. Leave me with her. I'll let you know when she's awake."

I'm about to protest, but James steps in. "Baxter's right. You're exhausted and need to rest."

"I can't rest! Jessica needs me."

James takes my hand. "Jessica would want you to be safe. Let Baxter handle this."

I'm angry and want to fight back, but deep down I know they're right. There's nothing I can do for Jessica now.

I sit next to her and lay my hand on the side of her face. "I love you Jess. I hope I made the right choice." I lean down and kiss her cheek. My tears make tiny wet spots in her hair.

Before James escorts me out of the room, I turn back to Baxter. "Will you be okay? If she's feral? Do you need help?"

Baxter shakes his head. "No. I've done it in the past, I can do it again."

I nod my head and walk out the door.

Thank God Baxter can handle it. I certainly can't.

As soon as I get to my room, I step into a hot shower to wash off all the blood and dirt. I tell James to throw my clothes away, I don't want them anymore. I stand under the water, replaying the events in my mind. I would love to stay in here for the rest of the night and let the hot water calm my nerves, but there is more to be done.

When I turn off the water, James is waiting for me with a fluffy, white towel. He dries off my back, then my shoulders, and works his way down my body. It's not a sensual gesture, it's a loving one. When he's done, he brings over my bathrobe.

"Thank you," I tell him as he ties the belt around my waist.

He kisses my forehead. "I'm here for you. In any way I can be."

We embrace for a few minutes, my head resting on his chest. Eventually, I stand straight. "We better get downstairs."

We walk into the conference room of the Guard Operations Center ten minutes later. Willa is sitting with Frank and Elias at the table. She is devastated.

"I've known Jessica since she was a little girl. I feel like I've lost my own child," she weeps into her hands. Elias holds her tight, showing the first sign of affection he's displayed since I met him.

"How do we tell Beth?" I ask, tears in my eyes again. "We can't tell her over the phone."

Frank nods. "I sent someone to get her. We know where she's staying."

The waiting is brutal. Whitney eventually joins us and we re-tell the story.

"Jessica will be a vampire now?" Whitney asks in shock.

"Yes," I answer, "if she survives the change."

Whitney sits back in her chair. "This is crazy. Absolutely crazy."

None of us can dispute that.

"Why don't you go up to bed Chloe?" James offers. "I'll wait down here and come get you the second anything happens."

I shake my head. "I can't. No way I'll be able to sleep."

A couple hours pass with no word. We're all basically sleeping with our eyes open.

"Alright," Frank says after a while, "let's move into the breakroom. There are a few couches in there, and we can all stretch out. Maybe get some shut eye."

The breakroom is empty, the Guard members cleared out to let us in. I sit next to James on one of the couches and lean against him. Whitney shares a couch with Frank, while Willa and Elias take up residence on the third.

"What if she's feral?" I ask James quietly.

"She won't be," he whispers.

"How do you know?"

"Jessica is strong. Quiet, but strong."

I hope James is right, but there's no way to predict what Jessica's reaction to the change will be. I'll feel awful if Baxter has to kill her, not just for myself, but for him too. I saw the look on his face when Gregory tore her throat open. I also saw the gentle, loving way he gazed at Jessica as he held her hand right before her heart stopped.

Killing Jessica would destroy him.

James hums softly as he strokes my hair. My body finally relaxes and I doze off.

Jessica

I scream, the pain is horrific. I grab my throat, worried what I'll find. To my surprise, it's smooth and not bleeding. And come to think of it, the pain is gone.

I open my eyes and immediately close them. The lights are blinding. I slowly open my eyes again and try to sit up. I'm in a bright, white room I don't recognize. My body moves sluggishly. I'm tired and a little achy. I'm not wearing the same clothes I was in earlier and my shoes are gone.

What happened?

Where am I?

How did I get here?

The walls are covered with white pads. There's a closed door with a tiny window to my left. There's no point in trying the door, I'm sure it's locked.

I continue scanning the room and stop on a man crouched in the corner. His face is dirty and he's covered in blood. He is watching me carefully. In his right hand he holds a wooden stake.

I speak, my voice gritty. "Baxter?"

Chloe

I'm not sure how long I've been asleep when a Guard member charges into the breakroom.

"Elias!"

We all jump. My eyes focus and I realize it's Jeremy.

"What is it?" Elias asks blandly, stone faced as usual.

"Baxter needs you downstairs, now!"

I stand. "I'm going too."

Jeremy puts his hand up to stop me. "Baxter said only Elias can come. Everyone else should wait here."

Elias is gone in a flash, literally. I flop down on the couch. Baxter asking for Elias can only mean one thing.

I put my head in my hands and start crying. "She's dead! Baxter had to kill her!"

James rubs my back. "Shh…you don't know that."

"Why else would Baxter want us to stay here?"

"She might be fine Chloe," Willa says. "Baxter may want another vampire to help him get Jessica acclimated."

Willa and James are right, I need to calm down until I know the facts. We all settle back into the couches, waiting anxiously. Jessica has turned, whether or not she's feral remains a mystery.

For what seems like an eternity, we all sit quietly and wait. Elias finally comes back upstairs.

Frank jumps up. "What's going on? Is Jessica alive?"

Elias shakes his head. "No, she's not."

My heart stops.

"But she is very much undead." Elias smiles. He actually smiles.

"Don't do that!" Whitney yells at him. "You scared the shit out of me!"

"So she's okay?" I ask.

Elias nods. "Yes, she's fine."

I'm so relieved, I feel like I can breathe again. "Can we see her?"

Elias hesitates. "You can see her, but you'll be shocked. Prepare yourselves."

I nod. "We're ready."

Am I though? Am I ready to see Jessica the vampire?

"They're in the conference room." Elias walks over and extends his hand to Willa. "Ready my dear?""

Willa nods and stands. "Okay everyone. Let's put on brave faces."

I take James's hand as we walk toward the conference room. I'm nervous, I don't know what my friend will be like now. We stop at the conference room door.

"You go first Chloe," Willa says.

Gee, thanks.

After a deep breath, I turn the door handle and push the door open. Here we go...

My eyes water when I see Jess. She looks the same as she always has. Baxter cleaned her up as best he could and put her in the clean clothes I brought down. There is still some blood in her hair, but nothing a shower won't fix.

She is in Baxter's arms and smiling up at him. While it's nice to see, it's unexpected, to say the least.

Why is she already so affectionate with Baxter? Then she turns to look at me. I expect vacant, dead eyes. Instead, her eyes light up.

"Chloe!" she exclaims, and before I know what's happening, her arms are around me. I'm forced to step back from the impact of her hug.

"You, you know who I am?" I ask stupefied.

She pulls away, her hands still on my shoulders. "Yes! I remember!"

I look at Baxter in disbelief. "She remembers?"

Baxter smiles and nods.

"How is that possible?"

Everyone streams into the room behind me and Jessica gives them all hugs. They look as shocked as I do.

"It's very unusual for vampires to remember their human life," Elias explains. "However, it has been known to happen when the person is a supernatural. The Reader, Elliott I believe his name is, told Jessica she has a bit of witch blood in her. It must have been enough to secure her memories."

Jessica beams. "Can you believe it?"

"No, no I can't," I answer truthfully.

"Are you hungry?" Whitney asks.

I roll my eyes. Good ole Whitney.

Jessica laughs. "Not really. Baxter gave me one of his cow hearts. It wasn't as bad as I thought it would be."

Whitney crinkles her nose.

I give Jess another onceover. "How do you feel? Are you okay?"

"Yeah. Weird, but okay."

Elias interrupts the reunion. "You need to get to Paris as soon as possible."

"Paris? Why?" Whitney asks.

Baxter takes Jessica's hand. "I need to register Jessica with the Council. We will get in a lot of trouble if we don't."

"Use our private jet so you don't have to wait to set up travel arrangements," Willa suggests. "I don't want any issues with the Council."

"Wait a second," I turn to Elias, "aren't you on the Council?"

"Indeed I am. But there is a Registration Clerk. There are documents that need to be completed and filed with her."

"Vampire red tape. What can you do?" Baxter jokes.

"Are you coming back?" Frank asks. Of all of us, he looks worse for the wear. I would be too if the person I'm in love with was murdered in front of me, and then reanimated as a supernatural being.

Jessica glances at Baxter. "We haven't talked about it, but I'd like to come back."

Baxter squeezes Jessica's hand. "We'll be back. I want to travel around Europe for a while first. Show Jessica my home in England, things like that."

Willa smiles. "Of course."

We stay and talk for a few more minutes before Willa tells us it's time to go to bed. I hang back as everyone else starts to leave.

I tell James quietly, "I want to talk to her for a second. I'll be right up."

"Sure," he says before giving me a kiss.

"Can I have a minute with Jessica?" I ask Baxter.

"Absolutely." He turns to Jess. "I'll start packing."

Jessica watches Baxter leave with a look of pure love and happiness on her face. "He's really happy you know. He was afraid to love me before, I was too fragile. He's not scared anymore."

I shift my weight, not sure how to respond. "That's great."

"Who would have thought a tiny amount of witch blood would end up meaning so much?"

"I'm sorry," I blurt out.

Jessica's eyes widen. "For what?"

"For not protecting you. For letting Gregory get to you."

Jessica walks over and pulls me into a hug. "None of this was your fault."

"Do you hate me? Did I make the right choice?"

Jessica steps away from me. She hesitates before answering. "I don't hate you Chloe. You're my best friend. You did what you thought was right."

"I was afraid of losing you Jess," I try to explain.

Jessica smiles. "I understand. It will all work out for the best."

I note that she doesn't come out and tell me I made the right choice, but she isn't angry with me. This is probably the best I'm going to get. Our eyes meet for a moment. She is undoubtedly different. Just how different remains to be seen.

"Well, you better go and pack. I don't need the Council knocking on my door. We're running out of room."

Jessica laughs and gives me another hug. "I love you Chloe. Everything will be fine."

"I love you too Jess."

One second she's in my arms, the next she's gone. This will take some getting used to.

Chapter Fourteen

Jessica

I spend my first two weeks as a vampire traveling through Europe with Baxter. We're visiting fantastic places I've only read about - the Eiffel Tower, the Roman Coliseum, and the canals of Venice.

The first thing we did when our plane touched down was check-in with the Registration Clerk. She is a nice woman who will perpetually appear to be in her early forties. She helped me fill out the necessary paperwork and told me how to maintain the proper legal documents throughout my existence.

I was shocked when she said, "Every five years you will receive a new birth certificate with an updated birth year."

"I will?"

"Yes. Your age will never appear suspicious."

"What about my social security number? Will I get a new one as well?"

"We have an understanding with the U.S. government. Just make sure you file your taxes every year," she says with a wink.

Legalities aside, I'm coming to terms with my new "lifestyle." I tried my best to look optimistic and happy for Chloe the night I turned. When we were in quarantine, Baxter told me how hard the choice was for her.

In a lot of ways, I was happy. I was thankful to be alive and with my family and friends. I was excited about my relationship with Baxter and what being a vampire would mean for us.

But there were things I struggled with. I will never be able to have children. I'll never eat regular food again. And I will outlive all my loved ones. It's impossible to wrap my head around the fact that I may exist until the end of time. Literally.

I didn't tell Chloe I was okay with her choice, because I wasn't. Not at that moment, anyway. But the longer I've been a vampire, the more I've accepted it.

I may never have children, but Whitney and Chloe probably will. I will be the best aunt those kids have ever seen!

I'm not able to eat food anymore, but I don't miss it. Turns out drinking blood isn't so bad. In fact, it tastes kinda good. There are no cravings for the things I used to eat.

A couple days ago, I sent Chloe my first text since I left:

You made the right choice ☺

I meant it too. I wasn't saying it to make her happy. I'd rather be a vampire than miss out on the life I have now.

Her response was immediate.

Thank you ♥

"Two more days in Spain. Where should we go next?" Baxter asks over breakfast.

We switched it up this morning. Instead of our usual cow hearts, we're drinking pigs' blood. Variety is the spice of life!

"What are my options?"

"We could head toward Germany and Austria."

"Or…"

Baxter smiles. "We can go to my place in England."

I put down my glass. "I say we go to your place."

"Cheers to that!" Baxter says before downing what's left in his cup.

"I talked to my mom last night while you were at the butcher."

"Oh yeah? How did it go?"

My mom is having a hard time with everything. I didn't get the chance to see her before I left for Paris, and I feel guilty about it. I wasn't ready, and I'm pretty sure she wasn't ready to see me either. The first time we spoke she was hysterical. But every time I call, it's a little easier for her.

"She's doing better."

"We can head back to New York City after we spend a week or two at my place," Baxter suggests.

I smile. "Yes, I'd like that."

I wait until it's 9:30 a.m. in New York before I call Chloe.

"Hey globetrotter!" she answers.

"Hola chica!"

"Don't tell me…you're in Spain."

"Si!"

Chloe groans. "I got a 'C' in Spanish. Don't say anything too complicated."

I've only been in Spain for a day, but I'm nearly fluent in Spanish. Baxter wasn't kidding when he said vampires pick up local languages quickly.

"I'll keep it in English."

"Good! So what's up?"

I tell her about our plan to return to New York City in a couple weeks.

"Yay! Will you be staying for a while, or just a quick visit?"

"Not sure yet."

"Okay, no rush. Take your time. We've got things handled here."

Chloe agreed to let me take an extended leave of absence. I want to be in New York with her and my supernatural extended family, but traveling with Baxter is an amazing experience. I'm not quite ready to settle back into my "normal" routine yet.

I worried Baxter wouldn't be happy about moving to New York, but he is thrilled. "Wherever you are, there I'll be," he told me.

I end my call with Chloe and track Baxter down on the balcony of our hotel room. I walk up behind him and give him a big hug.

He rubs my arm affectionately. "It's beautiful out here, isn't it?"

I look out over the city of Seville and the Guadalquivir River. "It's gorgeous."

We walk through Seville and take in all the city has to offer. I'm still adjusting to my new walking speed. Occasionally Baxter will tug on my hand to let me know I need to slow down.

It's funny, when I used to envision myself traveling the world, food was involved. Exotic cuisines, food from street vendors, delicacies not available in the States, and fancy desserts from pastry shops. I've traded all of that for the handsome vampire beside me. I think I got the better end of the bargain.

After Seville, Baxter and I visit his home in England. As it turns out, we're only there three days when I get the call from my mom.

"Jessica, you need to come home."

Chloe

Frank and I are in the gym. Today it's high-intensity interval training. Whitney was working out with us, but she bailed during medicine ball tosses. Apparently, we throw too hard. Now she's sitting against the wall playing on her phone.

James is out west again. It sucks when he leaves, but there isn't much we can do about it. I offered to go, but he turned me down.

"Don't come out this time. I'll be really busy and you'll be bored. I want to plan a long stay so I can show you around."

234

I don't know much about James's home in the west, and I want to see it for myself. I also have no idea what he does every day. I should get a handle on that too.

Frank and I are on our second set of squats when Sherman comes into the gym. "You're needed downstairs immediately." His usually stoic voice is panicked.

"What's going on?" I ask as we head for the elevators.

"It's Willa. There's been an incident."

Frank's face tightens. "An incident? What kind of incident?"

"We're not sure yet."

As soon as the elevator doors open, Frank and I run through the lobby. Whitney and Sherman are somewhere behind us.

I push through the door and yell to Sherman, "Which way?"

"Left!"

Frank and I turn left and run as fast as we can. We're nearing the boundary of our wards when I see a group of people huddled together. I hit the brakes and catch my breath as Frank parts the crowd. I gasp when I reach the last row of people. Willa is on the ground, her eyes shut and her body still. Elias and Bane are both on their knees beside her.

"What happened?" I ask frantically.

"This woman," Elias points behind him, "tried to attack Willa!"

I turn to see another person on the ground. She is face down in a pool of blood. Her brown hair is plaited in a neat braid. Anger rises within me. It's Nina.

Frank catches my attention when he says, "I think she's had a heart attack. We need to get her to a hospital."

For the first time since I met him, Bane speaks. His voice booms. "We've already called 9-1-1."

As if on cue, I hear sirens.

"Get out of the way!" I yell at the crowd. "Move!"

Of course none of them do, too entranced with the drama.

I get down on my hands and knees next to Willa. "Willa, if you can hear me, help is on the way. You're going to be just fine."

An ambulance comes to a stop behind us and the paramedics weave their way through the crowd. We get out of the way as the EMTs swarm Willa and Nina.

They immediately begin CPR on Willa and get her moved onto a stretcher. Her body looks so frail. When they load Willa and the gear into the back of the ambulance, Bane asks me if he can ride with her.

"Yes. Go with her. Keep her safe."

"Understood." He climbs into the ambulance, his huge frame making for a tight squeeze. Just before they shut the doors, I see him take Willa's hand.

The ambulance drives off, its sirens blaring.

Another set of EMTs work on Nina. They roll her onto her back. I don't need a medical professional to tell me she's dead. Her eyes are glazed over and staring straight up at the sky. There's a huge dent in the top of her skull. I don't know how it happened, but she took one hell of a blow to the head.

I listen as Elias gives his statement to the police. He and Willa were on their daily walk when Nina approached them out of nowhere. Elias tells the police he couldn't hear what Nina said before she attacked Willa, but I know this is a lie. Elias can hear a butterfly flap its wings.

When Elias is done giving his statement, I round up our group. I've got Whitney, Sherman and Elias, but I can't find Frank. I finally spot him on his phone near a lamp post. I run over and tug on his arm. He swats me away.

"Hey!" I say to him, completely disregarding the fact he's on the phone. "Let's go! We need to get to the hospital."

He takes his phone away from his ear and sighs. "That won't be necessary."

"What do you mean?" I hiss. "Let's go!"

He puts his hand on my shoulder. "Willa's gone."

I take a step back. The city starts swimming. The people and buildings become a watercolor painting. The Earth tilts and my legs give out from underneath me.

Jessica

Baxter and I catch the first flight home.

I learn the hard way that vampires cannot cry. My face contorts in anguish, but no tears roll down my cheeks.

"Willa lived a long life. Her legacy will remain," Baxter says, doing his best to console me.

It's surreal. What happened to my life? It was all so different a month ago.

I stand outside the building in New York City staring up at my home. So much in my life has changed, yet it is the same.

Baxter squeezes my shoulder. "You ready?"

I nod. "Yes, I'm ready."

Baxter holds the door open for me and I step inside first. Three Guard members stand in the lobby chatting near the receptionist's desk. I expect double takes and odd looks, but they act the same as they always have.

"Hey Jess!" one of them greets me. "Welcome home."

After I mumble a shocked "hi guys", the men return to their conversation as if there is nothing new to see.

"That went better than I expected," I say when we're in the elevator.

"They know you're still in there Jess. They're supernatural beings too. They understand how this works."

I am pleasantly surprised again when I track down my mom in the kitchen. She is standing with her back to me, focused on a giant pot on the stovetop.

I steady myself. "Hi Mom."

She turns to me and breaks out in a giant smile. "Jessica!" She puts her slotted spoon down and wipes her hands on her apron. She pulls me in for a big hug. "I missed you so much!"

I return her embrace, careful not to squeeze too hard. "I missed you too."

She stands back and gives me a onceover. "You look wonderful Jess, just wonderful."

"So do you. The California sun did wonders for your skin."

"Well thank you! It was a nice trip, but I'm glad to be home."

I'm relieved my mom has conquered whatever fears she had, but there is still one more person to convince – Whitney. I call her room from the kitchen phone.

"Hey Beth!" she answers in her cheery voice.

"It's me Whit. Jessica."

"Oh, uh, hi," she stammers. "I didn't realize you're in the building."

"I just got here a little while ago. I'd like to come see you. Is that okay?"

"Um, sure," she says after a pause. "Better yet, I'll come down and meet you in the kitchen."

I'm disappointed Whitney doesn't trust me to come to her suite, but I'll take what I can get.

"Give her time," Mom assures me. "She'll come around, I promise."

"I hope so."

When Whitney walks into the kitchen, my mom excuses herself. "I'll give you girls some space."

"Why don't you stay Beth?" Whitney blurts out. "I mean, you have something on the stovetop. I don't want it to burn."

Mom waves Whitney off. "My stew won't be done for half an hour. It's fine."

Whitney watches my mom walk out of the kitchen with quiet desperation.

"I won't hurt you Whitney, you're safe with me."

She turns to look at me for the first time. She scans my face. "You look the same."

"I am the same."

Whitney sits on a stool next to the kitchen island. "I know it's you in there, Jess. I really do. But I've always been afraid of vampires. It doesn't help that I don't know the truth about your kind. I was raised with books and movies that don't paint vampires in a very good light. It's hard for me to weed out truth from fiction."

I cautiously take a seat near her, but I leave space between us. "Ask me anything you want."

She considers her first question. "Do you drink human blood?"

"No, just animal blood."

"Do you kill the animals yourself?"

"No, we go to a butcher."

"Do you crave human blood?"

I shake my head. "No, not at all."

Her next question surprises me. "Are you happy?"

"Yes. I am."

She smiles. "Then I'm happy for you."

We talk a while longer about my new life, then I remember I have something for her. "Wait a second, I'll be right back." I make a dash for my room, grab the book from my suitcase, and return to the kitchen.

Whitney's eyes are wide. "How did you do that?"

I blush. "Super speed. Pretty cool, huh?"

"What is that?" she asks when she sees I'm holding a book.

"Here." I hand it over. "Read this. It's a good book about vampires in modern times. It was written by a Countess."

She scans the cover. "Huh, never seen it before. I'll check it out."

When I'm done convincing Whitney I won't kill her in her sleep, I go looking for Chloe. She's in the first place I look. I find her standing in front of her office window staring down at the city. She's wearing black sweatpants and a pink tank top, her hair in a sloppy ponytail. Only the top portion of her tattoo is visible, but I can tell her hawk has more gold in it than Willa's ever did.

Despite her power and abilities, my friend is broken. I don't need to see her face to know it.

"Just because you're a vampire now doesn't mean I don't know when you walk in a room," she says without turning to look at me. Her words are in jest, but her tone is filled with sadness.

I don't attempt to console her, she won't allow it. "I came to see if you need help with the funeral arrangements."

"Bane handled it."

"He did? Already?"

She nods. "Willa had a plot and a casket picked out. She left detailed instructions. There wasn't much to be done."

"Is there anything else I can do for you?"

Her eyes remained focused on the outside. "No."

"Are you hungry? Do you want something to eat or drink?"

"No thank you."

"Not even pizza?" I implore her.

She glances over her shoulder. Her blue eyes are dull, the purple smudges underneath them standing out on her pale skin. She smiles for a brief second, then turns back to the window.

"Close the door on the way out, will you?"

I'm being dismissed. "Sure. Call me if you need anything."

Her response is barely a whisper. "Understood."

I feel like I've been punched in the stomach. Losing Willa is hard enough, but I may have lost my friend too. Is her cold treatment temporary because of her grief? Or will she treat me differently now that I'm a vampire?

James relieves some of my concern when he stops by to see me a little while later. He looks almost as bad as Chloe does.

"Have you talked to Chloe?" he asks.

"I've seen Chloe, but we didn't really talk."

He frowns. "She's not talking to me either. She hasn't slept more than an hour at a time since Willa's attack."

"You know Chloe," I say, trying to make him feel better, "she keeps everything tight to her chest. She just needs to process what's happened. She'll be okay."

"I hope so."

I give him a hug. "I know so."

But two days later, I'm less confident. My attempts to liven her up have failed, and James isn't having any luck either. She spends her time in her office alone. When I stop in to see her, she hardly acknowledges my presence.

Today at the funeral, Chloe stared blankly at Willa's casket. She was a sedated version of herself. She didn't attempt to speak to anyone or pretend to be okay. The Chloe I know puts on a brave face. This Chloe doesn't seem to have one.

I'm worried this is too much for her. We're all grieving, but she's also dealing with the loss of her sister. Not to mention what Willa's passing means for her – it's all on her shoulders now.

"Chloe isn't doing well, is she?" Baxter asks on the car ride home.

I frown. "No, she's not."

Chloe

Four days have passed since Willa died.

I've watched our surveillance video of the incident at least twenty times. In it, Willa and Elias are walking down the sidewalk. Bane keeps some distance between himself and them for privacy. Willa pauses at the corner, likely strengthening the wards.

As Willa stands there, Nina runs into the frame. We know from other cameras that Nina was sitting on a bench across the street pretending to read a newspaper for most of the morning.

Nina grabs a hold of Willa's arm and shouts, "You should have been there! You could have stopped it! It's not…"

This is all Nina manages to say before Bane gets in between her and Willa. He wraps Nina in a bear hug and drags her away. Instead of going peacefully, Nina decides to fight. On the video, you see her poke her finger into the flesh of Bane's arm. When she does, Bane instantly falls to the ground. He twitches as if hit with a stun gun.

Meanwhile, Willa clutches her chest and falls to her knees. Elias panics, but reaches out his arms to keep Willa from toppling over. Nina makes a move for Willa again, a menacing look on her face.

Just as Nina is about to touch Willa, Bane (who is no longer twitching) grabs Nina's ankle from behind and pulls as hard as he can. Nina's legs give out from underneath her and her head slams onto the concrete. Hard. Hard enough to dent her skull. She never moves again.

The coroner determined that Willa died from a heart attack brought on by a stressful situation.

I arranged Willa's funeral per her directives, which she gave me a while ago. It was a small affair, she didn't want a spectacle. I invited her list of guests privately, then sent a mass email to the witch community advising them of Willa's death. I did not mention Nina's involvement, but I'm sure word will travel fast.

I had no intention of holding a public ceremony as Willa did not include it in her directives. However, requests poured in when people learned of Willa's passing. I received phone calls and emails from members of all the supernatural communities begging me to hold a public ceremony so they can pay their respects. Fearful people would attempt to attend the private ceremony and cause a spectacle if I did not have a public remembrance, I acquiesced to their wishes.

I asked Samantha, my former Coven Leader, to conduct the private funeral services this afternoon. She asked if anyone wanted to say a few words, but no one stood up. I could feel the weight of everyone's stares, all waiting on me to say something, but I'm not ready. I'll speak at the memorial service we're holding for her later this week.

We laid Willa's body to rest in a plot between her husband and daughter. One of Willa's wishes was that we stay to watch her casket as it was lowered into the ground. I'm not sure why she wanted this, but I followed her wishes.

"Rest in peace Willa," I whispered as I dropped a handful of dirt on her coffin. "I'll try to do you proud."

As I stood there looking over Willa's lowered casket, Elias came up beside me. "I've lost a lot of friends and family over the years. It never gets easier."

"No, it doesn't."

"Some hurt worse than others," he continued. "In this case, we lost a good woman. I'll miss her."

He walked off before I could respond.

After the funeral, I went straight to my office and shut the door. Ten minutes later, Frank interrupted my peace and quiet.

Without asking, he took a seat and started talking. He hasn't stopped talking since.

I'm staring out my window, wishing I was anywhere but here. I'm still in my black dress from the funeral, my hair pulled up in a bun like Willa used to wear. It hasn't sunk in yet that she's gone. I keep expecting to see her at the dinner table. A couple times I've thought to myself, "I have to see what Willa thinks about…" and then I realize I'll never be able to seek her advice again.

I am numb.

"Are you listening to me?"

I glance at Frank, annoyance written all over his face. I'm honest with him. "No."

He sighs. "I was saying we concluded our investigation into Nina's last days."

I give him the side eye. "Tell me."

This topic is a sensitive one for me. I'm upset Nina wasn't being watched in the first place. The Guard checked on her periodically for about a week after she left the hospital. When it appeared all was back to normal, they stopped going to her house. It kills me to know that if we'd kept surveillance on Nina, Willa would still be alive.

"She left her house four days before the attack. We thought she came right here to the city and stayed for a few days, but it turns out we were wrong. She was in New Orleans."

"New Orleans?"

Frank nods. "Yes. According to sources, she met with the High Priestess."

I snort. "She was resorting to voodoo, eh?"

"She tried. The High Priestess turned her away."

Voodoo practitioners are technically witches, but they don't consider themselves part of our community. There is no bad blood between us, they just decided to do their own thing years ago.

Many of the women in New Orleans who claim to practice voodoo are fake and only out to make a few bucks from tourists. But there are legitimate practitioners. They shy away from truly harmful magic, but they can give someone a wicked case of diarrhea.

Hearing that the High Priestess denied whatever request Nina made is a sign of goodwill, one I won't ignore. "Send Angelique a bouquet. If I recall correctly, she adores tiger lilies."

"Understood." Frank jots down my request, then moves on. "After New Orleans, she met up with a small group of women in Charlotte, North Carolina."

Frank slides me a picture of five women standing together outside an IHOP. Nina's mouth is open, the camera catching her mid-sentence.

"Who are the other four women?"

He frowns. "Three witches are from the Boston coven. They were on a road trip to Charlotte when Nina met up with them. Two of them were silent Nina supporters. The third woman from Boston was indifferent to Nina's issues."

I look at the picture again and one of the women is vaguely familiar. "And the fourth woman?"

"She is the Coven Leader of a coven in Vermont."

Ugh. Another Coven Leader off her rocker. Great. I give the picture back to Frank. "What was their meeting about?"

"We questioned this woman, Lisa Sunderman," he points to the woman in the blue shirt, "and she spilled the beans. She was upset about what happened between Nina and Willa and cooperated fully."

"And…"

Frank sits back in his chair and looks at his yellow notepad. "Lisa told us she was vacationing in Charlotte with the two other women from the Boston Coven. Lisa claims she thought they were in Charlotte to do some shopping. A girls' getaway."

Frank flips the page and scans his notes. "The women took Lisa to the IHOP. They told her they were meeting up with another witch who happened to be in town. Lisa obviously recognized Nina as soon as they got there and became suspicious."

"But not enough to skip the pancakes," I interject.

Frank nods. "She stayed for the pancakes and listened while the women talked about how unhappy they are with the new werewolf treaty."

I grunt. "These women and their werewolves."

"After breakfast, they stood outside for a few minutes. Nina mentioned she wanted to talk to Willa one-on-one. Nina was convinced Willa would see her side and make everything right. The leader of the Vermont coven encouraged her to just show up in New York City."

"Gee, thanks Vermont coven lady. What's her name?"

"Norma Katz."

"And where is Norma Katz these days?"

"At the moment she's being interrogated by the local Guard. It's safe to assume she'll be stepping down soon."

I steeple my fingers. "So they get Nina all riled up and then send her on her way?"

"Not quite. Lisa said Nina wasn't acting crazy or out of sorts. Nina told the women she planned to schedule an appointment with Willa. There was never any mention of attacking Willa or meaning her harm."

"What happened then? When did Nina flip the switch?"

Frank takes out another picture. This one also has Nina in it, but I don't recognize the other woman. They are sitting in the corner booth of what appears to be a rundown diner.

"Who is this?"

Frank sighs. "Antonia Sheep."

"Antonia Sheep? Barbara's mother?" I ask incredulously.

"Yes."

I've never met the mother of the woman who was supposed to be the Verhena. Barbara would be occupying my chair if the rogue wolves hadn't killed her.

I slide the picture back to Frank. "You're telling me Barbara's mother got Nina all fired up?"

Frank nods. "Antonia Sheep has been busy. She amassed a small following of witches who disagree with our alliance with the wolves."

I put my head in my hands. "Great, more people who hate me."

"The list is growing," Frank jokes.

I glare at him. "Do you think this is funny?"

His face falls. "I'm just trying to lighten the mood. I haven't seen you smile in days."

"What is there to smile about?"

"I know you're upset…"

"Upset?! Upset?! I'm fucking devastated!"

Frank clears him throat. "No more jokes."

"How dangerous is this group?" I ask attempting to get us back on track. "Are they planning on attacking me or are they just a bunch of women flapping their mouths?"

"We believe it's the latter. Antonia admits she was upset when she saw Nina. Antonia told Nina she should insist on meeting with Willa and to do so by any means necessary. But Antonia never intended for Nina to hurt Willa."

"When Antonia said 'by any means necessary', what exactly did she have in mind? To me, it sounds like she was encouraging Nina to be violent."

"I agree," Frank says, "but we spoke with the members of Antonia's group. They were planning on sending letters or starting a petition. They never intended to use violence."

"Oh my God, this is all so ridiculous. They don't even know what they're mad about. They just want to be angry about something."

"Every major decision you make will be met with resistance. You can't make everyone happy."

Indeed. It seems I can't make anyone happy.

"Keep an eye on the witches in Antonia's group," I tell Frank. "Make sure they aren't up to something. Also, schedule a meeting with Antonia. I will go to her, I don't want her anywhere near this building."

"Understood." Frank jots down more notes on his notepad. "Which reminds me, you need to strengthen the wards."

"I added it to my to-do list."

I stare out the window again as Frank starts talking about the day to day operations of the building. I'm listening to him, but he thinks I'm ignoring him again.

"Can you look at me while I'm talking to you? It would at least give the illusion you give a shit about what I'm saying."

I turn back to him. "I am listening. You just asked me if I've considered who I will use as a personal assistant while Jessica is gone."

"Well, have you?"

"No I haven't."

Frank sighs. "I sent you a list of potential candidates two days ago."

"I'm so sorry Frank," I say in a mocking tone. "I've been busy planning a funeral and dealing with the loss of my mentor and friend. Replacing my assistant wasn't at the top of my list."

His jaw tightens. "Do you think grief is reserved for you? That you're the only one in pain?"

I look away from him, tears forming in my eyes.

"Every single person in this building is grieving Chloe," he continues. "Everyone is crying, everyone misses her. But we're all doing our jobs. We're all making sure this place doesn't fall apart."

I flinch when he stands and slams his notepad down on my desk. "You can't wallow in your misery. You're too damn important. Get your shit together."

I stand up and yell back. "For what? So people can hate me some more? So they can try to kill me next?"

"This isn't about you and your ego," Frank fires at me. "This is about the greater good."

"I have done everything for these people!" I scream. "I have sacrificed, and lost, and given up all of my dreams. And they don't even care! They get to lead the lives they want. They don't give a damn about me."

Frank crosses his arms. "What do you want? A cookie?"

"No! I want out of this. Tell the universe to give another girl the Verhena brand. Let her come in here and do this shitty job."

"You're being absurd. Enough of this."

I cross my arms too, mimicking his stance. "I'm done."

"No you're not. Sit your ass down and let's talk about some of the things Willa left unfinished."

"Why bother asking me? I never make the right choice."

Frank rolls his eyes. "Chloe, you're sad. I get it, I do. But this is insane. Do you need me to pat your back or something?"

My temper flares. "Get out."

His jaw drops. "What?"

"Get...the fuck...out!" I shout at him.

He shakes his head. "No."

"Get out Frank," I hiss through gritted teeth.

"No," he says again firmly.

249

"Fine, if you won't leave, I will." I walk around my desk and head for the door.

Frank tries to stand in my way, but I push him so hard he falls into his chair. The momentum tips the chair completely over and he rolls backwards onto the floor.

I take this chance to run as fast as I can down the hallway. I need to let off some steam before I explode. I push open the door for the stairwell and run up the steps until I've reached the access door to the roof.

I run through the door and stop in the middle of the roof. Panting, I look around to make sure no one is standing close. Then I scream as loud as I can. At the same time, I shoot fire from my fingertips into the air. It feels so good to unleash my anger.

After a good ten seconds of screaming and releasing fire, I take a deep breath. A thick, black cloud of smoke fills the sky above me. My body trembles as I struggle to regain my composure. Hot tears stream down my face, my chest heaving.

Then I see it.

Willa's greenhouse. Her pride and joy.

I slowly walk toward it. Who's going to take care of her beautiful flowers? I killed a cactus my mom gave me in the fifth grade, I really don't think I can handle an entire greenhouse.

I open the door and step inside. The humid air is warm and strangely comforting. I shut the door tightly behind me and walk down the narrow aisle between the rows of flowers and plants. Plump red tomatoes hang from green vines in one corner. Lush plants with giant leaves fill another.

I fall to my knees next to a bush of beautiful red flowers.

"I'll try to take care of you," I tell them. "I probably won't do a very good job. Willa was much better at this than I am."

"I doubt that," a deep voice says.

Startled, I turn to see Bane sitting on a wooden bench in the back corner.

"Bane, I didn't know you were in here." I start to stand up. "I'll go."

"Don't go," he tells me. He stands and walks over to me. He's in the black suit he wore to the funeral. He kneels next to me. "Want to know her secret?"

"There's a secret?"

Bane smiles. "Give me your hand."

I put my right hand in his. His massive hand is warm and consumes mine. He lays my palm flat in the dirt in front of a plant with pretty pink flowers. He keeps his hand on top of mine.

"Now," he says, "tell the plant to grow."

I look at him skeptically, but do as told. "Grow," I say to the plant.

Nothing happens.

Bane pats my hand. "Do it again. Mean it this time."

I visualize the plant sprouting more beautiful blooms. "Grow," I tell the plant again softly.

I watch with astonishment as the plant grows upward and outward. Large, pink blooms pop open, yellow pollen bursting from the center. The flowers' scent fills my nose. I stare at the blooms with wonder.

Bane lifts his hand. "See, you can do it."

I smile, tears in my eyes. "Thank you."

Bane stays on his knees beside me. "Willa loved you. She didn't think there was anyone better suited for this job than you."

"Willa always thought the best of people."

"She's not the only one who thinks you're the right woman for the job."

I look up at him. "I'm an imposter Bane. All the decisions I make are wrong."

He shakes his head. "Not true."

Tears roll down my cheeks. "My sister is dead because of me. Willa is dead because of me. Jessica is a vampire because of me."

"None of those things are your fault."

"But they are! I'm the head witch in charge, remember? They died on my watch."

"They died on my watch too. And Frank's. And every other man in this building." He pauses before adding, "Willa blamed herself for your sister's death. She was afraid you would hate her when you came here. She wasn't sure you would stay."

"What?" I ask in disbelief. "How could she think that? She had nothing to do with Chelsea's death."

"Chelsea died on her watch," Bane explains, using my own logic.

"Oh." I never knew Willa blamed herself for Chelsea's death. I wish she would have told me.

"You will always blame yourself when something goes wrong. It's human nature, or witch nature, I suppose."

We sit quietly for a moment. I touch the silky petals of the flowers I created. "What are these?"

"Zinnias. They were Willa's favorite."

"Did she use magic on all of her plants?"

Bane smiles. Instead of answering, he puts his pointer finger over his lips in a "shhh" motion.

I laugh.

"She made me promise not to tell anyone. She had her own insecurities Chloe. No one is perfect. Don't put that expectation on yourself. You'll fail every time."

"Have you always been this wise?" I ask with a smile.

"Yes," he answers without hesitation.

I laugh again. A great idea pops into my head. "What are you going to do now? Are you sticking around?"

He shrugs. "I don't know yet. I've served long enough, I'll get to choose my post."

"Do you want to be my security guard and personal assistant?"

Bane raises his eyebrow. "What about Frank and Jessica?"

"They'll still be around, but Frank wants to have a stronger leadership position in the Guard. He doesn't want to follow me around everywhere I go. And Jessica will be traveling with Baxter a lot. I don't want her to feel tied down by her job." I look up at Bane hopefully. "What do you think?"

He smiles. "I'd love to."

I give him a big hug, or at least try to. I can barely get my arms around him, it's like hugging a wall.

"Thank you," I say as I stand up.

He smiles. "Thank you, Ms. Chloe."

I wipe the dirt from my knees. "I should get back downstairs. I left Frank high and dry."

Before I walk away, Bane takes an envelope out of the interior pocket of his suit jacket. "I was going to bring this to you later, but here you go."

Bane hands me the envelope and I look down at it. It has my name written on it in Willa's handwriting.

"What is this?"

"Willa asked me to give it to you."

I flip the envelope over, but nothing is written on the back. "When did she give you this?"

"Willa went to the doctor a few weeks ago. She knew her time was limited."

"What?" I ask shocked. "Why didn't she tell me?"

"She didn't want to worry you. She didn't want you to cancel your trips to the covens. Willa truly enjoyed watching you progress. She didn't want to get in the way of that."

"Wow…" I wish I knew Willa was ill, I could have said good-bye. I'm sad, but not surprised. Willa thought of everyone before herself.

Bane walks back to the bench and sits down. I say good night and give him his peace and quiet.

When I step out of the greenhouse, I see a group of Guard members looking over the ledge of the roof. Blue and red lights flash as sirens blare below.

"What's going on?"

They turn to look at me.

Marcus speaks up. "Our neighbor dialed 9-1-1. She told the dispatcher she heard a woman screaming and saw a fire."

The men all give me knowing looks.

I blush. "Oops."

Chapter Fifteen

I'm back in my office.

Frank's chair is upright, and thankfully, empty. I carefully open Willa's letter. I pull out a folded piece of paper and smile when I see Willa's pretty handwriting.

> Well, I guess I'm dead. Hopefully I was wearing clean underwear.

I can't help it, I chuckle.

> I'm sure you are sad, and that's okay. But don't be sad for me Chloe. I lived a long and wonderful life. I have a few small regrets, as everyone does, but I feel like I'm leaving the world a little better than I found it. How many people can say that? Despite being incredibly happy with the way my life turned out, I am looking forward to being reunited with my husband and daughter.
>
> My doctor tells me my ticker is going out. I don't know if he's right or not, but I did a few things to prepare for my death. In addition to this letter, I've written a small manual for you. It's nothing major, but it contains a lot of helpful information and things I've learned along the way. You can

255

find it in the top drawer of my filing cabinet. You'll know it when you see it.

I thought long and hard about what to put in this letter. What advice is the best to give? I was once told people remember things in threes. So here are my top three life lessons:

(1) Go with your gut;
(2) If everyone is happy with you, someone is lying; and
(3) Nothing is promised.

These were the hardest lessons I had to learn. If you master them early on, you'll save yourself a lot of second-guessing and heartache.

I know you don't believe it, but you are ready. I couldn't have asked for a better replacement.

I love you dearly. Take care of yourself.

Willa

P.S. If you even try to resign from your post, I swear to God, I will haunt you!

I laugh. "Where were you half an hour ago?" I ask out loud.

I take the steps down to Willa's office, anxious to see what she left behind for me. I turn on the lights and open the top drawer of her filing cabinet.

I find myself laughing again. The lone item in the drawer is a white, three ring binder with a giant piece of paper on top that reads:

CHLOE'S BOOK

As if that isn't obvious enough, the inside of the drawer is covered with post-it notes saying "Chloe, here it is!" with arrows pointing down to the book.

I take the binder out of the cabinet and sit on the white leather couch. I tuck my legs under me as I open it.

Introduction

I don't want to leave you high and dry, so I've left you a list of all the important people you should know throughout the supernatural community. Their names and contact information can be found under Tab #1.

I flip to Tab #1, and sure enough, there is a list of all the Coven Leaders, as well as leaders of the other supernatural communities. Telephone numbers, email addresses and physical locations are listed under each.

I turn back to the Introduction.

I've also left you common protocols and procedures used inside the building during emergency situations and during travel. This can be found under Tab #2.

I check out Tab #2. A lot of the information is useful, but some of it is just for giggles. For instance, under what to do in case of a fire, Willa has simply written, "Stop, drop and roll."

Tab #3 is probably what you are most interested in. I call this my "Successes and Failures" section. It was common for you to ask me, "What would you do if..." and "have you ever dealt with..." This section was a labor of love for me. I compiled a list of all the major decisions I made as the Verhena (the ones I could remember anyway). I described what the issue was, how I handled it, and the ultimate outcome.

After I finished my list, I was concerned about what my legacy will be. My failures list is longer than I would like. But then I looked at my successes list and I'm really proud of myself.

You'll notice the things on my successes list are limited to my professional endeavors. Please know, my biggest successes, and the things I'm the most proud of, can't be found on this list. Try to have as many successes in your personal life as you do in your professional life.

I turn the pages to the third tab, by far the biggest section of the book. I look at number one on Willa's "Failures List":

August 1998: received a telephone call from a witch in New Hampshire who was concerned about her Coven Leader. The CL was acting strangely after the loss of her husband in a car accident. I knew this CL very well and had spoken with her several times since her husband's death. I got the concerned woman's call late in the day and decided to wait until the next morning to

have the Guard check on the CL. When the
Guard arrived at the CL's home, they found
her hanging from a rafter in her garage.

Wow! Of course Willa felt awful about that one.

I skim a few of the other entries and they are more common situations, like in-fighting between covens.

I flip back to the Introduction. There is one last paragraph.

Tab #4 will help you with your everyday
life.

I hope you find this notebook helpful. If
not, take it up with someone else. I'm dead,
remember?

I flip to Tab #4. It contains the silliest things yet. The topics include: what not to have Beth cook; how to tell when Bane is in a bad mood; the re-stock number for toilet paper; and places I can buy a bathing suit for my nightly swims.

I wish there were more personal messages from Willa, but there aren't. I clutch the book to my chest and sit quietly. The time and effort Willa put into this book and her letter to me warm my heart and inspire me.

I get up and walk behind Willa's desk. It feels weird sitting in her chair. I pick up the phone and dial Frank's extension.

"Hello?" he asks tentatively. I'd be a little thrown off too if I received a call from a dead person's extension.

"It's me."

"Oh," he says with bite, still peeved with me.

"Meet me in my office tomorrow morning at 9 a.m."

"8 a.m.," he corrects me.

I sigh. "8 a.m."

"Training at 10 a.m." His tone is back to normal.

"Fine."

"Good night."

I smile. "Good night Frank."

This simple conversation lets me know Frank and I are good. He doesn't need to apologize to me, and I don't need to apologize to him.

I use a notepad on Willa's desk to make a list of things Frank and I need to talk about in the morning.

1. Renovating the 14th floor to accommodate separate living quarters for Jessica and Baxter (if they want to live here)
2. Renovating my floor to add additional living space
3. New assistant – Bane
4. Possible living quarters in Colorado
5. Continuing coven tours
6. Meet with Elias to discuss strengthening alliance with vampires
7. Meet with opponents of werewolf alliance
8. Office space for James in the building
9. My coronation

There's a lot more Frank and I need to discuss, but we can only talk about so much in one meeting.

I rip my list off the notepad and push in Willa's chair. When I do, the chair bounces back a little. Something is keeping it from sliding in all the way.

I bend down to look under Willa's desk and see a familiar sight – her white, fluffy bunny slippers. I smile as I pull them out from under her desk. Looking at their cute pink noses, I remember the first time I met Willa. She was in her pajamas and rocking these slippers.

I put them down on the floor and slide my feet inside. They are warm and cozy.

Is it a little gross to put on someone else's well-worn slippers? Absolutely.

Do I care? No.

I stand at the threshold of Willa's office and take a long look around. I can almost see her sitting in her desk chair, hands folded on her desk listening patiently as I go on and on about my problems.

"I love you," I tell imaginary Willa before I turn off the light and shut the door.

I take my bunny covered feet up to my floor. I left James in my room hours ago. He has a ton of work to do, and I wanted to give him space.

I walk in my suite and James looks up at me, a pile of paperwork on the desk in front of him.

His brow furrows. "Chloe? Are you alright?"

I catch a glimpse of myself in the mirror. I'm a straight up hot mess. My hair is disheveled, my mascara is running down my face, my black tights are covered in dirt, and I have bunny slippers on my feet.

I laugh. "Despite my appearance, I'm good."

James comes out from behind the desk and gives me a hug. "Where have you been?"

I don't know where to start.

"Let's see... I fought with Frank, a neighbor called the cops on me, I got a gardening lesson from Bane, and I had one last moment with Willa."

James smiles down at me. "So your usual."

"Pretty much."

He kisses my forehead. "Since when do you like gardening?"

Of all the things for him to focus on...

"Today. I'm going to maintain the greenhouse. I have a feeling I'll be good at it."

"You sure about that?" he asks with amusement in his eyes.

I gaze up at him and smile. "Yes. I've got this."

Acknowledgements

When I completed *Branded*, the first novel in this series, I felt like there was more story to tell. I was intrigued by Jessica, a human in a paranormal world. What would that feel like? Of course Chloe was telling me there was more to her story too. These characters were so strong for me, maybe the strongest voices I've heard as a writer. I think they're so near and dear to my heart because they are the first characters I saw all the way through until the end of the story.

Some have asked if I will write a third book. At the moment, my answer is "no." However, that could change at some point. Whitney is still a bit of a wild card, isn't she? We'll have to see if she invades my brain with a story to tell.

As always, thank you for reading my work. I can't tell you how much I appreciate it. And to my Aunt Cindy, for whom this book is dedicated, your time and attention to my books means the world to me. You are a smart, witty and well-read woman who has encouraged me to chase these crazy dreams of mine. Thank you.

To my readers – I can't thank you enough. The fact that you spend your free time with me is an incredible honor. I love hearing from you. You can reach me at nevabellbooks@gmail.com or on Facebook and Instagram - @neva_bell_books.

Made in the USA
Coppell, TX
06 October 2021